THE FIGHTING IBEX

THE FIGHTING IBEX

LEO PETERSON

ISBN: 978-1-78324-245-0

Published by Wordzworth
www.wordzworth.com

Synopsis

Victoria Shannon thought she was about to find true happiness living a fairytale life with her own real live Prince Charming. She now finds herself alone in the majestic Dolomites Mountains of Italy befriended by a compassionate hotel staff and several soldiers from both Italy and the United States. As the Cold War evolves around this group where allies are not trustworthy, and it becomes increasingly difficult to figure out who the real enemy is.

About the Author

The Fighting Ibex is the first of the Cold War Series is the creation of Leo Peterson who lives with his wife in the Southeastern United States.

This book is dedicated to Chris Weiser; Bull rider, climber, friend. Your word was your bond. Climb high.

Chris Weiser
9.30.1963 – 3.21.2021

CONTENTS

FOREWORD

The Cold War series is a work of historical fiction; the action of this book is set in the mid-1950s, when people and cultures all over the world were becoming more aware of each other. Whenever there are societal changes such as this, there will be friction. To accurately portray the times, I have included language that some readers may find offensive, showing the attitudes of several of the characters toward certain members of our society at the time. These attitudes were wrong in 1955 and are wrong now. But rather than pretend these attitudes never existed, I feel it is important to acknowledge their harmful impacts so that we can learn from them and create a more inclusive future together. Please enjoy.

PROLOGUE

MILAN, ITALY

MONDAY, JANUARY 3, 1955
8:30 PM

Captain David Alexander walked silently through the red-light district of Milan, with his lieutenant Daniel Lightner by his side. The two men did not like to speak, as they had no wish to draw attention themselves. Both were in civilian clothes beneath their overcoats. As far as any passersby was concerned, they appeared to be ordinary businessmen—possibly domestic, but more likely foreign—just looking for a little physical relief. It would be disastrous, Alexander thought, for two CID agents—tasked as they were with investigating felony crimes and violations of military law among United States military personnel—to be caught with prostitutes. For Lightner, the risk was dire; even a suspicion of his attraction to teenage boys would be enough to end his career.

Captain Alexander did not judge his partner. His own proclivity for teenage girls was perhaps less dangerous, but even he had to endure gossip and hurtful comments about him being unable to handle an adult woman—some of them from his (now ex-) wife. The marriage had lasted barely two years; the taunts had escalated to physical altercations until she decided she'd had enough, returned to the United States, and filed for divorce. In many ways, Alexander found it a relief; he was free to explore more frequent sexual encounters with young women. For Captain Alexander, desire was tied up with control, and at twenty-eight he believed he could control younger women better than those his own age.

The two men, in short, were well-matched. They worked well together, and kept each other's secrets. But Alexander was uneasy. He was uncomfortably aware that both he and Lightner were dependent on the discretion of Nick Ferraro, a Milanese local who, for lack of a better term, acted as their pimp, arranging all the affairs for the two men. Nick had also saved them both from being arrested several months ago; when the whorehouse where they were being entertained was raided by the *carabinieri*, Nick was able to get the two Americans out of there before the door came down. An arrest would have been devastating for both men, considering their roles in the army.

But it had become evident to the two soldiers that Nick expected something in return. Everyone has something they consider valuable—a currency, so to speak—and Nick's currency was information. Alexander's unit was assigned to monitor and dismantle the Italian black market in goods stolen from the US government. Medicine, firearms, and clothing were in high demand throughout all of Europe, which was finally emerging from the ravages of the war, and the Italian black market had established itself as the premier distributor of these items. Neither Alexander nor Lightner knew how Nick had become aware of their assignment, but it was plain that he knew—and that it was their investigative activities that had motivated Nick to cultivate their acquaintance in the first place.

Captain Alexander did not mind that, insofar as it went. Sharing a tip with a small-time crook like Nick did Alexander no harm. In fact, he welcomed it. The lackluster performance of his missions so far felt like a petty revenge on his superior, that big Black son-of-a-bitch, General U.S. Thompson. As far as David Alexander was concerned, Thompson was an uppity nigger, sanctimonious and behind the times. General Thompson did not realize that the world was changing; he insisted that the sovereignty of the United States would serve as the world's example going forward in the second half of the twentieth century.

But Alexander knew better; he came from wealth, and he understood that families like his had opportunities that lay beyond the bounds of the US government. The future lay with international corporations like his family's business empire. It was these corporations that would be controlling the world. The beacon of global relationships would not be any ideological bullshit about "sovereignty," but the almighty dollar. And the best part was that the American taxpayer would help foot the bill for the expansion of these businesses. Back in America, the standard of living was high enough that your average Joes never realized they were being taken for a ride by the very people they were electing—all of whom were in the pockets of rich and powerful families. And as for General Ulysses Sampson Thompson—he would wind up working for Alexander's family as a figurative house negro.

All Alexander had to do was to bide his time for another year. His activities in Italy, commanding the unit in charge of disrupting the black market, would give the top brass the perception that he was some sort of expert in addressing international crime. From there it would be a promotion to lieutenant colonel, a position in Army Intelligence, and a post at the Pentagon.

In the meantime, he would continue to deliver insincere accolades to General Thompson and his staff—especially his XO, Colonel Austin Hill, that scallywag—while making token arrests which would have minimal impact on the black market. Alexander smiled to himself as he and Lightner rounded the corner to stand before a nondescript apartment house. Lightner opened the lobby door, and without a word the two men began to ascend the stairs.

Nick Ferraro greeted them at the door of the fourth-floor flat. "Gentlemen! So nice to see you again! Please, come in." He was a small man, about five-foot-six, with his hair slicked back and a thin greasy mustache; his red floral tie blared against his black double-breasted suit and his black-and-white wingtips.

Alexander and Lightner removed their coats and hats. Tossing his fedora on the cheap end table, Lightner asked, "Is he here?" His voice was high and anxious.

"Yes, Mister Dan," Nick said. "Fabrizio is here, and he is waiting for you quite excitedly."

Lightner's face lit up in a smile. *Jesus,* Alexander thought to himself, *I think Dan's actually in love with this little hustler. Poor bastard.* He shook his head, then turned to Nick, eyebrow raised.

"Ah! For you, Mister David, I have a treat." Nick's thin mustache curled as he smiled. "Fifteen years old. Very attractive—and a virgin."

Alexander said nothing, but gestured for Nick to elaborate.

"An unfortunate child. Her father—he gambles, you see." Nick clucked his tongue. "He owes a sizable debt to some associates of mine, and there is no way he can repay. He has three other children, and he is concerned about their welfare. Poor Josefina! The father, he views her as a sacrificial lamb, if you will."

Alexander only nodded; but despite himself, he found he was becoming excited at the prospect. He had never had a virgin; even his ex-wife had had at least two lovers before him; Father had warned him about her. But now, he could hardly contain himself. He had not a single thought for the girl—her sad story, her trauma. He only knew he wanted her. Wanted the conquest, the feeling of power.

He allowed himself a tight smile and took a step toward the bedroom door; but Nick put up a hand. "And what do you have for me, Mister David?"

In some ways, this was the best part of the interaction; Alexander felt as if he was putting a thumb in the eye of that upstart, General Thompson, while keeping himself above the fray. "Word is there will be raids next week. Several locations. I don't have the details yet, but I'll get them to you by this time next week." He looked Nick dead in the eye. "But you're gonna have to give me something in return."

"And that is?"

"I can't keep showing up empty-handed. The brass will become suspicious. You're gonna have to give me something to bring back as a trophy. One of the lower-level operations."

Nick smiled. "I'm sure we can come to some arrangement." He took a small handbell from the table and gave it a jingle. The door to the bedroom opened, and the two teenagers came into the living room.

Fabrizio was a handsome youth; he came in happily, more than eager to spend an evening with the lieutenant. But the girl, Josefina, lingered in the doorway, frozen. Alexander looked her over; she was beautiful, as promised. No doubt Nick and her old man has explained what was expected of her, but even so she was plainly terrified. Poor kid, he thought; she probably expected she'd finish her schooling, then give it up on her wedding night—the whole happily-ever-after bit. *Funny how things work out, eh, girl?*

"Gentlemen," Nick said. "Enjoy your evening. I will return at midnight."

After Nick left, David Alexander took a quarter from his pocket and flipped it in the air. "Call it," he said to Lightner.

"Tails."

The quarter landed on the dorsum of Alexander's right hand. Heads.

"Amazing how you always win," Lightner drawled.

Alexander grinned. "Just lucky, I guess," he said. "I get the bedroom. You boys can have the couch."

He grabbed Josefina by the arm; she resisted, but not for long.

1

CORTINA, ITALY

THURSDAY, JANUARY 6, 1955
3:30 PM

Victoria Shannon was enjoying a cappuccino and biscotti on the patio of the Miramonte Hotel, overlooking the majestic panorama of the Dolomites. Once again, she felt she needed to pinch herself to know that she was truly here, that it wasn't a dream. She suddenly shivered: Yes, this was for real. The temperature was dropping, and though she was dressed for the weather, she cinched the collar of her red quilted ski jacket around her neck to keep the cold wind out. Her après ski boots were keeping her feet toasty. Ernesto, her ski instructor, had already taken her skis, poles, and Nordica leather boots, putting them in storage until tomorrow's lesson.

Weather permitting, she reminded herself. Ernesto believed that they were in for a blizzard. And why should she doubt him? He had spent nearly his entire life here in the Dolomites, and at forty-five, he was an authority, as far as she was concerned. Even her fiancé, Sebastian, would defer to the old mountaineer—which was a statement, considering that Sebastian had been born and raised between here and Zurich, Switzerland.

Victoria found her hands growing cold. She pulled on her black leather ski gloves; she'd been sitting on them, so they were warm when she put them on. Again, Victoria shook her head in disbelief. How did a twenty-five-year-old girl from Hell's Kitchen wind up here in Cortina?

Victoria had inherited her mother's beauty and her father's tall slender physique—a little small in the chest, perhaps, with slim hips but a well-formed ass, if she said so herself. Her dark brown hair framed a narrow face that matched her long slender body, with a small, upturned nose inherited from her father and her mother's bewitchingly dark, almond-shaped eyes. From her mother she also inherited a passion for nursing; she was accepted into the St. Vincent's nursing program at only seventeen, and was working as a surgical nurse within three years.

In 1950, the year of her mother's death, Victoria married a handsome surgeon named Joel Arron. Joel's story was the stuff of movies. In January of '42, halfway through his second year at Columbia Medical School, he ran off and joined the navy. He had told her that he felt he had something to prove to the world; when he volunteered, he put down on his application that he had only a high school education and was working as a shipping clerk for Macy's.

His family was so appalled that they literally disowned him; he never spoke to his parents again.

Joel served as a navy corpsman during the long siege at Guadalcanal from August 1942 to February 1943, winning the Purple Heart as well as the Navy Cross. Eventually the military brass discovered his true identity, and he was shipped stateside to complete his medical training under the accelerated program. He returned to the Pacific theater as a navy surgeon in 1945. After his discharge in 1946, he returned to New York and entered a formal surgical residency program at St. Vincent's, where he was well liked and considered a gifted surgeon. Joel was so in love with Victoria that he even converted to Catholicism so that they could have a Catholic wedding. She tried to reach out to his family, but they wanted nothing to do with Joel—or the Gentile bitch he was marrying.

The couple were married June 17, 1950. The first year of marriage was bliss; the young couple tried eagerly to get pregnant, but their efforts proved fruitless. It was in their second year of marriage that Victoria began to see Joel's dark side, his demons from the war. It started with bouts of insomnia—three or four sleepless nights in a row—and then the nightmares began. Joel began to relive the battles in his dreams; he would awaken crying and in a cold sweat. Victoria begged him to go get help, but Joel refused. To accept psychiatric help, in his eyes, would be to admit weakness.

During that same year, 1951, Joel was called up as a reservist during the Korean War, assigned to the USS

Constellation. When he returned in January 1953, things were worse. Joel began drinking to keep the dreams at bay—and when that stopped working, he turned to narcotics. The combination of sleeplessness, alcohol, and drugs brought Joel's Mr. Hyde to the surface—and Victoria endured her share of black eyes and split lips to show for it. In the morning it was always the same: the tears, the remorse, the pleas not to leave him.

Then, in late December of 1953, Joel's nightmare ended. Victoria was at home alone when the police knocked on her door at three in the morning. There had been an accident, they said. Joel had lost his balance climbing the stairs to the apartment and tumbled down a flight of stairs, breaking his neck. The coroner ruled that Joel was exhausted from his late-night rounds; he didn't even run a toxicology screening. With the coroner's report, Victoria was able to collect on Joel's life insurance policy of $25,000.

After Joel's death, Victoria lost all passion for nursing; there was no joy for her at work anymore, and in April of 1954 she handed in her two weeks' notice. On her last night of employment, a young stockbroker was admitted to St. Vincent's with an acute appendicitis. Along with the patient came several well-dressed compatriots. One was a Swiss named Sebastian Bossard. He was tall, dark, and handsome, with a slim, athletic build that radiated Old World charm. The gaggle of young men were raising a terrible ruckus in the emergency department; they seemed to see the whole episode as an adventure. Carrie Albright, the charge nurse, thought it would be impossible to rein in these fellows, but nonetheless sternly asked them to keep the commotion to a low roar. She was pleasantly surprised when they did. However, she had to arch her brow when the European guy gave Victoria his card, asking if she would dine with him the next night. Victoria declined, saying—truthfully—that she would be attending a going-away party in her honor.

Sebastian, ever resourceful, found the party's location on his own initiative and invited himself. He charmed the knickers off several of the other nurses, but continued to ask Victoria to dinner. Her colleagues couldn't blame her when she accepted. They had watched the dissolution of her marriage to Joel—make-up can cover up a bruise but not swelling—and the tearful aftermath of his death. So not only did the girls approve of her dining with this Don Juan; they encouraged it.

The next night, Sebastian took her to the 21 Club, and he made her feel as if she were the only woman on Earth. At the end of the evening, he walked her home. On the doorstep, she was overwhelmed with grief. Joel was barely in the ground six months, and here she was, out on date with a man she hardly knew; maybe she *was* a Gentile bitch after all. Sensing her discomfort, Sebastian only asked when he could see her again. She told him she was leaving to visit her brother's family in Seattle. He asked her to ring him when she returned, and she promised she would. With that he bowed, kissed her hand, and left.

It took nearly a day to get to Seattle by plane; it was Victoria's first time flying. The visit was long enough for the family to get reacquainted, but not long enough to get on each other's nerves. Consistency was the key for the Shannon household: Victoria was not going to be the cause of any strife, but she did spoil her two nephews, Thomas and John, as much as possible. She was genuinely happy for James and Colleen, and they hoped that someday she would find happiness.

When she returned, she waited two days before calling Sebastian—mostly out of fear that he had already forgotten her and moved on. She was shocked to hear him say that the waiting was killing him. When could he see her again? He almost sounded like a schoolboy asking a girl out to the high-school dance.

The next night he took her to see *Daddy Long Legs,* which she loved. Victoria was a sucker for romantic comedies, and this one fit the bill. They talked for hours about all the movies they had seen over the years; that's when they both realized they were both incurable romantics. More nights at the movies followed: *Marty*, *Seven Brides for Seven Brothers, Sabrina* (with which Victoria was beginning to identify, in some ways), and *Vera Cruz.* Victoria loved westerns, with the whole mystique of the strong, silent type who rode off into the sunset. Clearly, that was not Sebastian; besides being charming and Old World, he was opinionated and intelligent. She came to find out he was in the United States to get a better understanding of the American economy; his family's banking business was looking to break into the US market.

Unlike her, Sebastian could trace his family back to the late fourteenth century. It was reputed that his family were

Knights Templar who had escaped to Switzerland after the king of France disbanded the order because of its heretical practices—if you believed in that kind of stuff. Regardless, Sebastian came from a very wealthy family, and he made it clear that he wanted to share that wealth with Victoria.

Victoria found herself falling for Sebastian, who was two years older than she. One night, she invited him to the apartment for dinner. She made *coq au vin* and served it with a Beaujolais (the local liquor store owner helped her with the selection), along with French bread and salad. He could not pay her a higher complement than to sit there sopping up sauce with bread during his second helping. He would have gone for thirds, but she reminded him to save room for dessert—assorted Italian pastries and coffee.

As they sat on the couch after dessert, Sebastian commented, "Beautiful, professional—*and* you can cook. You're too good to be true."

Victoria began to sob.

"Did I say something wrong?" Concern and worry filled his voice.

"That's what Joel told me three weeks before he proposed to me," Victoria heard herself saying in between gulps of air, barely trusting her voice.

"I'm sorry, It's horrible that such a love story came to a tragic end."

"It wasn't quite the fairytale you think." Sebastian's eyes begged for an explanation. Victoria closed her eyes and began, "I don't want to speak ill of the dead, but he was violent and abusive."

"*Bastard!*"

"No, Sebastian. Joel suffered from battle fatigue. There are many soldiers that suffer with this. I can't fault him for that."

"But he did fail you?"

"He failed us. I asked … I begged him to get help." Tears began to flow more freely now. "He had too much pride, he saw it as weakness."

"Why didn't you change your name?"

"I … I convinced myself I was too busy, but deep down I knew it wouldn't last."

"I'm sorry," was all he said.

She cried even harder, burying her face in his shoulder, and began to beat on his chest. He took her punishment, her pain, until there was none left, and she fell asleep in his arms.

When Victoria finally awoke, it was dawn. She was still in his arms, wrapped in his jacket with her stocking feet tucked underneath her. She didn't know how long she had slept, or if Sebastian had slept at all. He greeted her waking with a kiss; she got up to fix coffee and breakfast, not knowing what else to do. He gobbled up breakfast and gave her another kiss on his way out the door. He would call her from work to check on her, he said, but now he had to go back to his suite at the Waldorf, clean up, and get to the office.

After he left, she showered, put on a dressing gown, and fell back asleep. It wasn't a restful type of sleep; she dozed on and off for the next several hours. Sebastian finally called around one o'clock, wondering if she was all right. She could hear concern in his voice. She assured him that she was fine, and he asked if she would like to see a movie that night; the new Hitchcock picture, *Rear Window*, had just opened. She agreed, and he arranged to pick her up at her apartment at six o'clock; they would have something light at the Waldorf after the show.

Six o'clock. That gave Victoria nearly five hours to get ready for a night that she hoped neither of them would forget. She went to the beauty salon, had her hair done into a poodle cut, and had her nails done in a vivid red. She selected a black sleeveless swing dress to wear with a black yarn fascinator instead of a hat. In addition to the black shawl, she took a black leather pocketbook large enough to carry all the supplies necessary for her diaphragm. When Joel returned from Korea, she sensed things were not the same, so she was fitted with a diaphragm—not that she used it all that much. Regardless, she was not going to bring a child into this world when there was so much personal strife at hand.

They very much enjoyed the movie; its frankness about sex between its unmarried characters seemed very daring to Victoria—and gave her an idea on how to convey her wants. After the movie, they took dinner in Sebastian's suite: two chef salads and a bottle of Pinot noir. About a half-hour after dinner, Victoria excused herself and went to the bathroom. She took off her dress and inserted the diaphragm. In *Rear Window*, Grace Kelly came out in a negligée; the best Victoria could do was to come out in her bra, panties, stockings, garters and high heels. She walked out in the suite's living room to a shocked Sebastian.

He was lost for words—at first. For an instant, Victoria thought she had gone too far; but then she decided to go for broke. She pushed her panties over her hips and allowed them to drop, exposing a pair of sensuous hipbones and a well-trimmed pubic area.

Sebastian swallowed hard. *Well, at least he hasn't run away screaming,* she thought, as she walked over to him and sat on his lap, kissing him passionately.

Effortlessly, he picked her up in his arms and carried her to the bedroom; she kicked off her heels as they went. Victoria could not remember ever feeling with Joel as she did that night with Sebastian. She would never forget that night as long as she lived.

The next morning, instead of walking out of the Waldorf feeling any shame, she held her head high because she was in love.

Since then, they had been inseparable. Every weekend was a new adventure as they discovered America together—at least the East coast. At Thanksgiving, one of Victoria's girlfriends hosted dinner for four couples at her apartment. Sebastian proposed that evening with a five-carat engagement ring. She said yes, of course, and dinner turned into a celebration.

Over the next six weeks, Victoria wrapped up all the loose ends in preparation for a move to Switzerland. Her friend Molly took over the lease on her apartment; she even bought all Victoria's furniture for a thousand dollars (though it was worth three times that; Joel had expensive tastes). That gave Victoria close to $25,000 in an account at the Bank of New York.

When she asked Sebastian what she needed to do with the money, he told her to keep it where it was for the time being; they would figure out what to do with it later. She did, however, take out $1,500 in traveler's cheques, just in case. He also assured her that they would take care of any visa issues when they finally got to Switzerland—but only after a two-week ski vacation in Cortina.

Sebastian bought Victoria a four-piece Samsonite luggage set and a new wardrobe, including a full-length mink coat. They celebrated midnight mass at St. Patrick's Cathedral and Christmas with her relatives, with a promise of the wedding plans to come soon. They celebrated New Year's Eve—the last day of Sebastian's contract with the firm where he'd been working—with a black-tie event at the Waldorf, then left on New Year's Day for Milan via London. They got to Cortina on the morning of January 3, where he bought her a complete complement of high-end ski equipment and clothing. The next day, she took her very first ski lesson with Ernesto Bianchi. She was truly living the life worthy of a fairy tale.

All these thoughts ran through her mind in the time it took her to finish her cappuccino and biscotti. She shivered again as the temperature continued to drop. It was time to go in, shower, and get ready for her knight in shining armor, Sebastian—who happened to be on the slopes reserved for expert skiers only.

2

CORTINA, ITALY—MIRAMONTE HOTEL

THURSDAY, JANUARY 6, 1955
4:00 PM

Victoria stepped in out of the cold and into the hotel proper, climbing the three flights of steps to the suite that she shared with Sebastian. As she closed the door to the suite, she realized she was not alone. Standing there, looking out through the glass-paneled doors of the balcony, was an older gentleman in a grey pinstriped suit.

"Can I help you?" Victoria asked cautiously.

He turned to face her, a warm smile breaking across his face. He appeared to be in his late fifties, with black-rimmed glasses, a gold watch fob, and black-capped lace-up shoes that looked handmade. "Miss Shannon, I presume?" he said in mildly accented English, then bowed at the waist. "I'm Martin Eisner."

It took her a moment to place the name. "Oh! You're Sebastian's family lawyer?"

Eisner raised his right eyebrow. He seemed surprised that she should know his name; but his smile did not waver. "Indeed I am," he said.

Victoria now smiled happily. "Yes, Sebastian told me we'd be meeting you. But I thought it wouldn't be until the week after next, when we got to Zurich."

"And why did Sebastian tell you we would meet?"

"To go over the marriage contract, of course," she said. "To protect his family in case of divorce—though heaven knows I'd never do such a thing."

The smile vanished from Eisner's face as if someone had flicked a switch. "*Blast that fool!*" he cried. Victoria, startled, took a step back. The suddenness of the outburst gave her a moment of panic such as she had not felt since Joel's death.

Eisner saw the fear in her face. "Forgive me, Miss Shannon," he said. "I was afraid it might have come to this, but to hear it confirmed …" He trailed off, and mopped at his brow with a handkerchief.

"Mr. Eisner, I don't understand—"

"Perhaps we should sit down and talk, hm?" said the lawyer, visibly attempting to as compose himself. "I have news to deliver, and my blood pressure to consider."

Victoria gestured, and they settled into the matching armchairs by the fireplace. Eisner sank back, while Victoria was on the edge of her seat.

"I'm sorry to inform you, Miss Shannon," he said, "but there will be no wedding between yourself and Sebastian Bossard."

"What do you mean?" She was caught between anger and confusion. "We love each other! He gave me this engagement ring!" She displayed her hand; Eisner regarded the ring with no more interest than if she'd held up a river stone. "He told me that he talked to his family, and they couldn't wait to meet me."

"He lied," Eisner replied. His voice bespoke controlled anger. "The Bossard family had no knowledge of you until a few days ago, when you arrived in Cortina."

Victoria's felt her lower lip begin to quiver. "I—I don't understand," she said, not trusting herself to say anything else.

Eisner shook his head. "Sebastian is arranged to be married, Miss Shannon. To Katrina Olafsson, daughter of one of the most prominent ship-building families in Sweden. It has been arranged for many years. It is beyond my comprehension why Sebastian has carried this cruel deception as far as he has."

She fell back, feeling more pain than she had ever felt during one of Joel's beatings. Tears welled up in her eyes. "I need to speak to Sebastian as soon as possible!"

Eisner handed her his handkerchief, "I'm afraid that is impossible," he said. "Sebastian's father Frederick collected him about eleven o'clock this morning. They should be in Zurich in about an hour, weather permitting."

"But why?" she cried.

"I wish I knew," he said, his voice somehow terribly weary. "Sebastian is … most impulsive. When he wants something—or someone—he pursues it, with no thought to the consequences. No thought to whom he inconveniences. No thought to whom he might hurt."

Victoria struggled to hold in a sob. A question burned inside her; she didn't want to know, but she had to ask. "Have there—Have there been others?"

Eisner closed his eyes. "Frederick Bossard, I am billing you double for this," he murmured. Then he turned his gaze to her. "Miss Shannon, it is not helpful to think this way. You will only upset yourself."

"I bet there were," she spat. "Society girls, am I right? Snobby horsey types looking to move a rung or two up the ladder."

He looked at her with eyes full of pity, and said nothing. Somehow that was the worst part.

"But I *love* him, Mr. Eisner," she said. "I would have walked through the fires of hell for him. And he—"

And then there were no more words. The tears came in earnest, in long wordless sobs. Eisner was decent about it; he didn't try to shush her or hurry her along. He just stared at his expensive handmade shoes and let her cry.

At last, Victoria had breath enough to ask, "Wh—What now?"

Eisner sighed. He pulled a manila envelope from his briefcase; inside were two folders, "Trust me when I tell you, Miss Shannon, the Bossard family is deeply sorry for all of this and wishes to make amends."

Victoria felt a growing sense of dismay.

Eisner showed her the folder; there was a cashier's check clipped to the inside. "This check is for 200,000

Swiss francs—approximately 45,000 of your American dollars."

Her eyes widened and her mouth opened as she looked at the check.

"There will be another check in the same amount once you are safely settled in the United States," Eisner continued.

A bitter smile appeared on Victoria's face. *You sons of bitches,* she thought. *You're buying me off. You want to make sure I don't hang around and cause trouble. This must be that Swiss efficiency I've heard so much about.*

Eisner opened the second folder. "This folder contains all the documents necessary for your return to the United States. Train tickets to Milan, first-class ticket air travel on Pan Am to London, then to New York—along with a letter, signed by me, extending you a line of credit and the Bossard's suite at the Savoy in London if your flight is delayed due to weather. Your suite here at the Miramonte is paid through the end of next week, along with your meals and ski lessons, if you so choose—although I imagine you will prefer to return the United States as soon as possible."

Victoria offered Eisner his handkerchief back. "Is there anything I need to sign?" she asked. "A contract? A restraining order?"

Eisner, reaching for the handkerchief, touched her hand just for a moment. "Miss Shannon, you have every right to be upset. You have suffered a great betrayal," he said. "But there are no more betrayals. No strings. No conditions. We only hope that you will accept our apologies and restitution, and be happy in your life."

Eisner's smile was warm, compassionate. Victoria wished she could find it comforting. "One last question?" she sniffed.

Eisner nodded.

"When exactly did Sebastian contact the family?"

"Two days ago. January 4."

"One call?"

"No," Eisner admitted. "There were several between Sebastian, his parents, and his grandmother. It took several hours."

Victoria felt her face growing warm. "And when was the decision made to 'collect' him, as you put it?"

Eisner closed his eyes. "That same day. January 4."

Victoria rose from her chair. "That son of a bitch," she said. "He lied to me! He told he was skiing all day!"

Eisner nodded his head helplessly.

Victoria's anger reached its zenith; she pointed to the bed without looking at it and shouted, "Then he *fucked me* in that bed the past two nights! Told me he loved me! That he would stay with me forever!"

Now it was Eisner's lower lip that was quivering.

Their eyes were locked; and then the rage and the sorrow all boiled over again. Victoria convulsed, doubling over at the waist, and began to cry uncontrollably.

Eisner went to reach for her, but she pushed him away. "Please leave, *now!*" She cried.

Eisner hurriedly gathered his things and marched to the door, his face red with rage. As he went, Victoria heard him mutter to himself, "Damn you, Sebastian Bossard, your father will pay *triple* for this one!"

Then Victoria was alone, hunched over and holding her stomach. She had never experienced pain as she did now. Yes, her time with Joel was painful; but she could blame that on the trauma of war, as it was with her father and brother. Losing her mother and aunt to cancer—that was just dumb luck. She could accept the unintended consequences of life. But this? This was intentional. The cruelty of it was too much. She felt as if she'd been a toy to a rich, spoiled little brat; and when he got tired of it, he broke it, leaving his parents and their servants the clean up the mess.

She screamed in rage and threw herself on the bed—the same bed where she had opened her heart and her legs to that bastard—and began to cry as she had never cried before.

3

CORTINA, ITALY—TOWN SQUARE

THURSDAY, JANUARY 6, 1955
5:00 PM

While Victoria cried herself into restless sleep, four mountaineers were in the bar of the Montana Hotel in the town of Cortina proper, attempting their second conquest of the day; not trying to summit some mountain peak—they had already succeeded in that for the day—but trying to win the hearts of four English tourists on a ski holiday. Judging by the receptiveness and body language of the women, their success was assured.

The women were all in their early twenties, from well-to-do families who had made their fortunes in rebuilding England after the war. Beatrix Schofield, a short but voluptuous young woman, nervously smoothed back her strawberry blonde hair and fished out a cigarette from her purse, waiting for Captain John Gillespie to return to the seat next to hers with another bottle of the house wine.

She glanced across the table at Marjorie Hastings, a tall brunette with hazel eyes and the self-proclaimed leader of the group; she was hanging on the arm of the oldest of the four climbers, Gigi. Lt. Colonel Giovanni Pasquale—"Gigi"—had black wavy hair and a thick black moustache. She always had a thing for high-ranking officers, thought Beatrix; she supposed they reminded her of her father. In any case, Beatrix had to admit that Gigi's moustache did make him look terribly gallant.

Stephanie Russell, a redhead, could not take her eyes off Major Antonio "Tony" Pagnozzi, obviously the strongest of the group—not quite as tall as Johnny, but much broader and thicker than the American captain. Tony's hair, too, was wavy and dark brown, with a well-trimmed goatee. Beatrix could not help but to think how badly Stephanie must have wanted Tony; she was biting her lip as she looked up at his chiseled, tanned face with dark brown eyes. Initially Beatrix had believed that Stephanie had interest in her Johnny, obviously the most handsome of the group; she was a randy little thing, and Beatrix had feared she might throw herself at Johnny. But after a few minutes of conversation between Stephanie and the personification of Hercules, Beatrix noticed that her nipples were poking against her sweater—a tell-tale sign that Stephanie had set her sights on Tony.

Beatrix had no such worries about Portia; she seemed happy enough to be with Jo-Jo, and that was all right with her. Major Giuseppe Novinonte seemed to Beatrix to be the most generic of the four mountaineers. That was Portia all over, she thought: always settling for whatever was left. It puzzled her, though. Portia Walker was clearly the most beautiful of the group—tall, with pale blonde hair, porcelain skin, and dark mysterious eyes—but the least assertive.

Still, Beatrix was content to let Portia settle for the dregs. She felt better knowing she didn't have to compete for the attention of the best-looking men. And knowing what was waiting for her back in England, Beatrix considered herself entitled to a bit of attention.

She'd struck gold tonight with Captain John Gillespie, an Army Ranger assigned to Camp Darby, near the port of Livorno in Tuscany. Johnny was tall and lean, with broad shoulders and long limbs. His light brown hair had been made even lighter by years in the sun; the sun had also tanned his handsome face, from which shone forth a pair of deep-set, cobalt-blue eyes. Johnny sat relaxed, comfortable in his own body. His posture spoke of confidence without a hint of arrogance. This, Beatrix thought, was a man who could satisfy her all night long.

The other three were Italian Alpini soldiers, considered by many to be the best mountain infantry in the world. For an American to be invited to climb with such a distinguished group spoke volumes about Johnny's abilities as a mountaineer. It was also apparent from the conversation that these four had seen action together during the Korean War; but they would not elaborate when pressed. Their experiences, thought Beatrix, must have been dreadful indeed.

Of the group, Gigi was the only one who spoke proper English. When he was ten years old, his parents had emigrated to England to escape Mussolini's fascist regime. Now thirty-five, he was the old man of the group. Gigi had joined the British Army after two years at Eton, and was recruited for the Special Air Service in 1941, serving with the infamous "Desert Rats" who harassed Rommel's forces in North Africa. He was part of the D-Day invasion, and nearly lost his life during Operation Market Garden in 1944. After Mussolini was deposed, he was sent home, working for the OSS to help root out the Nazis from northern Italy.

Tony spoke English, as well—after a fashion, Beatrix thought acidly—having been raised in New York City from the age of eight. Stephanie, at least, loved Tony's accent; "Did you hear him say 'coffee' just now?" she whispered to Beatrix. "Where that 'w' came from, I'll never know. Isn't it *darling?*"

Joining the US Army in 1942, Tony trained as a paratrooper, graduating from jump school at the top of the class. His fluency in Italian earned him a post alongside Gigi—who was two years his senior—clearing out Nazi strongholds in the Dolomites.

Both Gigi and Tony had maintained dual citizenship, and after the war they were able to transition to the Alpini to help improve Allied relations with the new Italian government. Afterward, the two men acted as liaisons between the Italians and their NATO allies.

The youngest of the crew, Jo-Jo, had joined the Alpini in 1944, after the fall of Mussolini, and worked his way up through the ranks, making major by twenty-nine—the youngest in the corps—after distinguished service in Korea.

All three Italians were built similarly, broader and slightly thicker than their American friend, but still very lean and fit. Of the three, only Tony was as tall as Johnny, but much stronger. They all had dark hair and olive complexions browned by the sun. To the Englishwomen, they were quite exotic—a welcome change from the pasty-white, bookish bores who constituted their usual social circles. The women made it abundantly clear that they were all looking for a temporary escape from their milquetoast life, and that these four could be their rescuers.

And none seemed so exotic as Johnny Gillespie: For if what he'd told Beatrix was true, his life was something out of an American movie. Born and raised in Wyoming, Johnny grew up riding and roping, doing all the things cowboys do. Indeed, the Italians affectionately called him "Cowboy."

Beatrix had settled on Johnny. Stephanie was hanging on Tony's arm, enthralled by his New York accent. As for Marjorie, she was getting cozy with Gigi. And Portia could not take her eyes off of Jo-Jo. Heaven knows how they were communicating—Jo-Jo had very little English—but then, none of them were looking for conversation. Besides, thought Beatrix, Jo-Jo's youthful features and warm smile were the sort of thing to make a girl feel safe. And if that's what Portia wanted … well, Beatrix wasn't going to stop her.

It was half past five, and stomachs were beginning to grumble. Bread, cheese, and cured meats could only go so far with this group. The bar manager looked conflicted. Their tab must have been enormous—Beatrix had lost track some time ago of how many rounds they'd put in—but he had made it known that any soldier who had fought with the Allies would never pay for a drink in his place. But still, they were bottomless pits, God bless them, and could destroy the evening's profits.

Gigi extricated himself from Marjorie's long arms and came to his feet, every inch the commander. "Friends," he said, "we mustn't wear out our welcome here." He nodded to the bar manager, who crossed himself. "Alfredo, you've been most generous, but we need a proper feeding! Dinner arrangements must be made. Jo-Jo!"

Jo-Jo excused himself to borrow the bar's phone; after a moment, he returned, reporting that the chef's table at the Miramonte Hotel awaited their party of eight.

Gigi assumed command of the unit as they gathered up their belongings and headed outside into the snow. He commandeered a horse-drawn sleigh, ushered everyone and their gear into the carriage, then jumped in front with the driver. Majestically standing up in the driver's box—much to the amusement to all involved—he seized the reins, shouting, "*Avanti!*"

As they charged forward into the night, Beatrix glanced over her shoulder to see the bar manager standing in the doorway, ceremoniously tearing up the check and scattering the scraps to the wind. And then they were gone in a roar of laughter and merriment.

4

CORTINA, ITALY—MIRAMONTE HOTEL

THURSDAY, JANUARY 6, 1955
6:10 PM

At about the same time the mountaineering group realized that they were hungry, Victoria awoke and went into the bathroom. She was horrified at what she saw in the mirror; her mascara was smeared, her eyes bloodshot. "God damn you, Sebastian Bossard, you no-good son-of-a-bitch bastard," she said. Then she turned away from the mirror, stripped off her ski clothes, and turned on the shower.

Soon—showered, made up, and dressed in a grey wool pencil skirt and black sweater—she stood in the living room trying to figure out what to put on her bare feet. She was trying to decide between a pair of black ballerina flats and the black stiletto slides she'd bought in Milan. After thirty seconds, she shook her head. Why was this suddenly such a chore? She had never had trouble choosing shoes before. A flight of unruly ideas raced through her brain: *Maybe I should go downstairs barefoot. Hell, maybe I should go down there* naked, *with just the slides. Or maybe in a garter belt, stockings, and heels—that sure got Sebastian's attention back in May.*

She laughed aloud, startling herself; she did not recognize her own laugh. It sounded almost psychotic. That shook her back into the here and now; she wasn't going to be carted off to some Italian mental hospital in a straitjacket. With a sigh, she decided on the slides, which accented her long, slender legs. With that, she proceeded downstairs to make arrangements for departure—to leave this hell that she once thought was heaven.

Victoria stopped at the hotel desk. The clerk, Marco, greeted her with a nervous smile and stated that Signor Agnolini, the general manager, wished to speak to her. *Great,* she thought, *they're worried that I'm going to go psycho on them.* But she smiled and told Marco that would be fine.

Mario Agnolini came out of his office and bustled toward her. Mario—he was "Signor Agnolini" to the staff, but "Mario" to his guests—seemed to embody the charm and hospitality the luxury hotel trade. He was small and wiry, but carried himself like someone much taller, his posture impeccable. His steel grey-hair was receding. Above his immaculately groomed mustache, a pair of gold-rimmed spectacles perched on his hawkish nose. He gazed on Victoria with admiration—a widower, Mario could never conceal his appreciation for beautiful women—but also with sympathy. He greeted her with both hands on hers, and asked her to join him in his office.

Before she could respond, the lobby doors burst open and the army contingent entered, their camp followers in tow. Boisterous greetings were exchanged, and Mario excused himself to usher them toward the kitchen. "You boys," he chuckled, eyeing the English girls on their arms. "You will ruin the reputation of this prestigious hotel!"

There was general laughter at this. Victoria watched the soldiers as the clerk and bellhop swarmed around them, brushing the snow from their outerwear. She remembered seeing them check in; they had arrived at the same time as she and Sebastian, all in their uniforms. The tall, Gary Cooper-looking one was in a US Army Ranger uniform, complete with jump boots and bloused trousers. She hadn't recognized the other uniforms; Sebastian had told her about the Alpini, the famed Italian mountain infantry battle group.

As they swaggered through the lobby toward the dining room, all four gave Victoria a healthy once-over as they passed. She didn't mind so much; then she saw Mario Agnolini giving the four a glare that could have frozen the very fires of hell, with the unspoken message *Hands off! This poor child has been through enough.* She almost laughed at the old man's gallantry. The soldiers turned their attentions back to the Englishwomen, who were all giggling with excitement, completely missing the fact their escorts' attentions had been briefly diverted.

Returning from the dining room, Mario led Victoria into his office. After seating her, he went around to his side of the desk asking her if she would like a drink. He produced a half-filled bottle of Johnnie Walker Black and two glasses. "Will this be all right? Or if you wish something else, I can call the bar and have it sent over."

Victoria pointed to the bottle and held up two fingers.

Mario seemed impressed. As he poured the drinks, he said, "I must apologize for the scene just now in the lobby. These soldiers—they're good men, even if they don't know how to behave." He passed her the glass, then sat back with his hands out in gesture of surrender. "Boys will be boys, you know."

Victoria sipped her scotch and smiled. It was easy for her to be gracious, for she sensed the old man would do anything for those "boys," even the *Americano*.

Leaning forward, Mario (switching to Italian, as he knew Victoria's comprehension was so exceptionally good) offered his condolences on her situation at hand. He and his staff were at her complete disposal, he said, and would be happy to assist her in any way.

"Thank you," Victoria said. "You've been very kind, Mario, but I think it's probably best for me to go as soon as I can.

"I understand, Signorina Shannon. And my people will take care of the tickets, the luggage—whatever you need."

"It's too late to make travel arrangements for tonight, I suppose. Would it be possible for me to leave first thing in the morning?"

"Of course," Mario said. "That was what the other two women did when—" He broke off suddenly, and his hand flew to his mouth.

Victoria's eyes grew narrow. "What other two?" she said in English.

Mario glared at his glass of scotch, as if it were to blame for his indiscretion.

"Mario," said Victoria, anger creeping her voice. "What other two?"

He grew flushed. "I should not have said. Forgive me, Signorina Shannon, for hurting you further. But the Bossard family—they should never have allowed this travesty to continue as it did. My anger got the best of me."

"You're telling me Sebastian has done this before?"

"For three years running." Mario gulped his scotch to steel his nerves. "The son would show up just after the New Year, always with a new woman, all with the promise of learning to ski."

"And all with the promise of marriage," Victoria said bitterly.

Mario could only nod miserably. "Then, after a few days, Frederick Bossard would come to 'collect' Sebastian, and Martin Eisner would clean up the mess."

Victoria was seething now, but held her tongue and gestured for Mario to continue.

"It's a wicked thing that has been done to you, Signorina Shannon, and I can only thank God you are a woman of strong character," he said. "I shouldn't tell tales, but the others—*ai!*" He gestured explosively. "The first, the Frenchwoman—she destroyed the suite before leaving. Fixtures, vases, paintings, antique furniture, all smashed to bits. The Bossard family just paid the damages and pretended as if nothing had happened. The Englishwoman, the second one—that was a sad thing. She was inconsolable, crying, hysterical. She simply could not get ahold of herself. A physician had to be called to sedate her. Two days later, she was still crying. We had to find an English-speaking nurse in the village to travel with her as escort back to England. When she got back, the nurse told us they'd put the poor woman in a hospital."

"And the Bossard family?"

"They paid for everything and trusted us to pretend it never happened. And—to our shame—we pretended."

Victoria shook her head in disgust. "It looks as if Sebastian is working his way west," she said. "I wonder where his next stop will be. Chicago? San Francisco?"

Mario could not stifle a chuckle. "Even now, you can see the funny side," he said. "God made you strong, Victoria."

"New York City made me strong, Mario," she said. "You needn't worry about hysterics. Women from Hell's Kitchen are not prone to hysterics."

The old man laughed out loud, and so did she. When he was done, he wiped his eyes. "I will telephone Ernesto now and cancel your ski lessons. He will want to say goodbye, at least."

"Who said I was leaving tomorrow?" Victoria said. She met his eyes with a defiant smile. "I will be staying on for the next ten days, as arranged, Signor Agnolini. I will keep my suite, and my skiing lessons. If the Bossard family wants to ruin people's lives and trust to their money to make it all right, then let them pay through the nose. I mean to enjoy the hospitality of your lovely establishment to the fullest."

"*Brava*," said Mario softly, and poured her another two fingers of scotch.

5

BOLZANO, ITALY

JANUARY 6, 1955
6:45 PM

The man who called himself Tommaso Cinzano followed his guide up the winding mountain trail toward the dim lights of a distant cabin. The going was hard. Tommaso was an experienced hiker, and had navigated the trails of the Southern Tyrol with ease; but winter hiking was something else again. The heavy snow made the footing treacherous. He walked with care in the gathering darkness, keeping his eyes on the figure of Fidelio, his guide, ten steps ahead of him.

They had met two days earlier, when Tommaso arrived in Italy at the city of Milan. The flight from Buenos Aires had been long and turbulent, and the customs officer had been scrutinizing his passport for an uncomfortably long time, gazing first at the document and then at Tommaso with suspicious eyes. A broad, stocky fellow with a shiny pink face had sidled up, seemingly out of nowhere. He looked freshly shaven, even faintly comical; but he moved in close and spoke softly in the officer's ear, and when he stepped away, Tommaso could just see him withdrawing his hand (surprisingly small and delicate for a man of his build) from the officer's pocket. The next moment, with exaggerated courtesy, the officer waved him through.

The stocky man fell into step beside Tommaso, picking up his second suitcase. "I am Fidelio Provenzano," he said, holding out his free hand for Tommaso to shake. His necktie reached only halfway down his broad chest.

"How much do you know?" Tommaso asked.

Fidelio gave a noncommittal shrug. "I have the information I need to do my job. I will be your guide to Bolzano, in South Tyrol. From there, I have arranged for another guide to lead you over the mountains to Innsbruck, Austria. Payment is all arranged. Come, I have a car waiting outside."

And so, after a night and a day in a safe house in Bolzano, they were making the trek to the small mountain cabin about three kilometers outside. Fidelio was broad and graceless, but he waddled through the snow seemingly without effort, like a penguin, pausing occasionally to let Tommaso catch up. The two men did not speak.

At last, as they came to the cabin, Tommaso spoke. "What is he like, this Alpine guide?"

"Aldo?" Fidelio waggled his hand. "What's to say? He's not much of a talker, but he's never lost a client." He raised his hand and knocked twice on the cabin door.

The door swung open to reveal a giant of a man, well over six feet. His full beard and shaggy hair made him seem even larger. His eyes were deep and brooding as he waved them in.

The big man's voice was unexpectedly gentle. "Did you bring the money, Fidelio?"

"Aldo!" Fidelio chided, unwrapping his scarf to reveal his ruddy face, fairly glowing from the cold. "After all these years, you still doubt me. It's an insult!"

Aldo just grunted, and gestured for the two men to be seated. The cabin was lit by lanterns, and the main room was furnished with a rude wooden table and four chairs. Tommaso could see a collection of steel spring traps, glinting faintly in the lamplight, hanging on one wall. A woodstove glowed in one corner.

Settling in a chair, Fidelio made introductions. "Aldo, this is Tommaso Cinzano. You will be guiding him to Innsbruck. Sooner is better. There's an extra 30,000 lire in it for you if you leave tomorrow."

"There's a blizzard coming," Aldo said.

"I am aware, but time is of the essence."

Aldo turned to Tommaso. "Do you have experience with mountain hiking?"

"Some," said Tommaso. "Though I must admit, it's been a while."

"When was the last time you traveled a high mountain pass in the winter?"

"Nineteen forty-two."

Something stirred in Aldo's eyes; but he only said, "It's 130 kilometers to Innsbruck. If we manage thirty kilometers a day, I can have you there by Tuesday."

Five days, then. "That's a hard pace," Tommaso said.

"It is. But it can be done, especially if we travel light. There are a number of mountain huts where we can stay along the way, so we won't need camping gear. Conserve your energy, do as I say, and we will both survive."

Tommaso nodded; but a look of doubt must have flashed across his face, because Aldo turned to Fidelio. "You'd better make it 50,000 lire," he said. "I may have to carry this poor son of a bitch most of the way."

Fidelio chuckled, but handed over the cash.

"That's the deposit," said Aldo. "The rest is due when I deliver him alive to Innsbruck. Fifteen ounces of gold bullion."

"That will be between you and my superiors," said Tommaso.

Aldo made a noise of satisfaction. "Do you have mountain boots?"

"Yes. I bought them in Argentina before I came to Italy. They're already broken in."

Aldo indicated his own clothing—coarse woolen trousers and a wool thermal undershirt. "You'll need an outfit like this for the journey."

"I have thick wool slacks and a sweater, but no long underwear."

"I have spares. They'll be big on you, but they'll keep you warm. Your overcoat won't do for the mountains. You'll need freedom of movement. Do you have heavy jacket?

Gloves? A proper hat?"

Tommaso shook his head no.

"I can sell you what you need. Wool socks, too."

"How much?"

"A thousand lire."

"Very reasonable," said Tommaso reached into his overcoat and counted out the money. "You embrace capitalism, I see?"

A sad smile came to Aldo's face. "Currency and power are what makes this world go round, whether I embrace them or not."

"Gentlemen," Fidelio said, pulling on his jacket. "I am pleased to see you getting on so well. Honestly, Tommaso, this is the chattiest I've seen Aldo in years."

"You're leaving?"

Fidelio wound his scarf around his shiny pink face. "My part of the business has concluded, my friend, and there's a hot meal and a pretty barmaid waiting for me back in Bolzano. I'll leave you two to make your final preparations. Good luck, Tommaso. *Ciao,* Aldo!"

After Fidelio was gone, Aldo closed the door behind him and looked at Tommaso. "Have you eaten?"

Tommaso shook his head.

"I was about to make dinner for myself. There's enough for two." He smiled faintly. "No extra charge."

"I would appreciate that very much, thank you. What are we having?"

"Wild boar with pasta," Aldo said. "Most of the people around here believe that it is my only occupation, you know." Tommaso gave a questioning look, and Aldo gestured to the traps. "I supply several of the local butchers with wild game. As far as they're concerned, I am a hunter and trapper. That allows me to keep to myself, and helps avoid suspicious eyes on my ... sideline, let's call it."

Tommaso smiled. "You're a smuggler."

Aldo shrugged again. "I move cargo and people from one place to another."

"Between Italy and Austria, you mean. Across national borders."

Aldo waved his hand. "The lines on the map are all imaginary, Tommaso. Only the mountains are real."

It was not the answer Tommaso had expected, but it struck him as perfectly satisfactory. "Well," he said, "I'm glad we understand each other. Is there anything I could do to help with dinner?"

"Yes. Put the water on."

6

CORTINA, ITALY—MIRAMONTE HOTEL

JANUARY 6, 1955
7:00 PM

While Victoria was enjoying her second scotch with Mario, the affair at the chef's table was proceeding apace. The first order of business was the discard of unnecessary layers; extra clothing would make it impossible to enjoy the feast. One by one, the revelers were ushered into the small bathroom just outside the kitchen where they relieved themselves of long underwear or sweaters and bodily fluids. For the most part, everyone was out of their wet, heavy leather boots and padded around the dining room in wool socks. The men were in wool shirtsleeves and trousers while the women opted for their ski sweaters and trousers.

Discarded clothing and boots were drying by the fireplace in the staff's common room, away from the kitchen, all arranged with great care by Jo-Jo and several staff members. What Jo-Jo had neglected to mention back at the Montana was that the chef's table at the Miramonte Hotel was always open to him; his uncle was the hotel's head chef, and he had worked in the kitchen himself as a boy.

It was decided to forego the antipasto; they'd been nibbling on the Montana's stock of bread, cheese, and salami for the past few hours. The group went straight for the pasta dish, which was pappardelle with duck ragù. Salad with winter greens came next, with a sorbet to cleanse the palate. The main course was roasted wild boar with root vegetables cooked to perfection; the long marinating process had rendered the boar tender and succulent, without a hint of gaminess. Dessert was a Napoleon, light and flaky, with espresso and grappa.

It was going on seven o'clock, and Victoria's stomach began to complain that there was nothing but scotch to fill it. She had taken up more the kind old gentleman's time than he could afford. She thanked Mario and let herself out, proceeding to the main dining hall. The other patrons seemed to stare—wondering ,perhaps, why such a beautiful creature was sitting by herself on this cold, snowy night. She ordered fettucine with bolognese sauce and a salad, deciding against wine with dinner. *A glass of wine after the scotch,* she thought, *and I just might be tempted to march myself over*

to the chef's table and steal that tall drink of water of an Army Ranger away from his little English girl. She stifled a laugh in her napkin, pretending to sneeze. What was happening to her? *Enough reflecting for one night,* she told herself. *Enjoy your dinner and see what tomorrow brings.*

As she finished dinner, she decided against dessert. There would be chocolate in the suite; the bed should have been turned down by now. As she entered the lobby, the four soldiers also made their way through; their camp followers apparently needed a moment to themselves. Four pair of eyes admired the long-legged beauty in her sexy slides as she made her way to the stairs. As she began to ascend the stairs, she thought she heard someone whisper, "*Bellissima.*" In the past, this would have caused Victoria to be mindful of the swivel in her hips; tonight, she smiled to herself exaggerated the swing. As she rounded the corner after the first landing, she distinctly heard one of them say, "*Brava.*"

The four men heard the women coming before they could see them, so their attention was focused again on the quest at hand. Marjorie had assumed leadership of the women, which complemented Gigi's role in this affair. "Gentlemen," she asked, all innocence, "how are we to get back to *our* hotel?" It was growing late. The lobby was empty. As if on cue, the cold, snowy wind set up a moaning outside.

The soldiers looked at one another. Suddenly Tony's sweet baritone sang out, "I really can't stay!"

Stephanie, affecting a comically gruff male voice, returned: "Baby, it's cold outside!" With that unstated message sent, the group paired off into their pre-assigned couples and headed to their designated rooms.

Johnny and Beatrix entered his room. He had just put down his pack and outerwear when Beatrix threw herself at him, wrapping her arms around his neck and her legs around his waist. She locked her mouth onto his for nearly a full minute, her tongue probing nearly to his tonsils. All Johnny could think was this young lady has been around the block a few times.

Beatrix unwrapped her legs from Johnny and dropped to the floor, stepping back from Johnny as she began to undo her boots. "Please tell me you have prophylactics?" she asked.

Johnny went into the bathroom and came out with several foil-wrapped condoms. Beatrix squealed with delight as she pulled off her sweater and began unfastening her ski trousers. She pushed both her trousers and panties over her hips and stepped out of the whole tangle, somehow leaving even her socks behind, and stood there bottomless as she began to unfasten her bra. Johnny swallowed hard as Beatrix stood there naked. She was small, about five foot four, but round and firm, with lush breasts and supple hips. She spun around so he could admire the rear view; he affectionately slapped her plump ass, making her squeal again. Then Johnny picked her up and deposited her on the bed. She giggled as he quickly undressed, hoping he had enough condoms.

For Marjorie and Gigi, the experience was completely different. Marjorie pushed Gigi back onto the bed fully clothed, then slowly took off her sweater. Next, she pulled off the ski pants and socks. A striptease, then. Standing there in her bra and panties she asked Gigi which should come off next. He indicated the bra and she complied. Lastly, she pushed the panties off and stood there naked to see if everything met with Gigi's approval. It did, and as he tried to get off the bed, Marjorie told him to sit where he was. He obeyed as she walked over to him and undid his pants, pulling both his trousers and underwear down around his knees in one smooth movement and taking his already erect member in her mouth. "*Dio Mio*," was all he had time to say as he climaxed in her mouth. Never had he ever experienced anything like this. After she finished, he removed the rest of his clothes and pulled her up into the bed, wondering what other tricks this vixen knew.

Stephanie had found a deck of cards in Tony's room. She shuffled them and dealt out five cards each for her and

Tony. The game was strip poker. Amazingly, poor Stephanie lost every hand. The sight of her sitting there naked made Tony's mouth water. She finally said that she only had one thing left to play for, and that was her virtue. They played one more hand. Oh drat—she lost that hand, too, and informed Tony he could have his way with her—which he did.

When Portia got to Jo-Jo's room, she was tense. She knew why: this was scandalous behavior. All four of them were involved with men back home. Why had she let Beatrix talk all of them into this? Yes, it was a casual fling, and would all be forgotten in a week from now, but there was something about this Italian that gave her the shivers. He was kind, funny and gentle—she was not afraid that he might hurt her. It was almost as if she was afraid that she might hurt *him.* This was someone she could easily fall for; his eyes spoke of empathy, as if he already knew her worst fears. Was she that transparent? None of the girls knew them—not even her parents.

The thought was absurd; she pushed it away. *Well,* she thought, *in for a penny, in for a pound.* She undid her hair and let her it fall around her shoulders. Jo-Jo kissed her then, passionately but tenderly on the lips, and she liked it. He went to embrace her, and she felt herself go tense.

"*Bella,*" he said, "is everything all right with you?"

"My shoulders," she lied. "They're sore from a hard day of skiing."

"Ah," he said. "I fixa." In one motion, he pulled off her sweater.

She stood shocked for a moment, arms crossed. He grabbed his shave kit from the dresser and pulled out a small jar of salve. "No worries," he said, smiling. "I fix." Coming around behind her, he moved her hair out of the way and expertly unfastened her bra. *He's done this many* times, Portia thought with an unexpected twinge of jealousy as she let the bra slip off.

The salve smelled of lavender. He rubbed some into his hands and began to massage her knotted shoulders. Portia moaned with a mixture of pain and delight as his warm, strong hands unkinked her tense muscles. Moving from the trapezius muscles, he made his way to the deltoids. She relaxed into the rhythm of his hands; she was beginning to enjoy this.

Jo-Jo motioned for her to lie down on her stomach, and he worked on her latissimus dorsa muscles. When Jo-Jo was done, he flipped her over, admiring her small but perky breasts. She liked the way he looked at her; it made her feel special and safe.

"Any other parts bothering you?"

"My feet," she said. "They're cramping and cold."

He pulled off her socks. Her feet were like ice. He applied more salve to his hands and began massaging the arches, the heels, restoring blood flow and alleviating the cramping.

"My legs, they are dreadful," she pouted, and he pulled off her ski pants and began to massage her legs. By the time he finished, she felt like putty.

Portia stretched like a cat. She felt as if she were glowing. "You're a miracle worker," she said. "I'm in your hands. Is there any other part of me that needs your attentions, do you think?"

A fiendish grin came to his face as he pulled off her knickers and dove face first between her legs. "Glory be to God," she cried out as his tongue worked its magic.

When Victoria got to her suite, she belatedly realized that the only bedclothes she had were sexy sheer lingerie. She did not have a set of pajamas or nightgown appropriate for a cold night alone; her only option was the long wool underwear. Hanging up her clothes, she put on the long johns and socks.

As she approached the bed, she felt nauseous and froze. She could not bring herself to sleep in that bed—not after the lies that were told in it. She pulled off the quilted comforter and settled in on the couch. Surprisingly, it was quite comfortable, and she fell asleep listening to the wind outside.

7

MILAN, ITALY—POLICE HEADQUARTERS

THURSDAY, JANUARY 6, 1955
10:45 PM

Lieutenant Dan Lightner sat in the interrogation room of police headquarters in Milan, pondering the end of his life as he knew it. Two *carabinieri* stood near the door, smoking, both glaring at him with unambiguous disgust. Lightner had not been given so much as a glass of water. He sat there with a bare table in front of him two empty chairs opposite him, a single bulb overhead lamp the only illumination in the room. The room was poorly ventilated, and the lingering smells—stale cigarettes, coffee, sweat, fear—defined its purpose. The message was clear: Cooperate, or else. CID were on their way, and it was plain that the local police were eager for him to be someone else's problem.

Lightner closed his eyes. He had been a fool to take such a chance, trying to rendezvous with Fabrizio outside of Nick's apartment. He just couldn't help himself. None of them understood—not David Alexander, not Nick, certainly not these cops. They thought he was a pervert. They thought he was dangerous—that he was *hurting* Fabrizio. Hurt him? Lightner would sooner cut off his own right arm. He was in *love* with Fabrizio. He knew in his heart that they belonged together for always—if he could only find a way.

He thought he'd found his chance. The school day had ended for Fabrizio when Lightner met him. They tried to be as clandestine as possible, assuming the building would be empty once Fabrizio's classmates had left for the day. Unfortunately, they were caught in the bathroom by a janitor who believed that Lightner was attacking the poor boy and restrained the lieutenant. The commotion alerted several of the priests who taught at the school and the police were called. Lightner was brought to the police station, fingerprinted, and booked. Once it was learned that he was a US Army officer, the police lieutenant informed him that the matter was going to be turned over to CID.

Two strangers stepped in with the police lieutenant: Americans, both of them, the suits under their coats marking them as CID. The *carabinieri* stood at attention, as did Lightner. The police lieutenant dismissed his men and, in accented English, told the two CID agents, "Gentlemen, he's all yours."

The shorter and older of the two stepped forward. "Captain Lucius Buckhorn," he said. His voice was not loud, but harsh. He indicated the other. "My associate, Staff Sergeant Ed Carter. Take a seat."

Lightner sat down. Buckhorn took a cigarette from a silver case, and offered one to Lightner; he declined.

For a moment, no one spoke. Buckhorn lit his cigarette and took a drag, then jabbed two fingers at Lightner. "Son, you are in a world of shit."

"I understand, sir."

"I don't think you do, lieutenant. I don't think you have the faintest inkling of just how deep in the shit you are." He tapped the ash off his smoke. "Let me explain the facts of life. That young man you were diddling in the latrine is the nephew of the local archbishop. Word is he's been tapped for cardinal, and will probably be in the Vatican by the end of the year. Very prominent family. The kind of family that can make things very difficult for the local authorities, and for the US Army. Are you starting to get the picture?"

Lightner was numb with shock. He'd had no idea. Fabrizio had never talked about his family. The school was prestigious, he knew, but he had assumed Fabrizio was there on an academic scholarship.

"The family has high expectations for that young man," said Buckhorn. "The last thing they want is a scandal like this. They are ready to press charges of rape." He crushed out the cigarette.

Lightner could not speak.

"Is it all coming together for you, Lieutenant?" Buckhorn said in a steely voice. "It's gonna be very hard for us to convince the Italian government not to lock you away for twenty years for child molestation."

"Rough customers in these Italian prisons," said Carter, speaking for the first time. He was a big man, heavyset, with a prominent gut. "Mafia types, a lot of them. None too fond of kiddy-fiddlers, the way I hear."

"Not to mention the damage this affair might do to the US mission here," Buckhorn went on, as if Carter had not spoken. "There are political factions that would love to see Italy pull out of NATO and have the United States government kiss their ass goodbye on the way out. Locals don't like when we fraternize with them. We're tolerated here, and that's on a good day."

"Ask me, the army's best off washing its hands of the whole thing," rumbled Carter.

Buckhorn said nothing; only fixed Lightner with a cool, contemptuous stare.

Lightner raised his head. "I have information," he said. "Valuable information. In exchange for a deal."

"Selling out your pimp's not good enough," began Carter, but Buckhorn raised a hand to silence him.

"I'm listening."

"Captain David Alexander."

"What about him?"

"He's a traitor."

"That's a serious accusation," said Buckhorn, settling back in his chair. "A very serious accusation, Lieutenant. You really don't want to add lying to superior officers to the child molestation charges, do you? I can honestly tell you that Leavenworth will not be any kinder or gentler to you than an Italian prison."

"I have proof."

Buckhorn leaned forward.

"Physical evidence?" asked Carter.

"Tape recordings and a notebook."

The two CID agents looked at each other. "Are these items in your possession?" asked Carter.

"Not at the moment," said Lightner. "But I can lead you to them."

Buckhorn nodded, and Lightner thought he saw just the smallest hint of a smile. "Let me make a phone call."

After Buckhorn made the call, they waited for nearly an hour. Lightner refused to speak any further, and after a while Buckhorn and Carter stopped trying to make him. Buckhorn smoked three cigarettes. Carter talked to the police lieutenant, who arranged for coffee to be sent up, and they drank and smoked in silence.

Shortly before midnight, Buckhorn ushered in a well-dressed civilian. "Lieutenant Lightner, this is Mr. Stetner of the US State Department. He would like to hear more about your story."

"I would like some guarantees," Lightner said.

"What sort of guarantees?" Stetner asked.

"Make this all go away."

Stetner sucked his teeth. "That's a very tall order, Lieutenant."

"Can you deliver?"

Stetner looked at him like a jeweler appraising a gem of doubtful provenance. "I've talked to army brass. If your information pans out, I am prepared to guarantee that you will serve no prison time, either here or in the States, after a dishonorable discharge from the army."

"Not good enough," said Lightner. "A general discharge, at least. I've earned benefits—"

Stetner's eyes went cold. "Don't push your luck, soldier. You should be grateful you're not facing a court martial. The best you're getting is a dishonorable discharge—and even that depends on just how good your proof is."

"Oh, it's good, Mr. Stetner," said Lightner with a tight smile. "It is very good."

"Captain Buckhorn," Stetner said. "Bring in Lieutenant Marini, if you don't mind. I'd like to have a little chat with him."

Buckhorn did as he was ordered; it was obvious Stetner was now in charge.

After a moment, the police lieutenant—Marini—knocked at the door. Stetner excused himself and stepped out of the interrogation room to talk to Marini in the corridor.

Buckhorn and Carter kept post by the door, staring at Lightner with frank loathing. The discussion outside was growing heated; both Marini and Stetner had their voices raised, but Lightner could not make out what they were saying.

After a few minutes, the two men came in together. "The lieutenant here has agreed to release you into our custody," said Stetner. "He is also placing two of his police officers at our disposal.

"Time to deliver, Lightner," said Buckhorn, handing him his coat and hat. "Tell us where we're going."

As Dan Lightner led the other five men to the apartment house, he felt his heart begin to race. His breath quickened, wondering if Nick Ferrara had already removed the evidence. The little son of a bitch had a paranoid streak: If word had gotten around that Lightner had been arrested, he would try to cover his tracks and run. They were in a race against time.

Lightner wondered if Nick had known about Fabrizio's family connections before he'd introduced them. It seemed unlikely. The boys and girls he had turned out over the last year had always been nobodies—common street hustlers, or poverty cases like Alexander's little virgin. No one that anyone would miss if things went bad; Nick was too careful for that. Fabrizio must have deceived Nick, just as he had deceived Lightner. He felt a little pang of heartbreak, then shook his head to clear it. He had no time to feel sorry for himself.

They were near the apartment house. Lightner looked up at the fourth-floor window and saw it still dark. Perhaps they still had a chance after all.

They entered the lobby, talking among themselves in English and Italian, making no attempt at stealth, and

Lightner immediately cast his glance up the staircase. On the landing, a figure was disappearing around the corner, partially obscured by the turn in the stairs. Lightner caught a glimpse of the shoes: black-and-white wingtips.

"That's the pimp!" he shouted. "That's Nick Ferrara, on the landing!"

Police and CID agents swarmed for the stairwell. Nick dashed full-tilt up the stairs. He had a two-floor head start; time enough, Lightner thought, to reach the fourth-floor flat, grab the evidence, and vanish out the window before they had a chance to break down the door. But one of the cops, a local *carabiniere* by the look of him, was bounding up the stairs two at a time, his sidearm already drawn.

Nick's key was in the apartment door when the first cop rounded the far corner of the corridor, with Lightner right behind. Nick was pale, and Lightner saw from his wild eyes that he did not mean to be taken alive. Nick crossed to the hallway window without pausing, wrenched it open, and exited to the cold night air.

"He's gone down the fire escape!" Buckhorn shouted. "Carter, cut him off!"

Lightner moved to the open window. In the half-dark below, he could see Nick creeping down the rickety iron steps as quickly as he dared, for they were slick with ice. As he went, he drew a small automatic from his raincoat.

"Carter, look out!" Lightner called. "He's got a gun!"

Nick glanced upward from the fire escape, locking eyes with Lightner for a moment in a glare of pure hatred. Then he leaped to the alley below. He landed hard; Lightner thought he might be injured, but he scrambled to his feet just as Carter charged around the corner, panting like a racehorse, pistol in his hand.

"Stop, or I'll shoot!" Carter yelled in English.

Nick ran. Carter, taking position in the mouth of the alley, fired once, catching him in the left arm. From the window, Lightner could see Nick, spun by the impact, falling back against the fence that cut off the alleyway to the adjacent apartment house. Then Nick raised his little automatic and fired blindly, sending Carter ducking for cover—only for a moment, but it was enough; Nick boosted himself, scrambled over the fence, and disappeared into the darkness.

Lightner felt Buckhorn's hand on his sleeve, pulling him away from the window. "Come on, lieutenant," Buckhorn snapped. "Leave that punk for the beat cops. You and I have bigger fish to fry."

Stetner stood in the center of the room, his hat in his hand, checking the layout of the apartment. He saw Buckhorn coming in from the corridor, leading Lightner by the arm, and nodded in satisfaction. "Secure the door! Nobody touches anything," he rumbled. "Not until Carter gets back with the pimp."

The *carabinieri* took position, one just inside the door, the other in the hallway. Stetner looked around the apartment. Bedroom, sitting room; half-bath, the sink spotted with rust; galley kitchen, unused, with liquor bottles on the sideboard and blank spaces where the stove and icebox would have been. The furniture was nicer than he would have expected for a whore's crib. The sofa, chairs, and ottomans were inexpensive, but well-made, with only the slightest hint of sag in the springs.

Stetner glanced over at Buckhorn; it was plain that he, too, was taking in the details. "Kept the place clean, didn't he?" said Buckhorn. "Floor swept, bar well stocked, bed made up nice and neat. Even a bookshelf for your reading pleasure."

"All the comforts," snorted Stetner. He looked at Lightner; the lieutenant was standing with his hands in his pockets, staring at his shoes. Overcome with shame, Stetner imagined—assuming he still had a shred of decency.

Just then Sergeant Carter appeared in the doorway, still out of breath.

"What happened, Carter?"

"The little greasy son of a bitch shot at me, sir," panted Carter. "I shot back. I think I hit him."

"And?"

"Then the little prick jumped the fence and took off down the other alley."

"And why didn't you pursue him, Sergeant?"

Carter patted his bulging belly. "Sorry, Mr. Stetner—but for the past ten years I've been married to an Italian woman who loves to feed me. My fence-jumping days are long gone."

Stetner was seething, but bit his tongue; he did not want to start a confrontation there with CID. "All right. If we're all secure, then it's time for Lieutenant Lightner to deliver the goods."

Lightner looked up, swallowed hard, and nodded.

"First, walk us through how you came by your infor mation."

"Yes, sir." Lightner came to a posture of attention, looking straight ahead. "We were last here with Nick Ferraro on Monday night, the third of January. It was myself, Fabrizio, Captain Alexander, and a fifteen-year-old girl. I didn't catch her name, but I know Captain Alexander was excited about having her because she was a virgin."

Stetner saw that the CID officers were staring daggers at Lightner. If he recalled correctly, Buckhorn had a fifteen-year-old daughter back in the states. "Continue, Lieutenant."

"Yes, sir. Captain Alexander took the young lady into the bedroom, which left Fabrizio and me out here."

"And?"

"Fabrizio said he needed to show me something." Lightner walked over to one of the ottomans and lifted off its top. Inside was a tape recorder, a reel of tape still spooled through.

"The boy showed you this?"

"He's a very observant young man," said Lightner. Buckhorn snorted.

Stetner knelt down to examine the recorder. He rewound the tape for a few seconds and hit play. A thin, crackly voice issued from the tiny speaker:

—raids next week. Several locations. I don't have the details yet, but I'll get them to you by this time next week. But you're gonna have to give me something in return.

"American accent," mused Stetner. Then to Buckhorn: "You figure it's Alexander?"

Buckhorn shrugged. "We'll need a full forensic analysis to be sure.

"It's him, all right," said Lightner.

"Well, Lieutenant, if we can confirm that it's actually Captain Alexander's voice on the recordings, we may have a deal."

"But there's more, Mr. Stetner." Lightner walked over to the bookshelf. He ran his hands over the books, feeling for something. When he found it, he tugged, and the spines of three books came away—a false façade, camouflaging a panel that opened to reveal a small cabinet. Stetner stepped over and looked in the cabinet. There were several more tape reels inside, at least a half-dozen.

"I'm quite sure if you listen to these tapes, you'll find other evidence of Captain Alexander giving details of the raids to Nick Ferrara."

Captain Buckhorn interjected. "And are *you* on any of these tapes, Lieutenant?"

Lightner swallowed hard. "I'm pretty sure I am, sir. And it's embarrassing stuff." Then he stood a little straighter. "But I'm not the one giving any details of Army activities."

"Anything else, Lieutenant?"

"Yes, Mr. Stetner." Lightner reached over the opposite end of the bookshelf and pulled out another book. It appeared to be a diary. He handed it to Stetner. "I can't read Russian," he said, "but I'm hoping you can."

Stetner began to leaf through the book. His Russian was rusty, but adequate to glean a few details. He looked up at Lightner. "We'll need time to analyze these. But if this information is authentic—" He slammed the book shut. "Yes, I believe we can make a deal. It won't be easy—that young man's family has some clout—but we'll see what we can do."

"Will you need a deposition from me, sir?"

"I'll talk to some of my counterparts at the FBI and let you know. Our first step is to clear up the paperwork back at police headquarters. You will be remanded to CID custody in the meantime, and not the local jail." Stetner looked at the lieutenant, seeing him for a moment as just a man in over his head, half-dead with fatigue and worry. "You've just dodged a very big bullet, son. And despite yourself, it appears you've done your country a great service."

Dan Lightner beamed; Stetner thought it was the most pathetic thing he'd ever seen.

"Get him out of here," Stetner growled. Carter nodded and grabbed Lightner by the collar.

Buckhorn sidled up to Stetner. "How should we proceed, sir?"

"Keep him locked down," Stetner said. "And put a tail on this Captain Alexander. I suspect we'll be taking him into protective custody before too long. I'll need confirmation from State, but it's plain that this Nick Ferrara—whatever his real name—is a damn sight worse than a pimp. He's spent a year cultivating two American officers as foreign assets."

Buckhorn whistled low. "Hell of a world," he said.

"Hell of a world," echoed Stetner. "To think that one of our biggest breaks in this cold war comes thanks to a couple of perverts who couldn't keep it in their pants."

8

CORTINA, ITALY—MIRAMONTE HOTEL

FRIDAY, JANUARY 7, 1955
7:00 AM

When Ernesto Bianchi walked into the Miramonte's dining hall, he spotted Victoria Shannon immediately. How could he miss her? Long and lovely, already dressed for skiing, she sat by a window, looking out at the snow, her breakfast on the table before her.

He settled into the chair opposite her. "*Ciao*, Victoria."

"Good morning, Ernesto." She gestured to her frittata and toasted bread with olive oil, already half-eaten. "Have you had anything?"

"I have already had breakfast, thank you," he said. A waiter materialized unbidden by Ernesto's side, carrying a tray with two espressos. "But there is always room for a cup of coffee."

Ernesto sipped his coffee, wondering how to begin. Mario had telephoned him with the news, of course, and he was enraged on her behalf. Personally, he wanted to smack that son of a bitch Sebastian in the face and throw him off a mountain. He could have managed it, too; though he was half a foot shorter than Sebastian and almost twenty years older, he was all muscle. His face was weathered, and he had callused hands, not soft from counting money all day. No one knew the Dolomites like Ernesto Bianchi. If he had taken it into his head to dispose of Sebastian Bossard, no one would ever find the body.

But that was impossible, of course. The Miramonte Hotel and the Bossard family had a long and nefarious history together. Regardless, the boy couldn't keep doing this to women, especially this one. She was kind and friendly to the staff, and her Italian was exceptionally good. She was a nurse, a professional. The other two—they were nothing. They had acted with arrogance comparable to Sebastian's own. Those two got what they deserved, he thought; but this one—he cursed Sebastian Bossard silently and sighed.

"I am happy that you decide to stay," he said in English. "Truly happy. You know I need to practice my English, and you are a very good teacher."

"It takes one to know one," she said.

He gazed at her warm smile. Sebastian Bossard had never deserved her, he thought. Victoria would have been perfect for his son Mauricio, who had died two years ago in an avalanche. They would both be twenty-five now.

Ernesto looked out into the snow. When his wife Esterina died of tuberculosis, he'd had to raise Mauricio from the age ten by himself, with some help from an elderly aunt. Mauricio grew into a fine, healthy young man; following in his father's footsteps, he had become an avid climber and skier. Two years ago, he was guiding four French tourists, novice climbers all, up a col approaching Tofana de Rozes when the avalanche hit. All five were lost, their bodies recovered the next day.

For a moment, he thought he heard Mauricio's voice; then he realized that it was Victoria's.

"Ernesto? It's snowing pretty hard," she said. "Will we be skiing today?"

"*Perdonami,* Victoria," he said. "You catch me daydreaming. I'm an old man, you know."

He saw questions behind her eyes, but she only smiled. "How am I doing so far?"

"Exceptionally, for one who has been skiing for only three days."

"Don't tease!"

"Signorina Shannon," Ernesto began, trying to sound like a pompous professor, "in all my years as a ski instructor, never have I had a student such as you."

Victoria made a face. "Answer the question, Ernesto."

He sighed. "You lack experience, of course, but you're truly negotiating your turns well. Most of all, you need to work on control on steeper terrain. Today will be a good day to work on that. It will also help to teach you to ski in different conditions."

Just then the army contingent came into the dining hall with their camp followers and were seated. Ernesto rolled his eyes. "Don't look now," he said. "Trouble." Victoria giggled.

Gigi, seeing Ernesto with the long-legged beauty, excused himself from the group. "*Ciao*, Ernesto!"

Ernesto stood and embraced the soldier, who he had known since 1944—a lifetime ago. "How are you, you arrogant son of a bitch?" he said in Italian—then cringed as he remembered Victoria was fluent in Italian.

"Well," Gigi said, finding it hard not to stare at Victoria. "I came to say hello, and to get a closer look at this apparition."

"And that?" Ernesto pointed with his head in the general direction of the table where everyone was sitting.

"Last night's conquest," Gigi beamed. "Once again the Italian flag was planted on foreign soil."

Ernesto snorted a laugh and Victoria giggled.

Gigi's faced reddened as the realization dawned. "You mean she speaks Italian? I was told she was an American!" He took off his hat. "Signorina, you have me at a disadvantage. The commanding officer has been caught with faulty intelligence."

Ernesto continued in Italian, "Signorina Shannon, meet Colonel Pasquale, the leader of that bunch of brigands over there."

"The pleasure is all mine," Gigi said in proper English, giving his most dashing smile.

Their eyes locked and Ernesto broke the moment with a cough, "Where are you climbing today?"

"Tofana di Rozes." Gigi returned to Italian, the mood broken.

Ernesto whistled and commented, "In this weather? Bad idea." Tofana di Rozes was where Mauricio died—and that was under ideal conditions. There was a blizzard coming; Ernesto could feel it in his bones.

Gigi was nonchalant. "We can always bivouac up on the rock shelf, if need be."

"Really?" Ernesto pressed. "What if the storm lasts for days? And what about the threat of an avalanche?"

"Perhaps you're right."

"How about the Ra di Valla?" Ernesto suggested, "It's well-protected."

"We did that yesterday."

"Yes, but not in these conditions," Ernesto responded. "The southeast col will be completely different in heavy snow. That's challenge enough for any mountaineer."

Gigi brightened. "A splendid idea," he said. Then he nodded toward the far table. "My friends are waiting," he said. "But I hope you will stop by our table before you go. I have an American friend I'd like you to meet."

Ernesto said they would, and he and Victoria reseated themselves. "You must forgive Colonel Pasquale," he said. "He's a good man, and a good soldier, but sometimes he simply cannot behave himself."

"Boys will be boys," Victoria said dismissively.

Ernesto grunted his approval and finished his espresso. "You will need more clothing and eye wear to protect you from the heavy snow. If you are finished with your breakfast, I have what you need at the ski shack."

"Let's go," she said.

"On the way, we'll say hello to Jo-Jo, Tony, the Americano and their—what is the word—their concubines."

Victoria laughed. She put on her ski jacket and headband and joined Ernesto as he marched over to the table full of brigands and their camp followers.

Tony and Jo-Jo jumped up to greet the old man—as did the Americano, who seemed to regard him as a living legend. Ernesto wasn't sure how he felt about being a museum piece.

The next few minutes were a flurry of handshakes and introductions; the soldiers introduced themselves to Victoria, Gigi introduced their good friend, Captain Johnny Gillespie. Tony introduced the Englishwomen to Ernesto and Victoria, Ernesto introduced Victoria to everyone else.

They were all eating bacon and eggs with pancakes. "Where on earth did you get all this?" asked Victoria.

"All courtesy of Captain Gillespie," beamed Gigi. "He came in from Camp Darby with his jeep piled high. A case each of pancake mix, bacon, and powdered eggs. along with a case each of Johnnie Walker Red, American cigarettes, and chocolate bars. The lad takes care of his friends."

Johnny shrugged. "It was a big deal me getting invited here, is all," he said. "I wasn't about to show up empty-handed.

As student and pupil walked out of the dining hall, the group finished breakfast; the ladies had to get back to town. As for the mountaineers, they resigned themselves to tackling Tofana de Rozes some other day. They would head to the col on the southeast side of Ra da Vila, knowing the old son of a bitch was right.

9

RA DI VALLA, DOLOMITES

FRIDAY, JANUARY 7, 1955
11:00 AM

The four mountaineers huddled together about halfway up the col. They had to shout to hear each other with the winds at seventy miles an hour. Discretion was proving to be the better part of valor; the group decided to descend before the weather got any worse. They glissaded down to where they had left their skis, finding them nearly buried, and headed back to Cortina.

Meanwhile, Ernesto and Victoria were retreating to the ski shack. Conditions were deteriorating quickly; there would be no more skiing this day. Toto, a sixteen-year-old who kept the shack in order and maintained the skis and equipment as a courtesy for the guests, took the skis from Ernesto and Victoria. Victoria was thankful for Ernesto's foresight in fitting her out with a hooded anorak and goggles. Without them, she could never have managed what little skiing they had done that day.

Ernesto looked out the window to the northwest. "Will they be okay?" Victoria asked, sensing the old man's concern.

"If anybody could, it will be those four," he said. "They have Satan's luck." Seeing Victoria shiver, he said, "But now I must ensure that my prized pupil does not become ill." The smile was genuine as he took her by the arm, guiding her to the hotel in the roaring wind and snow.

"What's your remedy for freezing?" Victoria sniffed.

Ernesto guided her toward the fireplace, where he took off her snow-covered boots. She felt her frozen toes begin to thaw, and opened her ski jacket to let in the warmth.

"Go upstairs and put on different socks and shoes, then return," Ernesto ordered. "I'll have a treat for you at the bar when you get back."

Victoria complied. When she returned Ernesto was sitting at the bar with a steaming mug and a tall glass of water. "Water first," he said. "Then the caffè Italiano."

Victoria sucked down the water; between the altitude and cold, she was dehydrated. She asked for another glass, drinking more slowly. Midway through her third glass, she had to excuse herself to the ladies' room—a good sign.

When she returned, she sipped the caffè Italiano; it was sweet and strong, with a kick. Ernesto ordered her a second coffee, along with a bowl of minestrone for lunch.

Satisfied, she pushed her bowl away. She yawned. "I can't believe I'm so sleepy after all that coffee," she said.

"It has been a hard day," said Ernesto. "You need rest more than anything. You should have a nap, then an early dinner. The soup will not hold you for very long."

"I like that idea," she said. Then, feeling suddenly awkward, she blurted, "Ernesto, would you join me for dinner?"

Ernesto smiled sadly. "Your offer is most kind, but I must decline," he said. "It would be inappropriate for a guest to dine with an employee at the hotel. More importantly, I have an elderly aunt—she is at home by herself, and is becoming feeble in the mind. She could easily become disoriented in the blizzard if she went outside to try and get firewood."

"Poor woman!"

"If anything should happen to her, I could never live with myself."

"I understand. I hope I haven't offended you."

"Not at all," he smiled. "It is only the difficulty of turning down an invitation from a beautiful woman."

With that, he departed to check on his aunt, and Victoria went up to take her nap.

While Victoria napped, the mountaineers had made it back to the Montana Hotel. The women were amazed at how quickly they recovered. When they entered, they looked like death warmed over, covered in snow, faces tinged with blue and ice-cold. Sitting by the fire and drinking what seemed like gallons of water, they were soon back to their old frisky selves, wanting to pick up where they'd left off last night.

But first, food! Between the four of them, they devoured a bowl of pasta large enough for twelve people, along with a loaf of Pugliese bread and two bottles of wine.

Beatrix piped up, "You fellows look like you're all ready for a siesta."

"Probably," Johnny countered. "Unless something else pops up." He smiled wolfishly.

"Right," said Beatrix, taking on Gigi's commanding tone. "It's now 1305 by my watch." She paced around as she continued. "I'm in room 36, Stephanie is right below me in 26, Marjorie is next to me in 34, and Portia is below her in 24. Gentlemen, at 1315 you are to knock on your respective doors and enter. Do you understand your mission?"

"Roger!" the four men answered in unison.

The women giggled as they ran up the stairs. The four mountaineers stared after them in disbelief.

"Why can't it always be this easy?" Tony asked.

"Maybe we're still on the mountain and having a delusional dream due to hypothermia?" Jo-Jo thought out loud.

"If that's true, then what a way to go," Johnny said.

"Right, chaps," barked Gigi, using an even-thicker-than-normal British accent. "Major Novinonte, please inform us when it's 1314."

Jo-Jo nodded.

"At that time," continued Gigi, "the first wave, consisting of myself and Captain Gillespie, will march double-time to our individual objectives. Thirty seconds later, the second wave, consisting of Majors Pagnozzi and Novinonte, will proceed to their individual objectives."

"Understood, sir!" they said in unison.

"Well done, Colonel," said Johnny.

"Best to leave nothing to chance, I thought," said Gigi.

At 1314, Jo-Jo announced, "Time!"

"Right!" Gigi ordered. First wave, double-time, *harch*!" He and Johnny began to jog up the stairs, followed thirty seconds later by Jo-Jo and Tony.

From somewhere behind him, Johnny heard Tony yell, "God save the Queen!"

Standing before room 36, Johnny knocked and entered. He smiled at what he saw; standing by the balcony door was Beatrix, wearing a sheer full length dressing gown with nothing underneath and a pair of gold-colored mules. She gave a little twirl.

Then Johnny was struck with a thought of horror. He smacked his forehead "Damn, I don't have any condoms."

"Not to worry, darling, I've put in my cap." Beatrix smiled.

Johnny looked confused.

"You'd call it a diaphragm, I think." Beatrix walked to Johnny and wrapped her arms around him. Time stood still as they kissed.

Suddenly, there was a knock on Beatrix's door. "Beatrix, darling, are you at home?" came a faint voice. A man's voice, British, slightly nasal. "It's Basil, darling. Will you unlock the door?"

The lovers looked at each other in horror. *Who is that?* Johnny mouthed.

My fiancé, Beatrix mouthed back. Aloud, she cried weakly "I've just gone to the loo, dear. I won't be a moment."

There would be time to be angry later, Johnny thought. His first order of business was to get out of sight until Beatrix could get rid of her fiancé. Without a sound, Johnny made his way out onto the balcony, thanking fate that he was still fully dressed and carrying his outerwear in a bundle. Beatrix exchanged her sheer dressing gown for a terrycloth bathrobe and closed the balcony door silently behind him. and went to greet her fiancé.

It was snowing heavier now, and the wind on the balcony was fierce. Johnny slipped into his sweater and anorak as he heard Beatrix say loudly, "Basil! You came to join me! How romantic."

"I couldn't bear it another minute without you, darling," said the nasal voice. "They're shutting down everything on account of the beastly weather. I had to pay the sleigh driver extra to bring me here from the rail station, the cretin."

"How dashing of you, darling," said Beatrix. "And how brave."

She was really laying it on thick, thought Johnny, as he pulled on his gloves and wool watch cap.

"I say, this place is situated up awfully high," said Basil. Johnny realized with horror that Basil's voice was drawing nearer to the balcony. "I've got a jolly idea to see what this blizzard looks like from this elevation."

"*No!*" shouted Beatrix. "The wind is just horrible. We ran into some mountain climbers in the bar. They warned us of the danger. You might be blown off the balcony."

Johnny knew he was running out of time; Beatrix was trying to buy him some—not for his sake but hers—but she couldn't hold out much longer.

"Mountain climbers, you say?" said Basil. "How frightfully interesting. Are they here in the hotel? Perhaps I might buy them a drink. I do so want to talk to them."

"I'll see what I can do," Beatrix said nervously.

"Now, I simply must see what the blizzard looks like from this height." Basil's hand was on the door latch.

Beatrix screamed, "*No!*", but too late. Basil was on the balcony. She followed him out; there was no sign of anyone.

"Most impressive," said Basil. "You're right about that wind, though, darling. I wouldn't want to be out in that for long. Let's go back in and get you in some proper clothes, eh?"

They stepped back inside and closed the balcony door behind them, neither seeing the climbing rope looped around the right side of the balcony's railing.

Johnny had fed both ends of his climbing rope around the railing, then climbed over the rail with his pack on his back and both hands on the rope. He had jumped off the railing just as the doors flew open. Relaxing the grip of his gloved hands on the rope, he let the momentum carry him safely onto the balcony below Beatrix's. He hoped he was correct in remembering that it was Stephanie's.

He landed with a thud on his feet and heard a familiar voice exclaim, "What the fuck?" Tony's voice. Yep, it was the right balcony.

"Tony, it's me," Johnny called softly, pulling the free end of the rope.

Tony opened the door and stared. "Johnny?" he said. He was wearing only the bottoms of his long underwear. "What kind of weird shit is Beatrix into now?"

"Her fiancé showed up, that's what happened," Johnny grumbled as he walked into Stephanie's room, the snow and the cold in his wake.

Stephanie was in the bed with the bottom sheet drawn up around her both for modesty and warmth. She stared without a word.

"Say again," Tony asked, both amused and annoyed. Johnny noticed that his long underwear bottoms were on backward.

"Basil, Beatrix's fiancé, just showed up." Johnny said, coiling up the climbing rope. "I had to rappel off her balcony to get here."

Stephanie began to laugh. "Oh, how like Basil," she said. "He follows Beatrix around like a lost little puppy. He's completely paralyzed without her."

"So, this was totally unexpected?" Tony asked her. "Can I expect *your* fiancé to show up, too?"

"I don't have a fiancé," Stephanie said. "Well, not technically."

"Sounds like you and I need to have a discussion," Tony grunted. "In the meantime, let me get dressed, and we'll grab the other two *ciucci* and head back to the Miramonte."

"No," shouted Stephanie and Johnny in unison.

"Why should everyone have to suffer because of my rotten luck?" Johnny said. "Besides, do you really want to leave this poor beautiful woman alone on a night like this?" He pointed to Stephanie, who was pouting pitifully. She had also absently let the sheet drop when she thought Tony might leave, exposing a pair of round, firm breasts that doubtlessly made Tony's decision less complicated.

With his rope coil and secured to his pack, Johnny gave the lovers an exaggerated and dramatic bow. "Proceed with you mission, Major," he said, the exited the room to the sound of laughter.

Reaching the lobby, he headed to the bar. Alfredo's face was shocked. "Capitan Johnny," he said, pouring out a scotch. "You must be a magician! When that Englishman came in, I thought you were done for."

"I didn't even get a look at him," Johnny admitted. "Big fella?"

Alfredo waved his hand. "Big sideways, maybe."

"Look like he could take me in a fight?"

"Only on a day when you almost die on a mountain."

"Well," said Johnny, gulping down his drink, "let's hope my luck holds."

He slammed his glass down on the bar, slipped four 100-lira notes into Alfredo's hand, and vanished into the blizzard before the old man could protest. It was, Alfredo said later, just like in the movies.

Once outside, Johnny strapped on his skis and began the mile-and-a-half trek back to the Miramonte Hotel. *Caught out in a raging blizzard,* he thought: *Why, it's just like being back home in Wyoming.*

It took Johnny nearly forty-five minutes to reach the Miramonte. By the time he got in, he was exhausted and freezing. Toto was in the lobby when he saw Johnny. "Capitan Cowboy," he cried. "Everyone, come quick! Captain Gillespie needs help!"

Toto grabbed Johnny's skis and poles and Pepe, one of the bellhops, came over with a small glass of brandy. Mario bustled out of his office. "What happened?" he asked. "Where are the others?"

"Everyone's safe," Johnny reassured him in Italian, sipping his brandy. "No search party needed. They're safe at the Montana Hotel with the Englishwomen from last night."

"So, what happened to the little spitfire you were with last night" asked Toto in Italian. "Why aren't you there?"

"Her fiancé showed up." Johnny drained his glass.

The small crowd—Mario, Toto, Pepe, and Carlo the bartender—all howled with laughter. Their relief was evident as they escorted him into the bar for more details—and more brandy.

A half-hour later, after two more brandies and a healthy amount of water, Johnny finished the sordid details his adventure. The group of listeners grew larger as he told the tale, drawing several regular patrons of the hotel bar. Several portions of the story had to be repeated as the group grew and staff members wandered in and out as their duties permitted.

"I think you are no more Capitan Cowboy," said Toto. "From now on, I think you are Capitan Batman!"

With his new title was secured with cheers and toasts in the annals of the Miramonte Hotel, Johnny bade the crowd farewell and went upstairs to rest. The trip had not been easy; his body had stiffened up. and he was exhausted.

10

CORTINA, ITALY—MIRAMONTE HOTEL

FRIDAY, JANUARY 7, 1955
4:00 PM

It was around four o'clock when Victoria finally woke. She felt well-rested, but stiff from sleeping on the couch; she still could not bring herself to sleep in that bed. Instead of taking a shower, Victoria decided on a bubble bath, soaking the soreness and cold out of her body. Afterward she washed her hair and redid her nails.

Again, she found it difficult to figure out what to wear. What *would* a jilted lover wear to dinner while on a ski holiday, surrounded by Italian two-legged wolves? Last night's outfit seemed to provoke a lot of interest from the patrons and the staff—along with some sneers from the female guests at the hotel. She wondered what they were thinking. *An Americana comes in with a rich Swiss playboy; he leaves with his father, and she stays.* The most logical explanation, she thought, would be that she was a high-priced hooker. *That's what they're thinking.*

She shook her head and decided on a tight black buttoned-down sweater, black-and-red plaid wool slacks, double-pleated and narrow at the ankles, and her ballet flats. Thus attired, she headed to the bar for a cocktail before dinner.

The bar was crowded, and all the tables were taken. There was not much for the guests to do with the blizzard raging outside. Questioning eyes followed her as she took a seat at the bar itself, which was mostly empty. She considered playing the role to the hilt by ordering a champagne cocktail, but decided to stick with scotch, neat. Carlo refused to pour her a well scotch, running instead to Mario's office to pour from his private stash of Johnnie Walker Black. *The glamorous life of a hooker,* Victoria thought. *Wonder what I should charge.*

She did not have to wonder long, as an overweight gentleman of about forty came up and started a conversation with her. His name was Silvio Brunetti, he said; he was a stationery and paper goods salesman. He had heard Victoria speaking both Italian and English and wished to practice his English, he said, as he leered at her cleavage. As he stared, Victoria saw his left temporal artery begin to pulse. *Hope I don't give Chubby here a heart attack,* she thought.

The question swiftly became moot as a shrill female voice shouted, "SILVIO!" It was Signora Brunetti, all five feet, two inches of her, standing at the entrance of the bar. She held two young girls by the hands, perhaps two and three years old, probably wondering why Mama was so angry. Marching into the bar with the girls in tow, she lit into Silvio with a tirade in Italian so rapid and fierce that even Victoria could not follow it. It reminded her of her mother when Tommy Sr. would come home from the bars at three in the morning. She did, however, understand when Signora Brunetti called her a *puttana*.

"*Basta!*" Victoria held up her free hand, pausing Signora Brunetti in mid-harangue. In her native Hell's Kitchen accent, she scoffed, "That's 'high-priced hooker' to you, signora," then saluted the loving couple with her drink,

Both the Brunettis now turned red and hastily left the bar, leading their children, Signora Brunetti loudly questioning the integrity of the hotel as she went.

Carlo, who has been chuckling behind the bar, applauded Victoria. The curious onlookers in the bar quickly returned to their own business.

"Any word on the climbers?" Victoria asked, remembering that the band of brigands had gone out in the howling storm.

"They're safe," said Carlo. "All over at the Hotel Montana with their English women." A look of sly amusement came across his face. "Well … *almost* all."

Victoria leaned on the bar. "Okay, Carlo—spill it. I can tell there's a story here. And with that crew, it's bound to be entertaining, at least."

While Carlo told Victoria of Johnny's misadventures, Johnny himself was stepping out of the shower, tired, angry, and disgusted with himself. Why did he always wind up in these situations? Three months ago, in Rome, it was the Scottish nurse married to the America MP sergeant; Six months ago, in Livorno, it was the American fashion editor whose fiancé was the nephew of some congressman from Kansas; and a year ago—

A year ago, it was Daphne. Daphne, the black-haired beauty with hazel green eyes. Daphne, the gymnast, five-foot-nothing in her socks. Daphne the graceful. Daphne the poised. Daphne, who had nearly gotten him court martialed—the reason for his last-chance exile to Italy.

Johnny had met Daphne Bridges in Lone Pine, California, while he was teaching a course in winter mountaineering and survival at altitudes, leading a group of army officers on a three-day trek on and around Mt. Whitney. Unfortunately, one of the lieutenants in the group broke his ankle during the final ascent and had to be carried off the mountain; heavy snows and wind wouldn't allow for a helicopter rescue.

These heroics led to media attention, and Johnny was enlisted for several interviews with local newspapers and broadcast outlets. This led to his chance meeting with Daphne in the green room of Lone Pine's radio station. She and several of her UCLA classmates were barnstorming Northern California and the Napa Valley on a goodwill tour to promote women's athletics at the high-school and collegiate levels. They talked for hours after their on-air interviews, and several of the lieutenants invited Daphne and her teammates for drinks that evening.

During their shared evening out, Daphne became infatuated. It wasn't even Johnny's good looks so much as his matter-of-fact attitude about the rescue. He made it sound like another day in the office. Finding out he grew up in Wyoming made it all the better.

Afterward, Johnny did not give it another thought—until Daphne showed up at the barracks a week later wanting to see him. He took her to dinner at the officer's club, and Daphne told him that she was working on her second degree in kinesiology, which insured her scholarship eligibility at UCLA. She would also be competing in Olympic gymnastics trials in November, vying for a spot on the US women's team for the 1956 games in Melbourne. She stayed the night, and being that it was Friday she wound up spending the entire weekend with him; miraculously, she had packed a suitcase, which pleased him very much.

This went on for four weeks, but went sour on the fifth weekend. They were out to dinner at a cowboy bar when Daphne's boyfriend Tom Reynolds, an assistant coach for the men's gymnastics team at UCLA, approached the couple. Johnny tried to explain to the irate Tom that he had no idea that Daphne had a boyfriend, but Tom wasn't listening. The man must have had a Napoleon complex, Johnny thought, because—although in excellent shape—he stood just five-four, and only became more enraged when Johnny stood up to his full height of six foot one.

Despite multiple attempts at reasoned reconciliation, it was evident that all Tom wanted to do was fight. He launched himself at Johnny, trusting his athletic physique to carry him to victory. Unfortunately for him, Johnny's easy-going demeanor was deceptive; he not only had the advantage of reach—he was an Army Ranger, a trained hand-to-hand combatant. The fight was short and decisive. When the dust settled, Tom was flat on the barroom floor, writhing in pain with a dislocated shoulder, calling Daphne a bitch and a whore. She stood there crying as they took him away in an ambulance.

Soon afterward, Johnny was called down before his superiors. Army brass were never happy when there was an altercation between an officer and a civilian, of course, but the circumstances here were especially troubling: Tom had been a likely contender for the men's US Olympic gymnastics team, and the shoulder injury was enough to disqualify him. An inquiry was launched. Eyewitnesses confirmed Johnny's account of the night in question, and ultimately no charges were filed; but UCLA faculty protested the decision as unjust, characterizing the incident as an example the military's fascist attitude toward American civilians.

To appease this vocal minority, Johnny was transferred to Camp Darby in Italy. He accepted the new assignment with a fatalistic shrug, especially given that Daphne had cut off all contact with him. She had seen him as nothing more than a welcome distraction—her final words to him had been "You put a smile on my face, Johnny, and that's it"—and his devotion to the military meant that they could never have a real future together.

So that, in his own estimation, was what women thought about John Meriwether Gillespie: a welcome distraction. Something to play with, until they became bored or someone made them stop.

Taking one last look in the suite's mirror, he had to laugh. "Here's to being free, single, and disengaged," he said aloud. Then he turned on his heel and headed for the hotel bar.

11

CORTINA, ITALY—MIRAMONTE HOTEL

FRIDAY, JANUARY 7, 1955
5:30 PM

Victoria was well into her second scotch at the bar when Johnny sat down three seats away. "Coffee, Carlo," he ordered, then turned to smile at her. "Miss Shannon."

Victoria nodded back. "Captain Gillespie," she said. Then, with a wicked smile: "Or should I say Bruce Wayne?"

Johnny's head dropped and he muttered, "Carlo!"

Carlo brought the coffee, protesting his innocence in the whole affair. Johnny took his cup and moved to the empty seat right next to Victoria.

In low tones, he murmured, "So, you heard?"

She leaned in and whispered: "Everybody has."

"Really?"

"Mm-hm." Victoria smiled her sweetest smile. "I believe it's going to make the six o'clock report on BBC radio."

He grinned at that. "Folks need to talk about something, I guess."

Victoria could not help marvel at how unconcerned Johnny seemed, how comfortable in himself, how relaxed in his simple button-down, well-worn khakis, and his cowboy boots. "Everyone loves a good story," she said. "Besides, what better way for two lonely Americans to break the ice in a foreign land?"

"I have a hard time believing you could ever be lonely, Miss Shannon."

For a moment, Victoria felt the pain of her loss freshly once more. But the moment passed; he'd meant it as a compliment. She gestured toward his coffee cup. "Care to join me in something stronger?" She regretted the words as they left her mouth; she was coming on too strong. *God, I'm new at this singles game.*

But Johnny, God bless him, rolled with it. "Anything stronger and I'll be asleep at the bar in fifteen minutes," he said. "It was tough going today. And if I took a nap now, I'd miss dinner." He shook his head, laughing. "Probably wake up at two in the morning starving, with nothing to eat except for the emergency K-rations I keep in my backpack. No, thank you."

"Johnny—" she began, then stopped herself. "Do you prefer John or Johnny?"

"Johnny's fine. And do you go by Victoria or Vickie?"

"Victoria, please. 'Vickie Shannon' sounds like someone on the jukebox." She shuddered. Johnny chuckled in agreement.

"As I was saying—Johnny—if I'm not mistaken, you're probably wondering what I'm doing in place like this by myself."

"The question had crossed my mind."

"Well, Johnny, it turns out I've got a pretty good story, too," she said. "If you have no other plans, let's see if we can find a nice quiet table in the back of the dining room. I'll buy you dinner and tell you all about it." She grinned. "If nothing else, it'll be better than K-rations."

Johnny readily agreed. The dining room required gentlemen to wear a jacket and tie for dinner, and Victoria was feeling underdressed in her plaid slacks and sweater; so, after finishing their drinks, they went to their respective suites to change, promising to meet in the lobby.

As she descended the stairs, Victoria was pleasantly surprised to see Johnny standing there in the lobby; he wore a navy-blue blazer with a crisp white shirt, gray double-pleated wool slacks with cuffs, black Italian loafers, and a tie striped in red, gold, and blue. He reminded her of some of Joel's friends who were members of the Yale Club in New York City.

If Victoria was pleased, Johnny looked stunned at her rapid transformation. Other women would take hours to go from skier to starlet, but Victoria had managed it in fifteen minutes. She was wearing a navy-blue long-sleeved skater dress with a floral print and a pair of black pumps, with her hair pinned up and her makeup immaculate.

Curious looks followed the tall American couple as they were seated, especially when the head chef, Giancarlo Pellegrino, came out to welcome them. Some in the crowd speculated that they must be movie stars trying to enjoy some free time between shoots, or absorbing some local color for an upcoming film.

Being that it was Friday, the hotel did not serve meat—only fish, in observance of Roman Catholic tradition. The antipasti consisted of dried figs with cheese, bread, and a nice Barolo wine. The second course was *Zuppa di Mare* served with a nice Rosé; the entrée was trout sautéed in a light tomato sauce, served with a Pinot grigio. While they ate, Victoria told Johnny about her life before and after Sebastian, including details of Sebastian's other conquests. She did, however, omit any mention of Joel's abusive nature; tonight was not a night to speak ill of the dead.

Johnny listened intently with an expression Victoria could not read. He did not ask any questions or offer opinions. By the time it was over, Victoria felt as if a large weight had been lifted off her.

It was not until dessert arrived—éclairs and cream puffs, served alongside cappuccino—that Victoria realized that she knew very little about her dinner partner. Boldly, she said it was Johnny's turn to talk about his life.

Johnny seemed reluctant to speak at first. "I'm the youngest of four, and grew up on a ranch that's been in the family for four generations. On my mother's side of the family, we can trace our lineage back to before the Revolutionary War. One of our ancestors may have traveled with the Lewis and Clark expedition back in 1803. That was the family story, anyway. My father's people, we're less sure about, but there was Scotch-Irish, German, Russian, French-Canadian—even Shoshone and Cheyenne mixed in there."

"A real Heinz 57 mutt, in other words," Victoria said impishly.

"And proud of it," Johnny smiled. "Patriot, mountain man, cowboy, and Indian all in one. Explains a lot, when you think about it."

"I'll bet," she snorted.

"My two older brothers—Stan and Horace—they fought in the Big One. They joined the 101st Airborne, both of them. Saw action at D-Day all the way through the fall of Berlin. They were mustered out in 1945, when our father died. He left the ranch to them, divided between the two. My sister Lucy had married one of the ranch hands. He's the foreman now."

"Keeping the business all in the family, then."

Johnny nodded, but he looked unhappy. "What you have to understand is that Stan and Horace are not only older than me—they're both much bigger than me. Even Lucy's as tall as I am. I'm literally the runt of the litter, and had nothing but hind tit to look forward to. Pardon my language."

She waved her hand. "Please. I was raised in Hell's Kitchen. I've heard worse."

"I had no stake of my own in the ranch. If I stayed on, it would be as an employee, taking orders from my older brothers for the rest of my life. Or I could try to make a living doing something else." He picked up his glass, then set it down again. "Don't get me wrong. I love my family, and help with the ranch when I can, but I need to be my own man. The army gave me a way to do that."

"Did you enlist right after high school?"

"Sort of. I applied to the University of Colorado and was accepted into the graduating class of 1948. History major. I was accepted into the Army ROTC program, which paid for my tuition, room, and board. That's where I really learned mountaineering, in the Alpine Club."

"Climbing in the Rockies?"

He nodded, his cobalt-blue eyes shining. "I'd been climbing since I was a kid. Our spread in Wyoming isn't far from the Idaho border, and I used to go out with my high-school friends to the Grand Tetons." He smiled. "We thought we were pretty hot stuff—but man, we were green as hell. Alpine Club is where I started learning the technical side of it. Not just rock climbing, but going up the ice. Winter survival. Different sets of skills. I had so much to learn, and I just ate it up."

Victoria gazed at him with a new understanding. "Did you get *any* studying done?"

"Well, between ROTC, climbing, and football—"

"Come on!"

"Mm-hm. Three years at tight end. Made starting team my senior year. After graduation, I qualified for jump school. I must have done all right, because they tapped me for Ranger school. That was 1949."

Victoria knew a thing or two about the army did things—her father and brothers had all served—and she knew Johnny must have done better than "all right." Only the best of the best were recommended for Ranger training. That he would play down such an achievement spoke volumes. "How did you wind up in Korea?" she asked.

"I was still at Fort Benning when the KPA moved south across the border. They sent me over in summer of 1950—me and a handful of other Ranger lieutenants." He looked at his glass. "That first winter was brutal, but with what I'd learned, I was able to keep my platoon healthy and safe. And I guess somebody must have noticed—I was promoted to captain and put in charge of a Ranger company specializing in mountaineering. See, the KPA were notorious for setting up emplacements on mountaintops and large hills, which allowed them to outflank traditional ground forces. Our job was finding routes to take out these mountain strongholds. In 1952, a joint operation was set up between my Ranger company and the Italian Alpini."

"And that's how you met your friends?"

Johnny nodded. "Gigi—with the moustache—he was our CO. He'd been a major when the war started. They bumped him up to lieutenant colonel and gave him command over a battalion of 500 troops, 400 Italians and 100 Americans. We acquitted ourselves pretty well."

"You don't have to be so humble, soldier," she teased.

Johnny grinned. "If I started telling war stories, Miss Shannon, we might be here all night. I'll just say the

Fighting Ibex won a lot of combat medals and kept our casualties very low."

"The Fighting Ibex? That's what they call the battalion?"

"Used to. The battalion was disbanded after hostilities ceased in 1953, and I was assigned to Fort Hunter Liggett in Jolon, California. That's where I served until being transferred to Camp Darby in Italy."

Victoria sensed there was more to Johnny's reassignment than he let on, but she decided not to press him. "That's quite the tale, Cowboy," she said. "You're a globe-trotter, all right. But isn't there anyone waiting at home? A Mrs. Gillespie, perhaps?"

A look of sadness came across Johnny's face. "There was, once," he said. His voice had lost its usual good humor. "For a while. A year. That was enough."

"I'm sorry," Victoria said, her cheeks burning with shame. "I didn't mean—I shouldn't have pried."

They sat there in awkward silence until Mario walked up, begging their pardon for the interruption—though in truth, Victoria was relieved.

"Ernesto has asked me to inform you that your lesson for tomorrow is cancelled. This blizzard—very dangerous."

"Of course," said Victoria. "How long will these conditions last, do you know?"

"Who can say? Another day, at least. Maybe more."

"Looks like our climbing party is grounded, too," said Johnny. "We were lucky to make it back alive today."

"Some more lucky than others," said Victoria under her breath, and was pleased to see Johnny's grin return.

"Such a shame," said Mario. "But we should not let bad news spoil the evening! Come, let me buy you both a nightcap."

Mario poured out the drinks himself; as he was pouring a third for himself, a low rumble was heard coming from the northwest. Johnny whistled to himself, and Mario made the sign of the cross.

"What was that?" asked Victoria.

"Avalanche," both men said absently.

Victoria began to shake inwardly. "Were there any other climbing parties out today?" she asked.

"Not that we saw," Johnny said.

"The Miramonte did not send any guides out today," said Mario, laying a reassuring hand on her arm. "I talked today to the manager at the Hotel Montana, and they too have grounded all their climbing expeditions."

"We were the only ones fool enough to try it," said Johnny. "And if we'd hadn't listened to Ernesto, well—"

"Everyone's safe now," said Victoria, with a great exhalation. "That's all that matters."

Johnny raised his glass. "We live and climb another day," he said. They all drank, and Mario bade the couple good night.

Johnny set down his glass and closed his eyes for a long moment. Victoria could sense the weariness he had been staving off all night crashing down on him.

"How ya feelin', Cowpoke?" she asked. "Reckon you still have enough giddyup in you to walk me to my room?"

He gave a sleepy smile. "Reckon I do, ma'am," he said, and offered her his arm.

Victoria leaned against him as they walked. She wondered at just how comfortable she felt around this tall, lanky cowboy, the personification of the romantic American West—quiet, capable, and determined, as comfortable out in the wilderness as she might feel in Times Square. Then she wondered to herself how he would find Times Square. That thought startled her; she wondered where it came from as they came to her door.

"Thank you for sharing your company this evening," he said.

"Better than K-rations?"

He smiled. "You bet."

"Will you join me for breakfast tomorrow morning?"

"Sure. I've got no other plans, what with this blizzard throwing a monkey wrench in the works." Then, suddenly, he gave a terrific yawn. "Just not too early, okay? I'm fixin' to sleep a good long while."

"I've got your room number. I'll call."

Her arm was still in his, neither wanting to break the link. At last, she slipped free. "Goodnight, Johnny."

After Victoria locked her door, she stepped out of her dress and hung it up. She stripped down naked and looked at herself in the mirror, shaking her head, wondering what would truly make her happy. With that thought she put her underwear, garter belt, and stockings into the laundry bag supplied to her by the hotel, stepped into her slides and dressing gown, and sat down to remove her makeup.

She was absently humming to herself when she heard another low rumble from off to the north. Another avalanche. She began to shake again. Tears were running down her cheeks; she tried to fight them back, unable to comprehend all the thoughts she was having. The wind picked up outside. The spacious suite felt claustrophobic.

Hardly knowing what she was doing, she took off the dressing gown and stepped back into the dress she'd worn to dinner. Without a second thought, she marched out of the suite and headed to Johnny's room.

She knocked twice, and heard Johnny's approaching voice inside: "So the three of you finally decide to report b—" Then the door swung open and Johnny—in his pajama bottoms, toothbrush in his mouth—fell silent, eyes wide at the sight of Victoria, teary-eyed and wearing a nervous smile.

With a mouth full of toothpaste, he invited her in. "Make yourself at home," he muttered around his toothbrush. "'Scuse me." He retreated to the bathroom, and she heard the sounds of running water and spitting. As he walked out of the bathroom he said, "I thought you were Gi—"

He fell silent again in mid-sentence, finding Victoria standing there naked, her dress pooled around her feet.

"I'm sorry, Johnny," she sniffled, "but I can't be alone tonight."

Without a word, he wrapped her in his arms. She began to sob uncontrollably, apologizing over and over again. He said nothing, just held her. They stood like that for a long time, until she cried herself out.

With the last of his strength, he picked her up in his arms and deposited her on his bed. Victoria crawled under the covers as Johnny dropped his pajamas, shut off the lights, and climbed in next to her.

In the dark, Victoria listened to the blizzard roar outside. She laid her head on Johnny's chest. "Thank you," she whispered, but he was already asleep. And a moment later, so was she.

12

THIRTY KILOMETERS NORTH OF BOLZANO

SATURDAY, JANUARY 8, 1955
12:15 AM

The man who called himself Tommaso Cinzano found himself in that twilight between sleeping and wakefulness. He was having a dream. He was back in Russia, marching through the snow and ice in the freezing wind, trying desperately to get back to Germany. He hated being cold. He couldn't catch his breath. His legs wouldn't move. How had he gotten so out of shape?

When at last he came fully awake, he realized that he was safe in a small bed under several blankets. He could hear the blizzard raging outside, and closer than that the crackle of a fire. He turned toward the fire and saw Aldo, stooped over a pot, stirring it.

"Finally," Aldo said. "I was beginning to worry. I

thought I had lost you and would not be able to collect my fifteen ounces of gold."

Tommaso sat up—and immediately fell back down on the bed; his entire body was wracked with pain. He also realized he was naked under the blankets.

"How did we get here?"

"What was the last thing you remember?" Aldo asked.

"We were skiing toward—I guess it was this hut, in that blinding blizzard, when you said that we had about three kilometers to go."

Aldo nodded. "I'll fill you in from there, but first, let me tell you," he said, "I warned you that it was a bad idea to go out in the blizzard."

"I understand. But it is vital that I get to Vienna via Innsbruck as soon as possible."

"You don't have the strength for this journey, Tommaso—nor the stamina. I guess living in South America, you've lost your resistance to the cold. Nineteen forty-two was a long time ago."

"I'll take your suggestion under better consideration next time." He gave Aldo a half-smile. "But you still haven't answered my question. How did I get here? And where are my clothes?"

Aldo sighed. "We were about a kilometer and a half from the hut. We were off our pace. You couldn't keep up. And finally, you began to become incoherent, and collapsed."

"And I suppose you carried me here?"

"If I had tried, we would both be dead," Aldo said. "No, Tommaso. I left you behind the rock outcropping, out of the wind, wrapped up in my jacket, then hiked to the hut as fast as I could. I found skis, and a sled, and came back to get you." Aldo shook his head. "I left you too long. You were soaked to bone and suffering from hypothermia. I had to get your clothes off and get you warm."

He pointed to the drying rack where all of Tommaso's clothes were. Tommaso managed a weak smile. "So, it seems like I owe you my life, Aldo."

Aldo only shrugged.

"This is something I do not take lightly, my friend."

"Am I your friend, Tommaso?" Aldo's face was expressionless. "I would think a friend would tell me his real name, at least."

Tommaso could say nothing.

"Were you in the *Wehrmacht*?"

There was nothing for it now but to tell the truth. "How did you know?"

"You said the last time you were in these mountains was the winter of 1942. The place was crawling with Germans then. And now you come to me from South America, eager to cross into Austria." He shrugged. "Not much of a mystery. Besides, you talked in your sleep while you were delirious."

"What do you want from me, Aldo?"

"You can start by telling me your name," Aldo said. "After that, tell me what you like. It might make you feel better."

He could not tell if the big man was baiting him or not; but, haltingly at first, he began to speak.

"Before I was Tommaso Cinzano, my name was Wolfgang Bauer. And as you guessed, I was in the Wehrmacht. Demolitions. Italy was only where it started. After Italy, they sent me to Stalingrad. Six months, our army froze and starved and bled." He stared into the middle distance.

Tommaso—that is, Wolfgang—now looked at Aldo. "I was evacuated from Stalingrad in February. They brought me back to Germany, you see, because they knew—the Führer, and some in his circle—they realized the war could not be won. They let the fighting drag on in Europe, although they understood that it was lost, because they were buying time. They had a contingency plan." He laughed weakly. "Oh, yes, they had great plans for me."

Wolfgang fell back on the pillow. "My mouth is so dry," he said.

"You're dehydrated," Aldo said. He rummaged in his pack for a bottle of water. "Drink slowly. You'll make yourself sick otherwise."

Wolfgang sipped from the bottle, swishing the water over his tongue, then took a long draught. "Some in the High Command had devised a scheme to establish a new Reich. A new Fatherland, with headquarters in South America. My talent in demolitions, they thought, could be useful in laying the foundations. I was smuggled out of Germany to Lisbon, then sailed to Argentina with false documents. That was when I became Tommaso Cinzano."

"They sent you to prepare the way for this new Reich?"

"They made me an assassin," Wolfgang said bitterly. "Between 1945 and 1947, on orders from Berlin,

I orchestrated several car bombings that took the lives of multiple South American dignitaries—not only in Argentina, but in Paraguay and Uruguay. Politicians who had been deemed enemies of the New Reich, who might stand in the way of its foundation."

"And after 1947?"

Wolfgang shrugged. "The orders stopped coming. My contact stopped coming around. I never heard why. I thought perhaps my superiors had been found out and arrested." He drank again. "To be honest, I was relieved. I hated what they had done to me, Aldo. I was a soldier. I fought honorably in the war. But they had turned me into a killer for hire."

He raised the bottle again and was surprised to find it dry. "But still I waited until I was sure. For two years, there were no orders, no contact. I thought that, at last, I was free. I left Argentina. Settled in Paraguay. I have lived a very, very quiet life. Married a local woman. We have two daughters. I was happy."

"But they found you again."

Wolfgang closed his eyes. "They did. Or their successors did. It doesn't matter. The organization to which I swore an oath, the organization that made possible my life in South America, has called me back into service. My talents, they said, were required for some of the political maneuvers they have planned for Austria."

"Could you not have refused?"

Wolfgang looked at him meaningfully. "They did not leave me a choice," he said. "My family."

Aldo was silent for a very long time. At last, he asked, "How do you feel?"

Wolfgang narrowed his eyes. "Will you kill me now, Aldo? Now that you know what I am?"

Aldo shook his head. "I promised I would deliver you alive to Innsbruck. I keep my promises." He sighed. "That's the only moral code I've ever needed. Are you hungry?"

"I'm still thirsty more than hungry."

Aldo grunted and retrieved a second bottle filled with water. As Wolfgang gulped it down, he became aware of a delicious smell. "What are you cooking?"

"Soup. Nothing much. Just chicken bouillon with pastina. You need the salt—you sweated like a pig while we were trekking here. Once you've had your fill of that, I've got some prosciutto, cheese, and bread. And we have dried figs for later."

Wolfgang found the courage to try to sit up; and though the pain rippled through him, he succeeded. He pulled the blankets around him. "Are my clothes dried?"

They were. While Wolfgang slowly dressed, Aldo ladled out the soup.

"So," said Wolfgang as he sipped the bouillon, "what is the plan?"

"We wait," said Aldo. "You will not survive trying to travel in this blizzard. I don't care what your superiors want, they have to take into account this type of traveling during winter."

"I still don't understand why they wanted me to make the journey now, rather than wait for spring."

"Safer for them," Aldo said. "It's less obvious. It's easier to smuggle things across the border this times of year." He gave a tiny smile. "After all, only fools would brave these mountains in winter."

Wolfgang rose to his feet and tried to stretch. He was sore all over. His left quadriceps cramped up, and he stumbled against the table. Aldo helped him sit down, and with strong hands worked away the cramp. "It will be several days before you can travel," he said.

Wolfgang lay back down and stared at the ceiling. "I don't know if I can make the rest of the journey."

Aldo let out a sigh. "We will make it."

"How?"

"We'll lighten your load," Aldo said. "I'll carry the equipment for both of us on the sled, so that all you have to do is ski. If you have difficulty, you can climb on the sled."

For the first time Wolfgang saw Aldo as he was—a man born and bred in these mountains. He hobbled over to his backpack and reached into the inner lining; with his knife, he undid several stitches of one of the inner seams. There were ten gold sovereigns sewn into the lining—1931 King George British gold sovereigns, part of the cache he had smuggled to South America. Each was worth approximately 550 US dollars. He handed one to Aldo, "I know I owe you my life, but please accept this as partial payment."

Aldo looked at the coin with apparent disinterest, then slipped it into his pocket and began slicing prosciutto onto a round of bread. "Here," he said. "You need to regain your strength."

13

CORTINA, ITALY—MIRAMONTE HOTEL

SATURDAY, JANUARY 8, 1955
2:35 AM

Victoria awoke with Johnny's right arm still around her and her head on his chest. It was still dark; she did not know what time it was, but she had to pee. Slowly she extracted herself from Johnny's embrace and tiptoed toward the bathroom. The blizzard was still raging outside, casting an eerie glow in the room. The room was cold, and she shivered. In the half-light she saw Johnny's long underwear shirt, a Henley, on the drying rack in the corner, and put it on. It was bigger than she anticipated, and scratchy, but it warmed her up. Best of all, the shirt carried Johnny's scent. She found herself becoming aroused.

She closed the bathroom door behind her. What was she doing? This wasn't her. A little over a year ago, she was highly competent nurse recognized for her achievements, married to a well-respected surgeon; despite his demons and the abuse, there might have been a chance to turn things around. Maybe if she had gotten pregnant, or if she had been a little bit stronger, or if Joel had swallowed his pride and gotten getting the help he so desperately needed … *Too many maybes,* her brain countered. She sat on the toilet and buried her face in her hands, fighting the tears. For six months she had been happy. Just three days ago, she'd thought she was going to live happily ever after in Switzerland with a fairy-tale life. Now here she was in halfway up a mountain in a snowstorm, sharing a bed with a complete stranger. How had her life become this disaster?

Then a new realization dawned on her. *I'm rich,* she declared to herself. *I'm fucking rich.* She ran the numbers in her head; with what had been promised her by the Bossards, she would have approximately $120,000 by the time she returned to New York. Considering she made $4,500 for 1953, she felt like J.D. Rockefeller.

The thought was exciting and frightening at the same time. *What am I going to do with my life? With all that money?* Then she remembered the words of her good friend Clair Richardson, a fellow nurse who was now doing aid work in the Sudan: *Sometimes, Vic, you've gotta live for the moment—because we plan, and God laughs.*

Clair had told that to her the night before she left for Africa. A few years older than Victoria, she considered herself very independent and unconventional. She was not married but had several lovers, and had refused a few marriage proposals in her time—the last being from one of Joel's colleagues, a married surgeon named Tom Borden, who was ready to divorce his wife over his affair with Clair. But Clair refused to be responsible for the failure of Tom's marriage, believing that this was not the way to have a healthy relationship. With the nursing administration unhappy with both her and Tom, Clair signed up for the medical mission to the Sudan; it was, she said, her penance for her wicked ways.

Victoria got off the toilet, washed her hands, and steeled herself. *I am rich,* she thought, *and I am free. If there were ever a time for me to live for the moment, it is now. There will be time to decide what to do with the rest of my life. There a plenty of people back in New York who make their living advising rich folks how to handle their money; I won't have to figure it all out alone. But for now, I am rich, and I am free, and I am going back to Johnny's bed.*

Johnny had rolled onto his left side, facing the windows; Victoria crawled back in on the opposite side, spooning him with her right arm over his torso for both warmth and comfort; she was asleep within in a minute.

When Victoria next awoke, she was on her right side and Johnny was spooning her. Something strange and hard was pressed against her back, and she realized that Johnny had an erection. A wicked thought came to mind: *I'm really going to enjoy that in me later.* She stifled a laugh, not wanting to wake Johnny up. However, Johnny came around on his own.

He sat up. "What time is it, d'you know?"

"It's dawning so somewhere between six-thirty, seven o'clock."

He stood and stretched, then headed into the bathroom. Victoria watched him ago, taken once again by how at ease he was with himself and his surroundings. He carried himself with the serenity of a man who was enjoying a stroll down a country lane, rather than naked in the company of a madwoman.

When he came back, Victoria was sitting up in the bed. She wore no makeup, and there was a lock of her hair that continually fell into her face, refusing to stay in place. The Henley hung awkwardly, exposing her left shoulder. "I must look like a fright," she said.

"On the contrary," he said. "I think you're the most incredible woman I've ever seen."

She noticed he was becoming aroused. "I might have something to fix that for you," she said, slipping out of the Henley. She was enjoying the wolfish grin on his face as he made his way back to the bed.

Johnny had only one condom, left so they would have to make it last. The only way to do that was several bouts of complementary oral sex and different positions. Two were new to Victoria. One was sort of the missionary position with her legs over his shoulders and him on his knees. The other was doggy style, which unlocked a sensation in her she had never felt before. As he squeezed her hips, Victoria had multiple orgasms, which was also a new experience for her; she lost count after four.

They finally climaxed together with her on top; Johnny arched his back, lifting her up, going deeper inside her as he did. When they finished, both were ready for sleep. As she fell out of consciousness, Victoria's last thought was *I hope this room is soundproof.*

They were awoken by the telephone. Johnny was on his back, with Victoria lying across his chest. How long they had been passed out, neither knew.

Johnny picked up the phone with his left hand, "*Pronto?*"

"Hey *sfachime*, what the hell you still doing in bed? It's after eight." It was Tony.

"Late night," drawled Johnny. "And a lot of drinking, because of the multiple debriefings I had to do about yesterday's escapades. Apparently, it made the six o'clock BBC report." He grimaced as Victoria pinched his left nipple.

Tony laughed. "Yeah, that was pretty crazy. Anyhow, it looks like the snow is starting to taper off, so we'll be heading back to the Miramonte soon. By the way, the girls want to have another feast at the chef's table tonight."

"Enjoy yourselves," said Johnny.

"Yeah, well, here's the skinny—Basil wants to meet you."

Johnny nearly dropped the phone, although that may have been from Victoria pinching his left nipple again, harder this time. "Why, so we can compare notes on Beatrix?"

"Yeah, I understand if you don't want to come." Something in Tony's voice made Johnny wonder if someone was putting him up this.

You should go, Victoria mouthed, then pointed to herself: *And bring me along.*

That familiar wolfish smile crept across Johnny's face. "You know what? On second thought, I'm in."

"Really? You don't mind being a—what, a seventh wheel?"

"No, let me see if I can scrounge up a date." Johnny grimaced again as Victoria now bit his right nipple.

"What aren't you telling me, Cowboy?"

"Tell you when I see you. What time will you be here?"

"We're leaving in two, three hours. How about lunch at one?"

"Sounds great. *Ciao.*"

"*Ciao.*"

"Well," said Victoria, rolling out of bed and stepping into last night's crumpled dress. "This promises to be interesting. You know, the other night I had thoughts of stealing you away from that chubby little blonde Beatrix." She smiled sweetly.

"I might have been better off if you had," he said. "Breakfast?"

"Yes, I'm famished."

"Fifteen minutes?"

"Make it a half-hour," she said. "That was one hell of a ride you just gave me, Cowboy. I need time to work the kinks out." She kissed him, a long, lingering kiss on the lips that carried the promise of more to come, then let herself out.

I'm dead, Johnny thought as he made his way to the shower. *I died last night up on the Cabrini Pass in that avalanche; my body is buried under tons of snow and now I'm in Heaven.*

14

CORTINA, ITALY—MIRAMONTE HOTEL

SATURDAY, JANUARY 8, 1955
1:15 PM

Johnny was sitting in the bar alone. The boys had gotten back to the hotel after noon, and wanted to shower and shave before lunch. Johnny and Victoria had enjoyed a hearty breakfast of pancakes, bacon, and eggs with copious amounts of *caffè latte.* It was decided that Victoria would make a grand entrance at half past one; it was Johnny's job to keep the trio guessing for as long as possible. Victoria was enjoying herself tremendously as she threw herself into living for the moment.

At last, the Alpini came in together, dressed, like Johnny, in khakis and button-downs, with loafers in place of his cowboy boots. "Well, if it isn't the Batman!" cried Gigi. Johnny took a bow and the comrades embraced.

"Who told you?

"Pepe gave us the news when we dropped off our skis at the shack," said Tony. "So, who's the mystery woman, Cowboy? You escape from Beatrix's bedroom and land in someone else's?"

"Wait!" Gigi commanded. "Sorry chaps—we'll take this up later, but first formalities must be observed. Carlo!"

The bartender came over immediately. "Colonel?"

"A bottle of the Johnnie Walker Black, if you please," Gigi ordered in the thicker version of his English accent.

Carlo returned with five glasses, asking if he could be permitted to join the observation, which he was.

The glasses were filled and raised. "To live and climb another day," Gigi toasted.

The five drained their glasses, then stared silently out at the heavy sky. The toast was more solemn than anticipated. The avalanches of last night were fresh in their minds. Johnny thought of Ernesto—the pain he must be feeling at the loss of Mauricio, and the debt they owed the old mountaineer. "Leave the bottle, Carlo," he said.

Gigi, casting about to lighten the mood, once again took command. "Now! Captain Gillespie, tell us: Who is the mystery woman?"

The four sat down as Johnny refilled the glasses. "Well, fellas, it's like this," Johnny said. "You know I always say—you can trust me with yer life, just not yer money or yer wife!" He grinned.

Just then, Victoria walked in, wearing a yellow short-sleeved turtleneck with black cigarette slacks—a grand entrance that would have rivaled anything either Joan Crawford or Bette Davis could do. Gigi looked at her, then at Johnny, and the dots connected. "You dog!" he whispered.

"Hello, gentlemen," Victoria sang. "Thank you for letting me attend your dinner party tonight." She smiled sweetly.

All four stood smiling; as Victoria greeted each in turn, Gigi murmured in Johnny's ear: "She would have been a great conquest, Cowboy—but if she brings you happiness, I accept defeat gladly."

While they chatted, Jo-Jo ran to the kitchen to see what was available for lunch. They settled on veal cutlets with sautéed spinach, and Jo-Jo ordered Chianti for the table. During lunch, most of the attention was focused on Victoria. She regaled the Alpini with tales of her life in New York. Tony had grown up in the Riverdale area of the Bronx and attended Dewitt Clinton High School on Mosholu Parkway; he and Victoria shared a passion for the Yankees, and both were hoping for Mickey Mantle to have a breakout season that year.

The "brigands" were all so charming and kind that Victoria found it easy to be open with them. When it came to her life with Sebastian, though, she fell back on a lie, saying that the ski trip had been a last-ditch effort to save the engagement but there was nothing there. She didn't care if they believed her; she was quite sure that the Italians had heard the truth about what happened. It was just that reliving it would be painful right now, and she was enjoying everyone's company—especially Johnny's. The men were all attentive and courteous; they made her feel special. What truly shone through was how deeply dedicated they were to one another.

She knew the four of them had a close bond forged in the fires of war. She wondered if Dad and Junior had formed the same type of bonds before they died. Joel had lost two close friends from boot camp in Guadalcanal; how much of an impact had that had on him in the long run? She shuddered to think what Johnny would be like if one of these three died in battle—then put that thought out of her head, resigning herself to the fact that she would probably never see Johnny again after next week. *Live for the moment, Vic,* she told herself.

Over a dessert of assorted cookies and espresso, Victoria asked, "What's the dress code for tonight?"

"I reckon on wearing what I've got on now," said Johnny.

"Informal is fine," said Jo-Jo. "We'll be in the kitchen, not the dining room, so no tie and jacket. It gets warm in the kitchen, you know?"

"Still," said Gigi thoughtfully, "it's probably best to telephone the ladies and let them know. It wouldn't do for anyone to be over- or underdressed." He shot Johnny a sideways glance. "Heaven knows we wouldn't want anyone made uncomfortable."

"I'll call them," said Jo-Jo. "And I'll let you all know if there's any change in plan."

"Capital!" barked Gigi, clapping his hands. "Right-o, chaps—and lady—I believe a siesta is in order. I have a feeling it's going to be a late night for all." He stood, and gestured toward the stairs. "We'll meet in the bar at half six. Cheerio."

Two hours later, Johnny was naked in his bed, lying on his back and smoking a cigarette. Victoria lay with her head on his chest, absently playing with his chest hair. Raising her head, she reached over and took the cigarette out of his mouth, took a healthy drag, and put it back in Johnny's mouth. He took one last drag, then stubbed it out.

The smile on Victoria's face masked the tug of war in her emotions. *Live for the moment,* she repeated to herself. *Live for the moment.* But it was hard. There was something magnetic about the handsome army captain, something she could not place. It scared and excited her all at once. More than that, it made her wonder about the future.

Returning to bed after a trip to the bathroom, she noticed a bomber jacket hanging in Johnny's closet. She pulled it out and examined it. On the right shoulder was the Far East Air Forces Fifth Air Force patch; on the left shoulder was Nineteenth Bombardment Wing patch, with a smaller patch signifying that the owner flew B-29s during the Korean War.

Victoria pulled the jacket off its hanger. On the left breast she saw another, circular patch; this one was red and black. In the center was a satyr—a mythical creature, half-man and half-goat. The creature had the head of an ibex with its long-curved horns, grimacing, the torso and arms of a man, but the hindquarters of a beast. The creature was firing a machine gun as it climbed up rocky terrain. The legend above the satyr read "The Fighting Ibex." Below was the Italian motto *In Alto e in Avanti*—"upward and forward."

"When were you in the air force?" she asked.

"I never was," Johnny said. "I won that in a poker game when I was on R-and-R in Tokyo, three years ago."

Impishly, she put the jacket on; the shearling lining made her naked skin tingle. On his dresser she noticed an Ansco Commander folding camera with a built-in flash.

"Don't tell me you won this in a poker game, too?"

Johnny nodded.

In the inside jacket pocket, Victoria found a pair of aviator sunglasses. She held them up. "Poker?"

"Poker."

She put them on, and then a wicked thought occurred to her. Reaching into the closet, she pulled out his military brimmed cap and put it on. "You any good with that camera?" she said as she stepped into the black high heels she had worn to lunch.

Johnny nodded again, breaking into a grin.

"Well, start snapping away before I change my mind," she commanded, walking toward the door for a better shooting angle.

For the first shot, Victoria stood wide-legged with her back to Johnny, the lower part of her nates exposed under the jacket; her head was turned over her right shoulder, and she looked over the top of the aviators with a seductive smile on her face. For the second shot, she wrapped herself if the jacket and faced him, bent at the knees and waist, puckering her lips. Her third pose found her sitting on the small hotel desk, the armless chair off to the side, legs crossed right over left, one high-heeled shoe dangling; she was leaned forward, bracing herself with her palms on the desk, smiling seductively. For the fourth shot, Victoria faced Johnny, legs wide, and let the jacket drop off her shoulders, exposing her breasts. For her fifth pose, Victoria took the jacket off and stood with her back to Johnny, naked but for her heels and the captain's hat, with the jacket slung over her left shoulder and her right hand on her hip.

"That's the last frame," said Johnny. He sat back sat in the armless chair, looking quite exhausted. Victoria put the jacket back on, walked over to the chair, and straddled Johnny with her long legs.

"This is the promise, Captain Gillespie," she said. "If you tell anyone, or show these pictures to *anyone*—including the Three Musketeers—I will personally cut off your balls and nail them to the bar at McSorley's Ale House."

"Promise," said Johnny. Then he wrapped his strong arms around her waist and—with her legs still wrapped around him—scooped her up, sunglasses, jacket, hat, and all, and deposited her on the bed.

15

CORTINA, ITALY—MIRAMONTE HOTEL

SATURDAY, JANUARY 8, 1955
6:30 PM

Johnny came into the bar at half past six, alone. About an hour previously, Victoria had decided she did not like the outfit she had on; Johnny could not find anything wrong with her lunch outfit, but Victoria claimed woman's prerogative and went back to her suite to shower and change.

As Johnny entered, he saw everyone else already present, including Beatrix and her fiancé. He was surprised when he finally got a look at Basil; the Englishman was nearly six feet tall, narrow in the shoulders but with a sizable waist and backside. He had a long nose with a slight hook to it—more effective for looking down at people, Johnny supposed—and unruly brown hair, thinning at the front. He was wearing a light brown tweed suit with blue sweater vest and a white button-down shirt, with expensive calfskin Wellington boots. A weak chin and a scrawny neck completed the picture. *Poor bastard,* Johnny thought to himself.

"Captain John Gillespie," Johnny said extending his hand. Basil's hand in return was soft, and Johnny was afraid that he would break it if he used his normal grip.

"Lord Basil Leighton, Baron of Castleburn, at your service, Captain," Basil sniffed. "The pleasure is all mine." He gave a little smile. "I've heard so much about you, 'Cowboy.'"

"I'm sure you have," Johnny grinned. Beatrix laughed nervously, and everyone else giggled. All the women were similarly dressed—double-pleated slacks, matching blouses, and heels.

"Did I say something funny?" Basil asked.

"Naw, Basil, the joke's on me and my clumsy ways," Johnny said disarmingly. "I'm just a hick from Wyoming, and here I am in Continental Europe talking to real live nobility. If the folks back home could only see me now!"

"Excellent, excellent!" Basil smiled thinly. "I believe drinks are in order. Oh, bartender?"

As Carlo approached, Basil asked, "And where is your companion for the evening, Captain? Or may I call you Johnny?" He gave a haughty laugh. "Or do you prefer 'Cowboy," perhaps?"

"'Johnny' is fine, Your Lordship. And as for my date, she'll be down in a minute." Johnny held his hands up helplessly. "Woman's prerogative."

"Fine, fine. But none of this 'Your Lordship,' eh?" Basil winked. "I get enough of that at home. Do call me Basil. We're all friends here—let's keep the night informal and intimate, shall we?"

"Let's," Johnny agreed, as Carlo took the drink orders. Basil went with a gin martini and the girls decided on champagne cocktails, while Johnny and the Three Musketeers had their old standby—scotch, neat—with Johnny ordering an extra glass for Victoria.

"A woman's prerogative! How true, how true," Basil nattered. "Beautiful creatures, aren't they? Always trying to please us."

"Hear, hear," Johnny exclaimed grandly.

Beatrix shot Johnny any icy stare, while Tony seemed to be seized with an inexplicable coughing fit; Stephanie pummeled his back rather harder than was necessary.

"Beatrix tells me you're a real live cowboy—is that true?"

"Yep."

"Do you have a six-shooter?"

"Of course."

"Amazing." Basil's eyes lit up. "A Colt Peacemaker?"

"Nope. A Navy Colt, 1852."

"But surely that's a cap-and-ball revolver!"

"That's right. My gun belt can carry three extra cylinders."

"Where's the holster on your gun belt, here?" Basil pointed to his right hip.

"Nope, I holster it backwards off my left hip," said Johnny making a motion of drawing the gun from his left across his body to his right.

"Ah, the cross-draw!," said Basil. "Like Wild Bill Hitchcock?"

Johnny smiled, but didn't bother to correct him; to be honest, Basil's enthusiasm was starting to win him over. "Sort of," he said. "Ol' Wild Bill carried two in a sash wrapped around his waist, but backwards."

Basil's eyes were wide. "Amazing," he said. "And a rifle? A Winchester, I suppose?"

"Nope, a Henry with the octagonal barrel."

"What caliber?"

"Forty-five-seventy," Johnny drawled. "I like things to stay down when I hit 'em." Johnny drawled.

Basil whistled softly. "That's a big bullet. What's your range?"

"It runs outta gas around two hundred yards, so you keep your shots under that."

At that moment, Carlo came to deliver the drinks. Before he could hand them around, something across the bar caught his eye and he loudly blurted, "*La Madon'!*" Everyone turned to see; Victoria had entered the room.

She came in wearing a black sleeveless off the shoulder blouse; she did not have a strapless bra with her, so she went without altogether. She was still wearing the black cigarette pants, which fitted her snugly, and she had swapped out her black high heels for the slides she bought in Milan; they seemed to have a magnetic effect on both men and women, albeit for different reasons. Her hair was down, and she had vivid red polish on her fingernails and toes, complemented by a more subtle shade of red lipstick. To hell with the fact that a nasty cold front was pushing the remnants of a raging blizzard out of the area and temperatures were well below freezing—Victoria wanted to make a statement. Looking at the stunned faces around the bar, Johnny had to judge her mission accomplished.

Without a word, Victoria came up to Johnny and placed her left hand lovingly on his shoulder just below the neck. The room had fallen strangely quiet, with only soft sound of jazz playing on the jukebox. Then she broke the silence, extending her hand to Basil. "Victoria Shannon. Pleased to meet you."

Basil's eyes were as big as saucers as he bowed from the waist. "Lord Basil Leighton, Baron of Castleburn, at your service." He kissed the extended hand. Beatrix looked on, nostrils flaring.

"What happened to informal and intimate?" Johnny asked.

"Quite right, old boy," Basil laughed. "I forgot myself. All my duties at Cambridge and whatnot. Do forgive me."

"Think nothin' of it, Basil, ol' cuss," Johnny beamed.

"Old cuss? Good heavens! Does everyone back in Wyoming speak like you?"

"Naw, I speak English better than most."

Basil eyed him, half-smiling. "I believe you're pulling my leg, Cowboy."

"You caught me, Basil," Johnny grinned. "Can't pull the wool over your eyes, can I?"

Tony began to rub his forehead over his left eye; it seemed like he was developing a migraine.

Johnny offered Victoria the extra scotch. She made a show of a little pout. "What are the other girls drinking?"

"Champagne cocktail," Marjorie replied.

"Really!" Victoria squealed. "How wonderful! Can you get me one, Johnny, dear?" She smiled sweetly. "Us girls have to stick together, you know."

Gigi suddenly developed a cramp in his neck and set to rubbing it to work out the kinks.

As Johnny went to the bar to fetch Victoria's champagne cocktail, Basil asked, "Do you prefer Victoria, or Vickie?"

"Victoria, please, Your Lordship." She batted her eyes and smiled. "'Vickie Shannon' sounds like someone on the jukebox, don't you think?"

"Do call me Basil, please. Pleasantries have been established," Basil stated grandly.

"Thank you, Basil. What were you two talking about when I walked in?"

"Johnny was giving us the details of his cowboy accoutrements—six-shooter, rifle, that sort of thing. Quite an interesting fellow, your Johnny is, isn't he?" Basil seemed unable to take his eyes off Victoria. Beatrix was fidgeting terribly. "I'm sure you know he's quite the mountaineer, as well. Skied up here yesterday in that dreadful blizzard! Quite extraordinary. Did you hear about that, my dear?"

"Yes," Victoria said straight-faced. "I heard it on the six o'clock report from BBC radio."

Now Jo-Jo and Portia coughed; the cold was becoming contagious.

Basil looked shocked. "Really?"

"I'm teasing." Victoria smiled sweetly, "Carlo and I made that up after we heard about Johnny's exploits."

Tony's migraine was getting worse.

Johnny returned with the champagne cocktail. Victoria giggled and raised her glass to the company, earning more flaring of the nostrils from Beatrix. "Basil was telling me you were telling everyone all about your cowboy accessories, sweetie. I'm jealous!" She addressed the group. "He hasn't even had a chance to tell *me* all about them. I guess things keep popping up." She took a sip of her champagne cocktail as Gigi and Jo-Jo began to cough simultaneously.

Johnny winked. "If you come to Wyoming, Victoria, I reckon I might put on the whole outfit."

"Oh, I would so love to see that!" said Basil gleefully. Beatrix now rubbed her head. Who knew migraines were contagious?

"That's not a bad idea, Basil," smiled Johnny. "Before you leave tonight, I'll give you the address and phone number to the ranch. Then, when I get back to the base Monday, I'll write the folks back home that if Lord Basil Leighton, the baron of Castleburn, ever calls, they'd better roll out the red carpet to you—*and* Beatrix."

"Marvelous, simply marvelous," Basil beamed. He smiled at Beatrix. "Perhaps we might go this summer, darling, as part of an extended honeymoon."

"Great," Johnny beamed, "I've got some stateside leave coming this summer. Maybe we can fix things so we can all meet in Wyoming."

Beatrix laughed nervously.

"Hey!" Victoria interjected. "What about me?"

"Why, Vic," Johnny said with his wolfish grin. "You'll always be a welcome sight to me."

Victoria put her hand on her heart and turned to Portia on her left. "He called me Vic," she whispered delightedly. Beatrix glared at her.

Basil seemed oblivious to the ocular feinting between Beatrix and Victoria, but Johnny was pleased to see Marjorie step in between them. "And what do you do in New York, Victoria?"

"I used to be a surgical nurse," Victoria said. "Up until about a year ago, when I met a Swiss playboy by the name of Sebastian Bossard, and thought I was going to live happily ever after in Switzerland."

Portia was intrigued. "What happened?"

"What usually happens with playboys," Victoria said nonchalantly. "I caught him with one of the chamber maids here in the hotel." Johnny could barely hold in a laugh. He was amazed. When he had met Victoria, just the night before, she was all raw nerves, wounded in a way no human heart should have to bear. And to see her now, just twenty-four hours later, telling tall stories about Sebastian, making him the butt of her joke—he wasn't sure just what it meant, but he took it for a good sign; given time, she would heal. Given time.

Careful, Cowboy, he told himself. *Almost caught you thinking this could be a long-term thing.*

The women (Beatrix excepted) were huddled sympathetically around Victoria. "Goodness!" Stephanie said. "Whatever will you do now?"

Victoria shrugged. "I came to Cortina to learn how to ski, which I'm doing. Then I'll go back to New York and figure it out from there," she said. "Sebastian may be a cad, but at least he left me financially sound, so I can figure the next part of my life without much worry."

It was generally agreed that Victoria showed great character in making the best of a bad situation. Beatrix continued to throw daggers, despite attempts by Stephanie and Portia to keep her cordoned off and engaged in conversation; she answered them in monosyllables, finishing her champagne cocktail and swiftly ordering another.

The conversation had turned to horses. Basil had a stable of thoroughbreds and enquired as to what Johnny had on the ranch.

"We ride Appaloosas, mostly. Some quarter horses, but most of us favor Appaloosas."

For some reason, this seemed to infuriate Beatrix; but Basil was intrigued. "A very hardy horse, the Appaloosa," he said. "Fitting for the harsh environment of Wyoming, I suppose. Not like our thoroughbreds. They demand rather a lot of upkeep, the spoiled wretches."

"Basil!" Beatrix exclaimed angrily. "Your stable is worth over two million pounds. I don't believe it's appropriate to call such noble and costly steeds 'wretches.'"

"Quite right, my dear," Basil said soothingly. "But it must be said, one of my thoroughbreds wouldn't last a week in that wilderness, whereas the Appaloosas thrive on it. I was simply commenting on hardiness of the breed, compared to what we ride. We do rather pamper our stock. The Appaloosa is bred to work."

Beatrix glared at him. "And what is that supposed to mean?"

"Simply that, if the chips were down, as they say, I'd rather have an Appaloosa than a thoroughbred."

"That's all well and good for the Americans—or the Italians," said Beatrix haughtily. "Naturally Johnny's horses are bred for work—that's what *he* does. It's his station in life." She drained her second champagne cocktail and snapped her fingers for a third. "*We* ride for leisure, which is what we do. There's no point in comparing the two."

Everyone around her had their eyebrows raised, but Beatrix seemed immensely pleased with her own observation. She rounded on Victoria. "What do you say, Miss Shannon?" Beatrix challenged. "As an American yourself, I imagine you have some insight.

"You have a point, Beatrix. Different breeds are made for different types of work. Johnny's Appaloosas serve a function, that's true." Victoria gave a disarming smile. "But working on the range, tending the ranch—of course it's hard work, but for Johnny, it's also the thing that gives him the greatest joy. Just as a life of leisure and elegance is a joy to you and Basil."

"Quite right my dear, quite right!" Basil spontaneously applauded. Johnny now had a proud smile on his face.

"Well, that's nice," Beatrix said, nonplussed. "At least we all know where we stand in life."

Marjorie rubbed her head; migraines were definitely contagious tonight.

Giancarlo came to the rescue, sweeping out of the kitchen to announce that dinner was served. As the group gathered their drinks and made to leave the bar, Gigi pulled Johnny aside.

"Your lady friend plays a dangerous game," he said in low tones.

"She holds her own, that's for sure," Johnny smiled.

"I'm trying to figure out a seating arrangement that will head off an all-out catfight," Gigi said confidentially. Then he winked. "Though if one does break out, I must admit—my money's on your long-legged brunette."

16

CORTINA, ITALY—MIRAMONTE HOTEL

SATURDAY, JANUARY 8, 1955
7:30 PM

The challenge of devising a seating arrangement, as Victoria saw it, was to have Basil and Johnny close enough to continue their conversation, while keeping Beatrix and herself from murdering each other and maintaining an alternating girl-boy pattern. Gigi, as resident tactical strategist, was entrusted with the task. His solution was to place Victoria at the head of the table opposite himself—rank had its privileges, she supposed—with Basil to her right and Johnny to her left. Beatrix was next to Basil, which cut off her direct visual contact with Victoria but left Johnny exposed. Portia was positioned to cover Johnny's left flank; of all the women, she was the best able to engage Beatrix and draw her attention away from Victoria.

Supporting Johnny's left flank was Jo-Jo; his easy-going manner and Italian charm also helped in absorbing some of the visual punishment she was unleashing on Johnny. Marjorie, seated on Gigi's right, provided aerial support by lobbing questions to Beatrix about the wedding plans and the extensive honeymoon. And to his left, Gigi placed Stephanie and Tony, who engaged in a flanking maneuver, drawing both Beatrix and Basil into a conversation about last year's World Cup that was held in Switzerland.

If there was a weak spot in Gigi's deterrence operation, Victoria thought, it was probably herself. She could not seem to help provoking Beatrix—and God help her, she was enjoying it. If she wanted to avoid an ugly scene, she would have to walk a fine line. She promised herself she would refrain from purposely needling Beatrix—but neither would she swallow any insults.

She just couldn't figure out Beatrix's anger—or her attitude. Did she feel betrayed by Johnny for moving on instead of pining for her? Did she feel she was selling out by marrying Basil? Was it all the above? *What the fuck is your problem, Lady Plushbottom?* she thought. *Soon you'll be the baroness of Castlebum or whatever—can't you be happy with that? You have to pretend that you were hard-done by this sweet, naïve man, too?*

Victoria's darkening mood was interrupted by the arrival of the meal; food always seemed to have a disarming effect on all. The antipasto was made up of olives, salami, and provolone with toasted bread and olive oil; throughout the night Chianti was served with the meal. The salad was a warm Castelfranco radicchio with vincotto and blu di bufala. The soup was minestra maritata, or "wedding soup"—a chicken stock with small meatballs and pastina. The main course was osso bucco with polenta. Dessert was a chocolate Amaretti cake with a choice of espresso or cappuccino.

As predicted, Johnny and Basil dominated the conversation. They talked mostly about history; Basil was working on his doctorate, which impressed Johnny significantly, and was writing a dissertation on the impact of the Black Plague on Europe—not only from a medical point of view, but economically and socially, with an eye to finding lesson that would be applicable to mitigate future epidemics. As they talked, Victoria thought of her Zia Marie. She closed her eyes and offered a silent prayer.

Her sorrow must have shown on her face, because Basil suddenly asked, with concern in his voice, "My dear, are you quite all right?"

"Yes, thank you. I'm sorry," Victoria said. "I lost an uncle and cousin to the Spanish flu in 1918. It was before I was born, of course, but I think of how I never got to know them, and of the people they left behind—" She trailed off, feeling vulnerable now. Johnny gently took her hand.

"It was a dreadful time," Basil said softly. "Anywhere between twenty to fifty million people dead—we may never know how many, precisely. It actually caused a statistical decrease in overall life expectancy." He shook his head. "And what of your aunt?"

"She survived the epidemic," Victoria said. "She lived with my family until her death in 1944. She practically raised me. I think she was the bravest woman I ever knew."

"You must have loved her very much," Basil said quietly.

"I did."

"Then let her courage and kindness live on in you, Victoria, and you will honor her every day of your life."

He laid his hand on hers for a moment and gave little squeeze. Victoria smiled gratefully; she was beginning to realize that Basil was more than the upper-crust clown she had taken him for. Then he gave a little chuckle of embarrassment and changed the subject. "And what about you, Johnny, old boy? What is your forte in history? The American Revolution? The US Civil War?"

"Neither," Johnny said. "I've always been partial to the westward expansion of the US—from the moment Daniel Boone founded what eventually become Boonesborough in 1775, through the Lewis and Clark expedition, to the establishing of the Republic of California in 1846."

"Really!" Basil eyed Johnny curiously, "I know so little about that time period. What do you find so fascinating about it?"

"It allowed for exploring of the unknown. The size of the United States was doubled, allowing access to immigrants for farming and creating great opportunities for commerce and industry. Of course, there were some negatives. Displacing the native peoples, expansion of slavery—hell, even the War of 1812."

"An interesting conflict, that one," said Basil. "The rules of engagement were most unclear. You do realize that Britain had surrendered three weeks before the last battle of the war?"

"What?" Stephanie asked.

"Yes, my dear," said Basil animatedly. "The peace treaty had been signed in Belgium three weeks before Colonel Jackson led his men against the British forces camped outside New Orleans. But news of the agreement had not yet reached American shores." He shook his head. "A tragedy, really. All those men perished, simply because they didn't have any modern means of communication."

"It was still a decisive battle, though," Johnny countered.

"How so?"

"Well, let's say the British forces had ended up capturing New Orleans. Now, treaty or no treaty—d'you reckon the Crown would have just given it back?"

Basil thought for a moment, then smirked. "One supposes not."

"And with the British controlling New Orleans, they would have controlled the Mississippi—giving them a stranglehold on the United States, which was still in its infancy."

"There would have been economic collapse."

"To the benefit of Britain, which would have wound up holding the reins again," Johnny said. "So even with the British surrender, their overall objective of weakening the US would have succeeded. In other words, the US might have won the war but lost the peace."

Basil smiled. "Touché, old man," he said. "Not only are you an historian—in my estimation you'd make a damned fine politician, as well. Bravo!"

A murmur of approval ran around the table—until Beatrix rose to her feet, her nostrils flared. "Right! Well, this is all nice and chummy," she declared. "But I'm afraid Johnny and I have a rendezvous to keep. Come, Johnny."

For a moment, the table froze. A collective cringe ran through them all. At last Basil found his voice. "Beatrix!" he exclaimed. "What on earth are you talking about?"

"Johnny and I were having a splendid little affair," Beatrix said, as coolly as if she was talking about the morning's newspapers. "We were having a marvelous time until *you* showed up and ruined everything—you, and that skinny trollop over there."

"That's a *high-priced* skinny trollop to you, sister," Victoria said matter-of-factly.

"*Fine*," Beatrix shouted. "No matter how high your price, Basil can afford you. And since he can't keep his eyes off you, he can shag you tonight, while I say a proper farewell to my Johnny before I have to fuck off back to jolly old England and live the life of an ornament in some musty manor house!"

Beatrix looked about the room, seeing as if for the first time the hotel staff gathered around in curiosity. Basil looked as if he'd kicked in the guts by one of his thoroughbreds. A cloud seemed to cross Beatrix's face; she looked like a woman waking from a dream. Her lips moved, but all that came out was, "I—I—I—"

Suddenly, Beatrix covered her mouth his one hand and ran for the ladies' toilets.

"Excuse me," said Portia; and rising from her seat, she ran after Beatrix.

Basil ran his hand through his hair. "It all falls into place," he said expressionlessly. "Once again, she's made a fool of me."

He buried his face in his hands and wept. The party froze, helpless to do anything but look on in sympathy. Victoria was silent, but seething inside.

After a while, Basil got ahold of himself. He took a deep, shuddering breath. "Forgive me," he said shakily.

"This isn't the first time?" asked Victoria.

"No." Basil sniffled, trying to compose himself. "The last was an Irishman by the name of Liam O'Donnell. He was the family chauffer. The affair was … not discreet." He laughed. It was not joyful sound. "The servants likened their behavior to a couple of dogs in heat."

"Jesus," Johnny whispered.

"Several weeks ago, this O'Donnell suffered two broken legs and was dismissed." Basil cleared his throat. "I have him hidden away in a flat in the City of York."

"Mighty generous of you, old sport," Gigi murmured.

"A tactical move, Colonel, not a humanitarian one." Basil smiled ruefully. "It's the sort of thing I learned when I was working counterintelligence during the war."

There were surprised looks all around the table. "Oh, yes," said Basil. "I did some dangerous and intriguing work back then. I wasn't always the inept bookworm you see before you today."

"I don't think that's the truth of you now," said Johnny softly. "It's a sort of disguise you wear, isn't it? When you want people to underestimate you."

"A secret identity," said Victoria, with a sideways glance at Johnny. "Just like Bruce Wayne and Batman."

"Nothing as fanciful as that, I'm afraid," said Basil, with a sad half-smile. "But I made my share of enemies during the war, especially among the communists. After the Iron Curtain went up, I was recruited for a post with MI-6." He sighed. "I turned them down. I'd had enough of the whole dirty business. I decided to pursue a more benign occupation, and went into academia."

He paused to sip his espresso with grappa. "With my dissertation well in hand, I decided—at the ripe old age of thirty-five—it was time for me to take a wife. I happened to come into the orbit of one Mortimer Schofield, guardian of a niece of marriageable age." He set his cup aside. "He's a most ambitious man, Mortimer. And my life has been on a downward trajectory ever since—at least until now."

Just then, Portia returned to the kitchen. Her face was pale. "Victoria," she said.

Victoria looked up curiously.

"There's something terribly wrong with Beatrix," Portia said. "I know she's been no friend to you, but please—as a nurse—will you help me?"

Without a moment's hesitation, Victoria rose to her feet, with the three Englishwomen close behind.

17

CORTINA, ITALY—MIRAMONTE HOTEL

SATURDAY 8, JANUARY, 1955
8:45 PM

The four women crowded into the tiny bathroom. Beatrix was sitting on the toilet with her slacks and panties around her ankles, her arms folded over her knees and her head resting on them, out cold. Expertly, Victoria hoisted the shorter woman and supported her while Stephanie and Portia pulled up her panties and slacks.

"What happened?" Victoria asked, settling the unconscious Beatrix again on the toilet seat and shaking her gently.

"She got sick in the toilet, washed her hands, rinsed her mouth out, then sat down to pee," Portia said. "She was saying she couldn't do this anymore, that she hated everyone. Then she buried her face in her arms and began to cry. It was only a few moments ago that I realized that she'd fallen asleep."

"She's not coming around," Victoria said. "We need to get her somewhere private, so I can take a proper look." She turned to the others. "We'll have to carry her. Stephanie, go get Tony. He's the strongest of the group. Portia, ask Jo-Jo if there's a service elevator we can use. Marjorie and I will stay with Beatrix."

The two women left with their assignments. Any feelings of anger that Victoria had toward Beatrix were now replaced by pity; she knew of too many women trapped in loveless marriages because their families all thought they knew what was best.

A few moments later, Tony peered around the corner. "What do you need from me, Nurse? Jo-Jo is commandeering the service elevator."

"Pick her up, please. We'll take her to my suite."

As they stepped out into the hall, Victoria saw the whole dinner party present, along with several members of the staff, waiting for an update.

Victoria sighed. "All right, people. Essential personnel only—Basil, Tony, and Jo-Jo. The rest of you—head to the bar. Once things are settled, we'll join you."

Hefting Beatrix effortlessly in his arms, Tony looked at Victoria with some admiration. "Looks like you've had experience with this sort of thing," he said.

Victoria broke out her best Irish brogue. "Oh, Tony darlin', compared to the drunk ward on St. Patrick's Day at St. Vincent's, this is nothing." She grinned and turned to follow Jo-Jo to the elevator.

When they got to Victoria's suite, they were greeted by Mario Agnolini, who was accompanied by a serious-looking woman who looked to be in her forties, wearing a maid's uniform.

Tony smiled. "*Bona sera*, Carmella."

"*Mascalzone*," Carmella said, smiling as she did.

Tony deposited Beatrix on the bed as Mario introduced himself to Basil. "And this is Carmella Vecchio," he said. "Though not formally trained as a nurse, she served as a medical assistant during the war. She also has a substantial command of English."

"I can vouch for that!" Tony chimed. He went to put his arm around Carmella and was greeted with a thwap to the midsection; as he doubled over in mock pain, both were smiling with great affection.

"Mr. Agnolini," Victoria asked in English for Basil's sake, "do you have a first-aid station in the hotel?"

"Of course," Mario said. "And very well-stocked. With the number of dignitaries who stay with us, it's easier for the doctor to come here if the need arises, instead of them going to his office."

Victoria nodded, kicking off her slides and stepping into her ballerina flats. "Would it be possible for me to have a peek so I can maybe help keep this poor woman from having the worst hangover of her life?"

"Of course, you can, Miss Shannon."

"Great." Victoria handed Carmella her most modest

dressing gown and instructed her to get Beatrix undressed and into the gown.

Tony sidled up to Carmella. "Need any help with that?" he smirked.

She snatched up a book. "So help me, I will cleave your skull with this if you come in before I'm done!"

"Tony, why don't you just keep Basil company until I get back," Victoria begged.

"Your wish is my command, Nurse Shannon," Tony bowed formally. She rolled her eyes and followed after Mario.

18

CORTINA, ITALY—MIRAMONTE HOTEL

SATURDAY, JANUARY 8, 1955
9:30 PM

Victoria let out a low whistle when Mario turned on the lights to the first-aid station. There were two hospital beds, a wheelchair, IV poles, a well-stocked medicine cabinet and IV fluids. For a minute, Victoria considered having Tony move Beatrix down here, but decided it would be easier to take any gear she needed back up to the suite.

Victoria first secured two bottles of saline to an IV pole; from the medicine cabinet, she took promethazine, vitamin B-12, folic acid, and a multi-vitamin infusion. In the instruments cabinet, she found the needles and syringes she would need and brought them over the autoclave and turned it on to heat up for the sterilization process.

As the familiar hiss of pressurized steam kicked in, it occurred to Victoria how strangely calm she felt. All the night's emotions—all her anger, sadness, embarrassment—had faded away as her training and instincts resurfaced. Her thoughts were clear and focused, her mind cool and efficient. It was more than just "being good in an emergency"—lots of people could manage that; this efficient, analytical frame of mind, she thought, was what marked her as a *professional.*

She looked over at Mario. He was standing, silently watching her with eyes wide. He looked slightly dazed. "Are you all right?" she asked.

He shook his head as if trying to clear it. "I am dazzled, watching you," he said. "It's like watching a movie star working in the repair bays at the Formula One Grand Prix. Such skill, in one so beautiful."

She smiled. "Flattery will get you nowhere."

"Signorina Shannon, my job is to play host to the wealthy and powerful. Flattery has gotten me everything I have. But tell me, what has happened to the young lady?"

"What d'ya think happened?" She shook her head. "Beatrix is with Basil. Basil wants her, but she wants Johnny, I'm with Johnny, and Johnny wants me and I want him, so Beatrix began to drink." She blinked, scarcely believing her own words. *I'm with Johnny.* Did saying it aloud make it so?

"How much did she have to drink?"

"Three champagne cocktails, four glasses of Chianti, and two shots of grappa in her espresso," she said, checking the timer on the autoclave. Seeing the way he looked at her, she said, "Yes, Mario. I was counting."

He said nothing.

"I was angry at her," she admitted. "I wanted to get back at her for putting poor Johnny in such a spot. I wanted to teach her a lesson. But now—" She sighed. "Now I just feel sorry for her. It seems like she's being forced into this marriage."

"She does not love this Basil?"

"I can't figure it," she admitted. "Basil's no prize in the looks department, but he's all right. He grows on you, you know? He's growing on me, anyway. He seems like the kind of man who'd give Beatrix anything she wanted." She shook her head. "I don't know. He was about to explain everything, but then we heard she'd passed out in the bathroom."

Mario said nothing, but he raised one eyebrow as if to say *Is that all?*

Victoria growled in frustration. "Okay, Mario. You caught me. I was angry at Beatrix, angrier than I should have been, because there's something about Johnny Gillespie that I'm very attracted to, but I—I—"

Her tears came without warning. "God dammit, Mario," she shouted. "What am I even doing here?"

Mario's voice was soothing. "Right now, you are rendering aid to a sick woman while she is dealing with the demons of a broken heart. And you are probably wrestling with your feelings for Johnny, wondering if this is real or just a salve for *your* broken heart. You have every right to be angry." His brows lowered for a moment. "But still, I wish you would not take the Lord's name in vain."

Victoria laughed through her tears.

"Signorina Shannon, please take this advice," Mario said. "It comes from a man who has lived through the horrors of two world wars, the rise of fascism, and a world economic depression. Enjoy yourself, be careful, and do not make a commitment until you are absolutely sure."

"Thank you," she whispered.

The autoclave's timer chimed, indicating that the equipment was sterilized. Once again, Victoria was all business. Wiping the bottle of multi-vitamin down with alcohol, she drew up 1 cc of the mixture and injected it into the IV bottle, giving the liquid in the bottle a yellow tint. She did the same with the folic acid, then spiked the bottle with a needle attached to IV tubing and clamped it off. Next, Victoria loaded up one syringe with 1 cc of vitamin B-12 and another with 1 cc of promethazine.

"I understand the need for vitamins to help with a hangover," said Mario, "but promethazine—it is for allergies, isn't it?"

"It's also good for relieving nausea, which she'll have," Victoria smiled. "And it'll help her sleep." She then put the loaded syringes in a basin along with an IV needle, adhesive tape, gauze, and alcohol. She put several aspirins in a small manila envelope for good measure. It was then that she eyed a portable oxygen tank in the corner, replete with hose and mask. She checked; it was full. "Mario, may I bring this along?" she asked. "Oxygen helps with the hangover. Why, I don't know, but we know it works."

Mario gave his assent, and the two of them carried the medical gear to Victoria's suite. When they returned,

Carmella was sitting next to the bed; Beatrix was now in Victoria's dressing gown as instructed. Basil and Tony were sitting at a card table playing hearts. *Clever Tony*, she thought, *keeping Basil's mind occupied until we got back.*

Once the equipment was delivered, Mario excused himself. Victoria went straight to work, first injecting vitamin B-12 in Beatrix's right hip, then the promethazine in her left. Beatrix hardly stirred. Next, she quickly found a vein in Beatrix's left forearm and started the IV of multi-vitamin and folic acid, securing it with gauze and tape, then attaching an IV board to the arm and setting the drip rate to run the liter of solution in two hours. Last, she fastened the oxygen mask on Beatrix and set it to flow at 2 liters per minute.

She turned to Carmella. "She'll sleep for a while," she said. "After an hour, remove the mask and cut the flow."

It was agreed Carmella would stay with Beatrix and call down to the bar if there were any change in her condition. With everything secure, the three of them—Victoria, Tony, and Basil—headed for the elevator.

As they waited for the car, Victoria said, "It looks like you and Carmella have some history."

Tony smiled. "Yeah, she stitched me up a few times. You know. Back in the big one. Me and a lot of others." A faraway look came to his eye. "There were a lot of brave men in the fight in those days—and women, too!—who looked at Carmella as a mother, father, best friend, preacher, priest, and rabbi. She earned a special place in heaven, in those days."

The elevator doors opened. Tony seemed to have trouble trusting his voice. "C'mon," he said gruffly. "The gang's waiting."

19

CORTINA, ITALY—MIRAMONTE HOTEL

SATURDAY, JANUARY 8, 1955
10:30 PM

The trio walked into the bar and found the rest of their party gathered near the fire, drinks in hand. The men had scotches, and the women snifters of brandy, but they looked untouched. Victoria gave them an update on Beatrix's condition, and there was the sense of a collective exhalation.

More chairs were drawn in, and a round of drinks procured for Tony and Basil. (Victoria declined a nightcap, instead ordering coffee; she felt she needed to stay awake and sober, just in case.) Once they were settled in, Basil returned to his "tale of woe," as he put it.

"As I said, at thirty-five I thought it time to settle down and marry. Mortimer Schofield and I both sat on the board of a charity dedicated to the restoration of museum pieces damaged during the war. Two years ago, in the spring, he introduced me to his niece, Beatrix Schofield—a most agreeable young lady, when I met her. We soon became engaged.

"Initially, I believed Beatrix was infatuated with me—or at least, infatuated at the prospect of becoming a baroness." He smiled a sad smile. "I'm not unaware of my shortcomings, you know. Not much of a 'catch,' in some respects. But I could offer status, and comfort, and security. I thought that would be enough for her. But by year's end, she had cuckolded me."

"How did you find out?" Victoria asked.

"Little things. There was forever something keeping her from me. An appointment, a missed train, an urgent call from a friend. So many details that didn't quite hang together. I was trained in the intelligence services, my dear. I learned to spot a lie, and once learned it is a knack one does not lose." He hung his head. "It shames me to admit that when my suspicions were aroused, I asked for help from some old friends. People who were in counterespionage with me. People I could trust."

"You put her under surveillance?" asked Gigi.

"Nothing quite so sinister, Colonel," Basil said. "Simply checked out her various stories. And as I feared, the details simply did not add up. Had she not been so very indiscreet ..." He faltered. "It was unfair to my friends, really, that they should have to deliver such bad news."

Victoria pondered how hard it must have been for Basil to bring his suspicions to his friends in the first place, and the blow it must have dealt to his pride.

"When I confronted Beatrix with it, of course, she denied it," Basil continued. "That is, until I showed her the photographs. That's when she told me about Uncle Mortimer." He took a sip of scotch to fortify himself. "Her consent had been nothing but a fiction of his. She had told him from the start that she didn't want to marry me. And in response, he beat her until she complied."

The room fell silent for a long moment. At last, Tony murmured, "That rat."

"Indeed," Basil said. His voice was hard with anger. "Mortimer, you see, has his eye on a position in Parliament and was hoping to use my station to help him achieve that goal. My money would be most useful to him in that respect—and my family connections. Endorsements, that sort of thing. My words in the right ears would give Mortimer access to circles that he would find quite unattainable otherwise. By this point, though, Beatrix swore that it was over between her and Liam O'Donnell. She had broken it off, and repented, she said, and would marry me without reservation."

He took a long sip of scotch and closed his eyes. "Things were splendid until November of last year. More unexplained absences. More lies. I investigated once again, and found that she was once more carrying on with Liam.

"This time, instead of confronting her directly, I went to Mortimer." His eyes again brimmed with tears. Listening, Victoria had a sick plummeting feeling in her stomach. "A terrible mistake, in hindsight. But in the moment, I couldn't bear to speak to Beatrix. I told Mortimer the engagement was off, but he convinced me he would take care of everything. He can be most persuasive. The next I heard, Liam was in hospital with two broken legs. And Beatrix—" Basil's voice went cold. "Beatrix couldn't see me for three weeks. Because of 'migraines,' I was told."

"My God," said Marjorie. "None of us saw her for most of November. Do you mean to say—"

"It takes a few weeks for bruises to fade," said Victoria dully.

"That son of a bitch," Tony growled, turning red in the face.

"Easy, soldier," Stephanie cooed, rubbing the back of his neck.

"Too late, I realized the danger in which I had placed Beatrix. Mortimer had her hidden away at a so-called 'health spa.' I managed to trace her, using some of the skills acquired in my previous life." He shivered slightly. "I saw some dreadful things during the war, but none that shall haunt me like the sight of her then. What he had done to her."

Victoria trembled. Seeing this, Johnny pulled his chair closer. She gratefully took his arm.

"Beatrix was terrified," Basil continued. "Not of me, but of Mortimer. She had never seen him so furious. He had threatened not only Liam, but his sister, who was working as a housekeeper for a retired brigadier. Three innocent lives, held hostage to one violent man's ambition."

"What did you do, old sport?" Gigi asked.

"I did what I was trained to do, Colonel." Basil managed a half-smile. "I protected my assets while I went about dismantling this diabolical operation. Beatrix told me the name of the hospital where Liam was being treated. I arranged for Liam to be discharged to a convalescent home, but moved him to a flat in York City before he took up residence at the home. Some trusted colleagues of mine are tending to him there. I then made a clandestine offer of employment to his sister. She immediately resigned her post at the brigadier's, and is now working for one of my estates in Scotland—out of Mortimer's reach."

"It all must have been terribly expensive," said Portia.

Basil looked momentarily puzzled. "Yes, I suppose it must," he said abstractedly.

The rich really are different from me and thee, thought Victoria.

Johnny, who had been silent throughout, now turned to look Basil in the eye. "So, what now?"

Basil looked coolly at Johnny. Victoria felt a sense of creeping dread. "Well, Cowboy," he said. "Before I answer that, I have one question for you."

"Shoot."

"When did you find out Beatrix had a fiancé?"

"Yesterday afternoon, when you knocked on her door at the Montana Hotel. Not a moment sooner."

"Amazing," said Basil. "And you rappelled off the balcony, I presume?"

Johnny nodded, but with a question in his eyes.

"I spotted what looked like a climbing rope, looped around the balcony railing," said Basil. "But of course, with the snow, I couldn't get a close look. Rather dangerous, I should think."

Johnny shrugged. Victoria was impressed with his nerve.

"I was hoping to catch you there," Basil admitted. "I thought it would save the time and effort of another investigation. But it appears to have all worked out in the end." Basil sighed deeply and surveyed the group. "The engagement is definitively over," he announced. "In light of recent events, it is plain that Beatrix simply doesn't love me. I thought that I might win her heart by casting myself as her protector, but I see that I was wrong."

"But do you not love her?" asked Marjorie.

Basil sighed. "Even if I do, my dear, the point is moot," he said. "Love her or not, I cannot *trust* her. I shall continue to do all that is in my power to keep her safe and protected, but that is only my duty as a gentleman. Any marriage between us would be a farce, and I refuse to participate. My mind's made up. Tomorrow, when she's sober and lucid, I will go about setting the world aright."

Tony eyed Basil suspiciously.

"Do not worry, Major Pagnozzi," Basil assured him. "Mortimer Schofield will never raise a hand to Beatrix again. I shall see to that."

With that, Basil drained his glass. Rising from the table, he said, "Come, Victoria. It's time we relieve Carmella."

The rest of the group rose, exchanging goodnights. The girls had arranged to spend the night with the soldiers here at the Miramonte, and they were all going to ski together tomorrow.

After the others had gone their separate ways, Johnny took Basil and Victoria aside. He extended his hand to Basil.

"I wouldn't blame you if you smacked it away," he said.

"On the contrary," said Basil, shaking Johnny's hand warmly. "You acted without malice, and treated her kindly. That's all I can ask for myself, or for her. If anything, I'm sorry you had to get caught up in this." Glancing at Victoria, who was holding Johnny's free hand, Basil gave a mischievous grin. "In any case, Cowboy, I believe you've come out on top."

20

CORTINA, ITALY—MIRAMONTE HOTEL

SATURDAY, JANUARY 8, 1955
11:45 PM

Johnny accompanied them back to Victoria's suite. Victoria was glad; she would be busy in tending Beatrix, and Basil would need a friend by his side. Funny, she thought, to think of the two of them as friends; but watching Johnny's growing sympathy and admiration for Basil as he poured out his heart out—and not just Johnny's, but that of all the soldiers—there could be no doubt that he was now a part of their band of brothers.

In the corridor, they ran into Mario Agnolini. He was pleased to hear Victoria's prognosis for Beatrix, and told her that Ernesto would meet her in the afternoon, if she felt up to it. Victoria thanked him, wondering if she'd be in any shape to ski tomorrow.

The hardest part about relieving Carmella proved to be convincing her to be relieved. She volunteered to stay if necessary, and refused the twenty-pound note that Basil tried to give her as a tip. Victoria had to remind Carmella of her own medical credentials before Carmella was satisfied that Beatrix would be in good hands.

Before she went, Carmella pulled Victoria aside. Silently, she jerked her thumb toward Beatrix, then patted her own stomach, giving Victoria a significant look.

Victoria felt herself go pale. She looked over her shoulder to be sure the men had not seen; but they were safely in the doorway of the sitting room. Turning to Carmella, she gave a nod of understanding and said goodnight.

It was approaching midnight, and the first liter of IV fluid was nearly complete. Victoria switched over to the new one; Beatrix was still sleeping soundly.

Johnny and Basil sat at the card table, half-heartedly trying to start a game of gin rummy. Johnny was dealing the cards, but kept losing count before he got to ten.

"Honey, you must be exhausted," Victoria said. "There's nothing you can do here. Why don't you head back to your room before you fall asleep on your feet?"

"I reckon I might, at that," said Johnny, rising unsteadily. "I'm sorry, Basil. Today has been a bear."

"Think nothing of it, old man," said Basil. "Tomorrow we fight another day, eh?"

Johnny smiled sleepily. Victoria showed him to the door and gently kissed him goodnight. "Leave the door unlocked," she whispered. "I'll join you in a few hours."

She leaned against the doorframe, watching Johnny walk away, and let out a helpless sigh after he disappeared down the stairs. Closing the door, she turned to see Basil watching her with a sly little grin on his face.

"Ah, shut up Basil, will ya?" Victoria said with a smile. Basil struck a schoolboy pose with his eyes turned heavenward, the very picture of innocence. They both laughed—quietly, so as not to wake Beatrix.

Mario had sent up a coffee service while they were downstairs. *God bless that man,* thought Victoria; *he thinks of everything.* She poured herself a cup from the vacuum flask, black and hot, and gestured to Basil. "Please," Basil smiled. "Cream and sugar, if you don't mind. To hell with my girlish figure."

Victoria laughed as she handed Basil his coffee. "Ain't we the pair."

"A pair of what, I don't know," Basil countered, smiling.

"So, counterintelligence. Spy-catching, right?"

"Correct."

"Did you ever, uh—?" Victoria made a gun shape with her hand and mimed firing.

"During the war, you mean? More times than I care to remember," he said. "More men than I care to consider. With my family connections, I could have secured a position on the home front, but I thought I could best serve king and country on the front lines. I was with the commandos, with the amphibious force in Operation Chariot."

"The raid on St. Nazaire," Victoria said.

"The very same. We won the day, of course, but the cost—" Basil closed his eyes. "Six hundred and twelve of our lads sailed across the Channel. Only 228 made it home. The rest were captured or killed. I myself got out on a medical evacuation."

"You were wounded?"

Basil smiled thinly. "Rather badly, as it happens. I pulled through, as you can see, but my combat days were over for good. That was 1942. "

It seemed surreal to Victoria, that this ungainly figure—so bookish, so gentle—should also be struggling with such demons. So strange, and so unfair, that out of a whole generation of men, seemingly not a one was spared.

"It was then that I transferred to the intelligence services," Basil continued. "And as it happened, I was very good at the job. I say that not as a point of pride, but as a simple fact. But it didn't make this last escapade any easier."

"You played it masterfully," Victoria said. "Right down to the fake tears."

"Oh, the tears were quite real," he said. He must have seen the surprise on Victoria's face. "I was looking for solace after the war, my dear. I wanted nothing but to leave it all behind. I had no regrets about turning down a commission with MI-6. I shudder to think of what I might have become."

Victoria said nothing. Basil sipped his coffee, as if collecting his thoughts. When he spoke again, he was hesitant, choosing his words with care.

"The nightmares mostly stopped by 1950. My academic endeavors gave me purpose. I was rebuilding my life. I had been broken for so long that I had almost forgotten how it felt to be whole. But at last, it seemed I was on the mend." He sighed. "And I thought—perhaps selfishly—that marriage might be the thing to make me feel fully complete."

Victoria listened in silence. She thought of Joel; perhaps he, too, had been seeking solace from the horrors of war in marriage.

"I don't think you're selfish," she said at last. "Maybe a person needs to learn to love himself before he's really ready to love someone else."

"You're very kind," he said. "I'm a bit of work in progress in that regard, I'm afraid."

"Join the club," she smiled. "So what will you do now?"

"It's plain that Beatrix loves Liam O'Donnell, certainly more than she will ever love me. And so I will do everything in my power to help the two of them live happily ever after." He pondered for a moment. "Though the thought of enlisting Major Pagnozzi to give Mortimer a New York City sermon on civility toward women is—intriguing." He smiled. "Mortimer would soil his trousers the first time Tony cracked his knuckles."

Victoria laughed. "I'd hate to see the big guy throw away his military career over it, though," she said. "I'm pretty sure he'd get caught before he got out of London."

"You might be surprised," Basil rubbed his chin for a moment "Methinks there's more to the good major than meets the eye. Nothing substantial, mind you, but I suspect our Tony might have worked for your OSS at some point during the war. The colonel, too, I shouldn't wonder."

Victoria stared at him, incredulous. "Gigi and Tony? Spies?"

"Multilingual, dual citizenship, know how to handle themselves in a scrap." Basil ticked the points off on his fingers. "There's a profile, you see. And those lads fit it."

Victoria studied Basil's face for a moment. She could not tell if he was joking, serious, or just talking for the sake of talking. And because she could not tell, she decided to put the thought aside. "You think you know someone," she said, as if to herself.

"Indeed," said Basil. "That's why I've made it my policy to be an open book. But you, Victoria! What mysteries do you hold? What set of circumstance finds you her, on this cold, wintry night in Cortina, administering nursing care with such great compassion to drunken young women and wounded hearts alike?"

"Flatterer," she smiled.

"Guilty as charged."

"You're trying to change the subject."

"Heavens, I should hope so," he said coyly. "Is it working?"

It was. Victoria poured herself another cup of coffee and proceeded to tell Basil her story, more or less as she had told it to Johnny, and included the budding of their relationship. She worried that Basil would despise her for her loose morals—sleeping with a total stranger within days of her engagement being broken—but after his frankness earlier that evening, she felt she had owed him no less than total honesty. She told it all, and for good measure told him the full story of Johnny's escape from the Hotel Montana, including the acquisition of his new nickname.

Basil listened in silence, his face expressionless. Victoria watched him for any sign of judgment or jealousy. But in the end, he only smiled that sad smile of his; and then, in his best attempt at a New York accent, said, "Ain't we a pair!"

Victoria smiled and shot him a one-fingered salute. "I'm sorry, my dear," said he, "but the appropriate response to an Englishman is two fingers." He demonstrated, and she mirrored him, and they laughed much louder than intended.

They were still laughing when they heard a weak voice from the bedroom area. Beatrix's voice: "Where am I?"

They walked over to the bed. "How are you feeling?" Victoria asked.

It took a moment for Beatrix to recognize them. Then horror dawned across her face. Victoria supposed she couldn't blame her; her fiancé and her nemesis, looming over her. "Where am I?" she demanded. "And what have you done with my things?"

Basil smiled gently. "You've been unconscious, my dear," he said. "Fainted dead away during dinner. Victoria has been kind enough to lend us her suite for your recovery—and rendered you excellent nursing care, despite the fact that you were such a horror to her earlier in the evening."

Beatrix's lower lip began to quiver, and tears welled up in her eyes. Victoria shot Basil a dirty look; *Was that really necessary?* she thought. But then, who was she to judge the broken-hearted?

"Basil," she said, "why don't you stand outside for a moment? I'll help Beatrix make herself presentable."

The awkward moment broken, Basil smiled and complied.

As soon as the door closed behind him, Victoria began the work on Beatrix. It was at this point that Beatrix realized that she was hooked up to an IV. "What on earth is going on? What have you done to me? Why didn't anyone stop you? And where's Johnny?"

Victoria paused and looked at her critically. "What's the last thing you remember?"

"I was eating," Beatrix stated. Confusion began to creep over her face. "Some sort of—meat, I think?"

"When I worked on the drunk ward, we used to call it a blackout," Victoria said. "When a person has been binge drinking, the brain sometimes stops processing memories properly. You're still upright, walking around, eating and drinking, even carrying on a conversation. You still appear to be conscious of your surroundings." She was careful to stick to clinical language, but she could see the awful realization crossing Beatrix's face. "But to all intents and purposes, you are oblivious. And you don't even realize it until you sober up."

"Oh, God," Beatrix whispered.

"Assuming you checked out during the osso bucco," Victoria continued, "I'd say you've lost about a half-hour." She paused. "Are you sure you want to hear this now? It's—a little unpleasant."

Beatrix was trembling, but she nodded.

"We finished up dinner," Victoria continued. "Johnny and Basil were talking about history, mostly. And then, while we were enjoying dessert and coffee when you stood up and announced that it was time for you and Johnny to go off and have one last romp in the hay before you returned to your miserable life in jolly old England. Pretty much in those words."

Beatrix was ashen. "In front of Basil?"

"In front of everyone. Including most of the kitchen staff."

"Oh, *God*," she said again. "Where are Stephanie, Marjorie, and Portia?"

"They're with the boys. They're staying the night. It's nearly two o'clock now."

"And where is Johnny?"

"He is in his room," said Victoria firmly. "Waiting for me. I'm heading down there as soon as I take that IV out of you."

Beatrix offered up her arm, utterly defeated. "Good Lord, what will I do now?'

"My advice?" Victoria removed the IV board and pulled out the needle, putting pressure on the site with gauze. "Trust in Basil. Despite the way you've treated him, he's willing to help you and Liam."

"He told you about Liam and me?"

"Honey," said Victoria wearily, "he told us about *everything*."

Beatrix buried her face in her hands and began to blubber. Victoria rolled her eyes. She was tired; and after seeing the grace and patience with which Basil had borne her infidelities, she was in no mood for Beatrix's self-pity. She slapped Beatrix's hands away. Beatrix looked at her with horror, tears streaking her face.

"Snap out of it," she hissed. "It took three of us to keep Tony from going over to England and tearing your Uncle Mortimer limb from limb. Basil has experience with running secret operations. Put your trust in him, and you and Liam might just have a future. If you try to strike off on your own, there's a good chance that you're in for more beatings." She paused, weighing her words. "And you really don't want that, do you? Considering that there's a good chance you're pregnant."

Beatrix clenched her jaw. "Who told you?"

"There's a nurse of sorts who watched over you while I was gone," Victoria said. "Carmella. She's the one who changed you into my dressing gown. I imagine she figured it out from one look at your breasts." Beatrix closed her eyes and sighed, but Victoria went on. "She's seen more than her share of pregnant women—and so have I. How far along are you?"

"About two months," Beatrix said glumly. "I was hoping it wasn't true. But now it's obvious, I suppose. Does Johnny know?"

Victoria shook her head.

"And Basil?"

"No."

Beatrix reached out for Victoria's hand. She was trembling. "Miss Shannon," she said. "I know I have no right to ask, but—could you be here when I tell Basil?"

Vitoria sighed and said she would.

Beatrix managed a half-smile. "Can you ask him in, please?"

Victoria opened the door, and Basil moved swiftly to the bedside. "My dear Beatrix," he said. "How are you feeling?"

"Much better," she said timidly. "I believe I owe Victoria a debt of gratitude for taking such good care of me."

"Oh, yes. Yes, she's a credit to the nursing profession."

"I'm sorry for the way I treated you, Basil."

"You were only searching for happiness, my dear," he said. "As was I. It's only a pity it took us so long to realize we would not find it in each other."

"There's something else."

"Yes?"

"I'm pregnant."

Basil took a deep breath, then exhaled. "I don't suppose it's mine?" he asked softly.

Beatrix winced. "I'm pretty sure it's Liam's."

"I see," said Basil. He was silent for a moment, and when he spoke again his voice was rather husky. "Well, now the course is simple. I need to ensure a safe life for you, Liam, and the baby." He managed a smile. "Let that be one good thing that comes out of this, at least."

Beatrix began to cry freely. Basil cradled her in his arms, nodding to Victoria over her shoulder. Victoria nodded back, and left the room, closing the door behind her as quietly as she could.

The walk to Johnny's room was long and weary. Finding the door unlocked, she crept silently inside, stepped out of her flats, and undressed, crawling naked into Johnny's bed. She heard his drowsy voice: "Everything okay?"

"What're you doing up?"

"Waiting for you."

"Johnny, I'm exhausted."

"What? No," he said. "I just wanted to make sure you're all right." He wrapped his arm around her shoulders and cradled her head on his chest.

"Everything's fine, darlin'. Go to sleep."

Within in a minute, Victoria could tell from Johnny's rhythmic breathing he was fast asleep. *Ain't we a pair*, she thought—her last thought before drifting off herself, less than a minute later.

21

CORTINA, ITALY—MIRAMONTE HOTEL

SUNDAY, JANUARY 9, 1955
10:20 AM

Victoria slept. Victoria dreamed.

She was sitting at an outdoor café near Central Park, enjoying coffee and pastries with someone who looked a lot like Johnny. She was dressed, for some reason, in high boots and riding pants; her blouse was silk, but she wore a brown leather jacket over it. On the table, next to her coffee, was a pair of aviator sunglasses like the ones Johnny wore. Her companion—was it Johnny? She was no longer sure—had light brown hair like Johnny's, but much longer, with a bushy beard, and his face was much more darkly tanned. He wore a homespun shirt and buckskin trousers, and around his neck he had a necklace of grizzly bear claws. Next to him was powder-horn and an enormous muzzle-loading rifle.

It was the aromatic smell of coffee that finally pulled Victoria into full wakefulness. As she sat up, she was greeted with Johnny's smiling face. He was dressed already in his green shirt and khakis, along with his cowboy boots. "There you are," he said. "Nice to see you awake."

"Thanks," she said sweetly. She sat up, allowing the covers slip down around her waist, and Johnny handed her a cup.

Victoria was amazed not only at how comfortable she felt to be naked around Johnny, but how unfazed he seemed seeing her that way. With both Sebastian and Joel, there had always been a degree of modesty—a skittishness, almost—which she did not feel with Johnny. *I could get used to this,* she thought, and the thought frightened her, making the hair on the back of her neck prickle.

She took a sip of the coffee. It was strong and hot. "So, what's the plan?"

"Well," Johnny said, "I've already talked to Ernesto. He's willing to do a ski lesson with you after lunch." He handed her a plate of pastries. She had not realized just how hungry she was; but before she knew it, she had devoured two chocolate croissants.

"What time is it, anyway?"

"Ten-thirty," he said.

"Jesus *Christ,*" she exclaimed, then bolted the rest of her coffee. "Is Beatrix still in my suite?"

Johnny shook his head. "Apparently, she and Basil left early this morning."

"Left the Miramonte?"

"Left Cortina altogether, I'm pretty sure."

"Without saying goodbye?"

Johnny shrugged. "After last night, I'm pretty sure they're both embarrassed. Maybe it's for the best."

Victoria made a noise of assent, then climbed out of bed and started putting on her clothes. "Okay, then. I'll run back to my place, shower up, change into my ski clothes, and meet you for an early lunch. By the way, what are your compatriots and their concubines doing today?"

"They're going to be all together skiing. They figure we two can be left to our own devices. I'll see if Ernesto is interested in seeing just how well I can ski." He grinned. "I reckon that old boy's never seen how we do it in the Rockies. I might even teach him a trick or two."

Victoria stepped into her flats. "Maybe you could teach me a trick or two later," she said, and kissed him. "Meet me in the bar at about half past eleven."

When Victoria got back to her suite, she found two envelopes on the card table, both addressed to her, in different handwriting. The first, in an elegant hand that bespoke an outstanding private education, was from Basil. He thanked her for her professionalism and her kindness, and said he was counting on her discretion in such a delicate matter. He invited her to keep in touch after her return to the States, and enclosed several of his visiting cards. Victoria thought to herself that she should write Basil at the first opportunity; she had to update him on her whereabouts and to learn about his final plans for Liam and Beatrix. After reading his request for her discretion, though, she was glad she had not told Johnny that Beatrix was pregnant; that, for the moment, would have to remain privileged information.

The other note was in Beatrix's hasty scrawl.

Thanks so much for taking such good care of me even though I treated you in such a beastly fashion. I hope you can find it in your heart to forgive me. On your advice, I will be placing my complete trust in Basil to help and Liam and me in this difficult situation. All we can do now is hope for the best. Please tell Johnny I am terribly sorry to have hurt him, and wish him only happiness in the future.

Victoria put both notes in her pocketbook and placed Basil's cards in her wallet; then she showered and change into her ski clothes.

About an hour later, she met Johnny in the bar. He had changed into thick, heavy wool military slacks and shirt, both in green. On the chair next to him were his anorak, wool sweater, gloves, and glacier glasses. Victoria was wearing a red, white, and black ski sweater with her black ski pants, her feet encased in her snow boots. Lunch consisted of linguine with marinara sauce, a side salad, and bread. Chianti was served with the lunch. Neither one wanted to be stuffed before skiing, so they skipped dessert but enjoyed the coffee. It was about a quarter after noon when Ernesto joined them. There was a seriousness about him that Victoria had not seen before. He was cordial to Johnny, but she could tell that he was not pleased that he was there. Johnny politely asked if it would be all right to join them—after all, this was Victoria's time, and he did not want to interfere—and Ernesto pondered for a long moment before giving his assent.

Despite the clear skies and sunshine, the temperature was well below freezing. Victoria shivered as she reached inside her jacket and put on the headband, while Johnny donned his watch cap. Ernesto supplied Victoria with a pair of ski goggles, Johnny donned his glacier glasses, and they went over to the ski shack to retrieve their skis.

Johnny was amazed at how well Victoria was skiing; he could hardly believe that she had put on skis for the first time only four days earlier. He complimented Ernesto on his instruction capabilities; Ernesto, in turn complimented the captain on his skiing technique.

Victoria was pleased to see that Ernesto was beginning to warm to Johnny. It had finally dawned on Victoria that Ernesto's initial reticence was most likely an expression of his protective, fatherly nature. Unless—could Ernesto be *jealous* of Johnny? Did he see the younger man as a romantic rival? Victoria discounted the thought even as it surfaced; Ernesto (and Mario, for that matter) might like to flirt, but both seemed far too conscientious about their duties to their guests to ever engage in any impropriety. That said, Victoria resolved to be careful of the old man's feelings; she had no wish to jeopardize the friendship and bond she was forming with him, not even for Johnny's sake.

Again, the voice inside her head was questioning what kind of future she could have with Johnny. In just a week, Victoria would be heading back to the United States, and

Johnny was returning to Camp Darby tomorrow. She probably would never see him ever again, and the thought even frightened her more. Tonight, they would have to talk about this.

22

CORTINA, ITALY—MIRAMONTE HOTEL

SUNDAY, JANUARY 9, 1955
4:30 PM

Johnny, Victoria, and Ernesto finished skiing at about four in the afternoon. Johnny thanked Ernesto and invited him to join them for dinner tonight with the rest of the crew; Ernesto politely declined, stating that he needed to take care of his elderly aunt. Johnny and Victoria met the rest of the gang at the bar, where they were all enjoying cocktails.

Just as Gigi was about to order a second round, two enormous Negro soldiers walked into the bar. Gigi leaped to his feet and loudly called everyone to attention. With Pavlovian reflexes, Johnny, Tony, and Jo-Jo came to attention with Gigi, all saluting. Victoria and the other women, not knowing what to do, stood up also.

The two soldiers were obviously military police; the MP insignia was stenciled on their white helmets and armbands, and they bore white cartridge belts white holsters. Behind them was a Negro officer, older than the other two and not quite as big, but impressive in both size and bearing. Two stars shone on his utility cap.

Gigi broke into a wide grin. "General Thompson, sir! An honor to see you again."

The general returned both the smile and the salute "Colonel Pasquale," he said in a rich baritone. "It is always a pleasure to see an old comrade in arms. Please, introduce me to you colleagues."

Gigi made the introductions—first Tony, then Jo-Jo, and finally Johnny. General Thompson fixed Johnny with a critical eye. "Captain Gillespie," he said. "Your commanding officer and I were just talking about you yesterday."

Victoria whispered to Johnny, "You're in trouble."

The general turned his gaze to Victoria. "I beg your pardon, young lady?"

"My name is Victoria Shannon, General Thompson," she said. "And I would like to thank you for what you did for my family, some years ago."

General Thompson had the air of a man who was seldom lost for words—but Victoria had thoroughly wrong-footed him. "I'm sorry, Miss, but you have me at a disadvantage."

"My brother James was under your command after the war. And when our mother died, you were kind enough to cut through the red tape in order for him to come back home for her funeral."

Even before Victoria had finished speaking, a smile of recognition lit up the general's face. "James Shannon's little sister Victoria! Yes, yes!" He took her hand in both of his. "How is James? My condolences about your mother, I wish there were more I could've done in your time of grief."

Victoria felt an instant liking for the general. As she struggled to answer his volley of questions, several other officers joined the group. The first was another Negro, a captain, who stood about six feet tall, with a muscular athletic physique. "My aide de camp, Captain Samuel Rodgers," said the general.

He next introduced a wiry, rather intense individual with black-rimmed glasses. "And this is Lieutenant William Jefferson, my legal attaché. Just graduated from Harvard Law." Both officers were in utility clothing, like the general, and carried .45 pistols.

By this time Mario Agnolini had come to the bar. He greeted the general like an old friend. "General Thompson! So nice to see you again. And how are your lovely wife and daughter?"

"Well, thank you, Mario. We hope to return for a visit this summer."

"Please, let me know. We will make every accommodation necessary for you."

Then General Thompson's voice took a more serious tone. "I am sorry for the short notice, Mario, but I'm hoping you can accommodate me, my officers, and some special cargo for tonight. It appears the weather is turning bad again, and we cannot risk being on the road."

Mario let out a whistle. "I am so sorry, General. The hotel is full. We can make accommodations for the enlisted men in some of the outbuildings, but there are no suites available. Please accept my apologies. I can call down to the Montana Hotel to see if there are available rooms there."

"No need for that," said the general. "I will bivouac with the men tonight."

Upon hearing that, Victoria volunteered her suite to the general.

He raised an eyebrow. "Miss Shannon," he said sternly.

"Victoria, please."

"Victoria, then. It will be a sad, sad, day for the army—and a cold, cold, day in Hell—when Ulysses Sampson Thompson kicks a young woman out of her boudoir for his comfort." Chuckles rattled through the assembled officers, quickly arrested by the general's scowl. "However, given the circumstances, I will prevail upon Captain Gillespie to surrender *his* room for the evening."

"Sir, yes sir," said Johnny, saluting.

"But General Thompson," said Victoria, all wide eyes and innocence, "where will poor Captain Gillespie sleep tonight?"

Tony's migraine made a sudden return.

"I'll requisition a pup tent and sleeping bag for the captain, naturally. My understanding is that Captain Gillespie is an authority on winter maneuvers. I imagine sleeping outdoors on a night like this would be fine by him."

Johnny's attention posture was losing some of its enthusiasm.

"That being said, I must warn you, Victoria," said the general with a smile. "The good Captain Gillespie here is a mountaineer, and mountaineers by nature are quite nefarious. You may want to lock your windows in case he scales the building to your balcony!" Again, there were chuckles all around—although they were not particularly hearty from the Four Musketeers. Johnny in particular looked as if he had a toothache.

The two sergeants were sent out and inform the men about their accommodations. The general asked Mario if it would be possible to have an impromptu dinner for the officers, including Captain Gillespie, the Alpini, and their lady friends. Mario assured him that he would requisition one of the banquet rooms.

As the general was thanking Mario, the sergeants returned with several other soldiers, all carrying cartons of Marlboro cigarettes or Johnnie Walker Red scotch. "If you won't accept a fair price for our lodging," the general told Mario, "then this is the least we can do."

The MPs were storing the scotch behind the bar at Carlo's direction when another sergeant burst into the bar. He, too, was a Negro, though much smaller than the two other sergeants and a bit older. "Where is he? Where's the colonel? I need to see the colonel," the animated little sergeant cried.

Drawn by the commotion, Gigi wandered back into the bar. When he saw the sergeant, his face lit up with joy. "Izzy!" he shouted. "So good to see you again, my friend!"

The two men embraced warmly. "It's always a pleasure, Gigi, and you are a sight for sore eyes."

The general had entered the room. "Sergeant," he said. "What's all the rumpus?"

"General," Izzy said, saluting. "It's pretty cold out there, and my rheumatism's acting up." He was smiling brightly. "Do I have the general's permission for some tonic?"

The general returned his smile. "You may proceed, Sergeant Robinson."

Turning to Carlo behind the bar, Izzy said, "Barkeep, a bottle of bourbon, please. And if I'm not mistaken, I believe the rheumatism is contagious. Everybody in this room right now may be susceptible."

The general was chuckling, as were the officers and the MPs. "The floor is yours, Sergeant," he said.

"Thank you, General."

Carlo handed out shot glasses to all present, including the ladies, as Sergeant Isaiah "Izzy" Robinson began to pour out the bourbon while singing "My Old Kentucky Home."

As he was doling out the bourbon, Tony turned to Gigi. "Is this Izzy character actually from Kentucky?"

"I haven't the slightest, old boy," said Gigi. "Is Jersey City in Kentucky?"

"Never mind," Tony said, tending to his worsening migraine.

When all in the assembly had their drinks in hand, one last shot glass was placed on the bar and filled.

"Who is that for?" Stephanie asked.

Solemnly, Tony said, "For those that are not here today."

Izzy raised his glass high. "To live, and fight another day," he toasted.

The company returned his toast and drank.

Gigi was not yet finished with Izzy. "Sergeant, do tell me—how is Letizia?"

"She's fine, Colonel," Izzy grinned. "And the children."

"How many are they now? Three?

"Four now, sir. Giuseppe, Maria, Franco, and little Andrea, three years old next month."

"Where does the time go, eh?" said Gigi. "I say—do you still keep in touch with Corporal McAllister?"

"'Deed we do, Colonel. Matter of fact, me, Letizia, and the kids and heading to the highlands this summer for a week-long vacation. McAllister is a gamekeeper up there. Him and his wife Liz and their kids live in a huge hunting lodge. Plenty a room for all of us to stay."

"Excellent, excellent," Gigi said. "Please give them my warmest regards."

Izzy then turned to the group and made an announcement: "I just want to tell everybody here—if you ever are trapped in a bombed-out church with most of your soldiers wounded, and you're surrounded by the enemy, you definitely want this man in charge."

That's how you bait a hook, Victoria thought.

Izzy filled his glass again and leaned against the bar, commanding every eye in the room. "It all started at the end of Operation Market Garden, late September, 1944," he began. "General Thompson here was a colonel, back then, and our unit was providing support for the retreating forces. So night was falling as this skinny little British paratrooper shows up in our camp and very politely asked the colonel if there was any way we could come and help evacuate the rest of his company. Most of them were wounded, see, and couldn't be moved.

"Unfortunately, we were under strict orders not to advance any further, and the colonel had to tell poor Corporal McAllister that we couldn't assist. McAllister understood, but he did ask if we could at least spare some first-aid material for the wounded—which we did—and some ammunition, so's they could at least make a last stand. Now, we had a lot of captured nine-millimeter ammo we'd taken from the Nazis and we could spare it, and the paratroopers could use it because they shot those funny-looking Sten guns. The colonel really hated that he couldn't do more, but he loaded up Corporal McAllister with as much as he could carry and made to send him on his way.

"Now hearing this story, and realizing that this is one of the bravest little sons of bitches—excuse my French, ladies—I ever had seen in my life, I asked the colonel if I might volunteer to help carry some extra equipment, and volunteered my cousin Sammy Johnson to boot. The colonel wasn't happy, but he agreed it was the least we could do. So, we loaded up as much equipment, ammunition, first-aid supplies, and bourbon—for medicinal purposes only—as we could carry.

"Next thing we know, Corporal McAllister takes off like he just stole the hubcaps off of Mr. Roosevelt's limousine, with Sammy and me in hot pursuit. When we finally get there, the captain—Colonel Pasquale, I mean, Captain Pasquale then—he was giving encouragement, talking to his men like they were family. He was very thankful to the two of us for all the supplies we helped bring in, then told us we better get the hell out of there before the shooting starts.

"Well, Sammy and me look at each other and say, 'What the hell we supposed to do, leave these boys here and head back to defensive position? Leave these poor bastards to the Nazis?' Sorry, but Mrs. Robinson didn't raise her son to run when somebody was in need—and these fellas were in need, even if they did talk funny. The only regret was we shoulda brought more bourbon."

Victoria could see that Gigi was uncomfortable hearing the story, as was General Thompson.

"So, a couple of Nazi patrols were probing our defenses," Izzy continued, "when out of the wood comes the calvary. Colonel Thompson ordered three half-tracks and three half-tons full of buffalo soldiers to go in and evacuate these troopers. To hell with orders—buffalo soldiers never leave comrades behind, even if it meant a possible court martial for the colonel."

Victoria felt a lump in her throat, and trusted her voice just to say one thing. "General, my rheumatism is acting up. I believe I need a little more medicine."

Apparently, so was everyone else's rheumatism.

23

CORTINA, ITALY—MIRAMONTE HOTEL

SUNDAY, JANUARY 9, 1955
5:45 PM

Dinner was to begin at seven o'clock, with cocktails at six. The hotel was setting up an impromptu bar in the banquet room, open not only to the dinner guests—the general, his aide Captain Rodgers, the legal attaché Lieutenant Jefferson, plus Victoria, Johnny, Gigi, Marjorie, Tony, Stephanie, Jo-Jo, and Portia—but also for the enlisted men bivouacked outside.

Victoria was already dressed for dinner and putting the finishing touches on her makeup when there was a knock on her door. Standing there was General Thompson in his dress uniform, shoes highly polished, smiling confidently.

"General!" she said. "I thought we were going to meet in the bar for cocktails before dinner?"

"You're correct, my dear. But I was hoping to get a few minutes with you privately before the festivities started. May I come in?"

"Of course."

There was sherry in the suite, which the general declined, and a chair, which he accepted.

"So, James is doing well?"

Victoria nodded. "He's very proud of his work with the Bureau. He and Colleen both love Seattle, and the twins, Thomas and John, are growing up to be fine young men."

"That's wonderful. And you?" He leaned forward. "How long have you and Captain Gillespie been involved?"

Oh, hell, Victoria thought. *Now this kindly old gentleman is about to find out that I'm a slut.* But ignoring the sting of blood rushing to her cheeks, she smiled. "Actually, General, we met two days ago."

His eyebrows rose, ever so slightly. "Hm. I would have thought you two had been involved for a long while. You seem very comfortable together."

"You noticed that, too?" she said blithely. "I thought it was only me. Thank you, General, I couldn't put my finger on it until now."

"Hmmph!" rumbled General Thompson. "I believe there is more to this story. And I believe I will take that sherry now, while you tell me."

Victoria regretted her teasing tone. You don't become a two-star general in the United States Army—especially when you're a person of color—without being an astute reader of human character, she realized. She should never have tried to bareface her way out of this.

When in doubt, she thought, *tell the truth.* She poured out two sherries and launched into her story, from her first marriage straight through to the previous morning, sparing no detail.

The general listened mostly without interruptions, confirming he had names and timelines correct. When she finished, he sat there for a moment, as if lost in thought.

"I lost my first wife in 1942," he said, a propos of nothing. "She was diagnosed with pneumonia. Despite antibiotic therapy, the infection overwhelmed her defenses and multiple organs failed, leaving me a widower with two teenagers. Oliver was fourteen at the time; Rita was only twelve. They stayed with my wife's family while I was fighting overseas."

He stared into his sherry glass. "Oliver decided to follow my footsteps. He joined up after attending Norwich University. He was killed in Korea, three years ago." General Thompson's voice had grown thick with the struggle to keep his emotions in check. "Rita is now a medical resident at Boston Free Hospital for Women. She's engaged to be married—to Lieutenant Jefferson, as it happens."

"Your legal attaché?"

"A brilliant young man. They're looking to get married next year, if I can spare him long enough to grant him leave." He smiled. "I met my second wife in 1946," he continued. "I never believed in love at first sight before then, but it happened to us. Quite a similar experience to your experience with Captain Gillespie, I imagine, and his with you. People meeting us for the first time tend to assume we've been together for a lifetime, despite our obvious differences."

Victoria was momentarily puzzled.

"She's Italian," said the general. "A white woman, a Catholic, married to a Black American man raised in the African Methodist church. But from the moment I met her, she knew. And so did I."

He sipped the last of his sherry. "The heart is a strange organ," he said. "It pumps our life's blood through our arteries and veins. Yet it can dictate to us our emotions when it comes who we love—and who we don't. My advice—not that you asked—is this: Approach your relationship with your eyes wide open, seek wise counsel, and—whatever you do—please do not make any long-lasting commitments for at least a year."

Victoria smiled. She had not known what to expect from this conversation when it began, but her heart now brimmed with relief—and hope.

"My goodness: said the general suddenly, looking at his wristwatch. "It's 6:15 already! The perfect time for us to make a fashionably late entrance."

When Victoria and the general entered the bar, everyone was present, and all came to attention. "At ease," he announced, allowing everyone to return to their conversations.

The Three Musketeers were now in their dress uniforms, and the Englishwomen in cocktail dresses.

Lieutenant Jefferson was engaged in a conversation with Jo-Jo and Portia, talking about art. Portia had been working on a degree in fine arts back home at the University College London—the same degree that the lieutenant had received from Harvard prior to his stint in law school. Both were passionate lovers of the arts, especially the European classics.

Gigi and Marjorie were talking with Izzy and several other non-commissioned officers; it seemed to Victoria that Marjorie was enjoying listening to Izzy hold court. He knew how to hold an audience. She saw, to her mild surprise, that Izzy was drinking a Coke, as were all the other non-commissioned officers. Marjorie clung tightly to Gigi. Victoria wondered what her situation was back home in England; was she, too, promised to someone else?

At the bar, Victoria chose a dry white wine while the general decided to stick with sherry. Seeing Captain Rodgers in conversation with Johnny, Tony, Stephanie, and the two enormous staff sergeants, they wandered over.

"General," Tony greeted the pair. "Sam here was telling Johnny and me you're thinking about putting together a football team to play the air force this summer. Need an extra linebacker?"

"Hmmph. I may at that," said the general. "Captain Rodgers is going to be my starting halfback, and these two jokers"—here he pointed to the sergeants, both of whom wore Cheshire Cat grins—"are my offensive tackles. Yes, I could use another linebacker." Turning to Johnny, he said, "I read your dossier, Captain Gillespie. You played tight end for the University of Colorado at Boulder, is that right?"

"Yes, sir," Johnny said, taken slightly aback.

"I already have several outstanding tight ends. But I am desperately in need of a strong safety."

"I played both sides of the ball in high school, General," said Johnny. "I reckon I could make the transition."

"Good! How's your tackling?"

"Bronko Nagurski would be proud, sir."

Victoria rolled her eyes; the two sergeants snorted, which earned them a reprimanding glance from the general. "We shall see," he said. "Tryouts and practices will start in May, and the game will be in late August. Captain Rodgers will be in touch."

"Did you play football yourself, General?" Victoria asked.

"Columbia University, class of 1930. I was a starting offensive guard my senior year."

They talked about sports for a while, and everyone was impressed with Victoria's knowledge of football and how closely she followed both the New York Giants and Yankees. Tommy Senior's duties as an NYPD desk sergeant left him with time to take the children—including Victoria—to games on Sunday when they were growing up.

It was seven o'clock, and dinner was about to begin when another officer walked in—a colonel, with grey hair at the temples and golden eagles on his shoulders. Victoria saw something of Johnny in the way the colonel carried himself.

"Ah, Colonel Hill!" the general said. "Is everything situated?"

"Everything situated, sir," the colonel said. He had a slight Texas drawl. "The packages are secured. Guards are posted—I've arranged a two-hour rotation for guard duty because of the weather—and the rest are bunked down. The hotel has provided dinner for the enlisted men." He smiled. "Good luck trying to get 'em to eat army chow again, after that spaghetti bolognese."

"They've earned it, poor devils," said the general. Satisfied with the colonel's report, he turned to make introductions. "Colonel Austin Hill is my XO—a graduate of Texas A&M. He's been with me since the end of the war."

The general introduced them each individually. When he got to Victoria, Hill's face lit up in a grin. "Miss Shannon, it's an honor and pleasure to meet you. I remember your brother well. He's with the FBI now, am I correct?"

"Victoria, please. He's doing well, thank you. Assigned in Seattle with his wife and twin boys."

"Excellent, excellent. I remember meeting Colleen when they were engaged," said Hill. "Remarkable woman. She reminds me a lot of Maureen O'Hara."

Victoria smiled, but she was puzzled; to her knowledge, Colleen had never visited Italy while James was stationed there.

"General, may I borrow you for a few minutes?" Hill asked.

"Certainly. Excuse me, all."

As the general and colonel went off to a corner to talk business, Mario Agnolini walked in announcing that dinner was ready. While everyone was making their way to their seats, Colonel Hill excused himself to make a phone call.

24

CORTINA, ITALY—MIRAMONTE HOTEL

SUNDAY, JANUARY 9, 1955
9:00 PM

As expected, dinner was exquisite. The antipasto was traditional, with olives and soppressata; the pasta was rigatoni with ragù bolognese, and the entrée was roast goose. A robust Barbera accompanied the meal, and dessert was panna cotta with espresso. Victoria noticed that the general and his staff all limited themselves to a single glass of wine with the meal, and took their coffees straight; Johnny and the Three Musketeers did the same. While dessert was being served, Colonel Hill excused himself once again. When he returned, he gave a nod of approval to General Thompson.

After dinner, the guests were mingling, many not wishing the evening to end. General Thompson was a very entertaining and gracious host. He had time for everyone, including the Englishwomen, and took care to include them in the conversation. He and his staff were attentive, polite, and worldly.

Victoria was watching Johnny and Tony talk to Sam Rodgers, probably about football. She and Johnny really needed to have a talk about where things were going between them, she thought. She was enjoying herself in the moment—she was by no means eager to get off this roller-coaster—but Johnny was leaving in the morning. That was the reality of the situation, and they had not addressed it. The timing of this conversation would have to be perfect, and the right moment simply had not arrived. And now, they were running out of time.

The general cleared his throat. "Captain Gillespie. Colonel Pasquale. A moment of your time, please."

Johnny and Gigi excused themselves to a far corner of the room. After a brief conversation with General Thompson and Colonel Hill, both nodded. They then called Tony and Jo-Jo aside.

Victoria and the Englishwomen sat together, all wondering what was going on. At last, General Thompson came over to the, saying, "Ladies, we have to get an early start in the morning, and I need several minutes with your gentlemen friends before we retire." He gave a courtly bow. "So, I bid you good night. It has been a pleasure, but duty calls."

With that he and his staff departed for the rooms that had belonged to Johnny and the Three Musketeers. All four had given up their suites to the general and his staff. The Alpinis' gear was already packed and stored in the lobby; they were going to spend the night with their lovers.

Johnny walked over to Victoria, his face somber. "There you are," she said. "You promised you'd bring your stuff up to my suite after supper."

"It appears I've been temporarily assigned to General Thompson's staff for a joint operation between US forces and the Alpini."

"What kind of operation?"

Johnny shrugged.

"You probably couldn't tell even if you knew, could you?"

Johnny shook his head affirmative.

Victoria let out a long sigh. Fun and games were over; life had just gotten very real. She remembered James talking about the Italian black market, Nazi sympathizers, and communist insurgents. There were still American casualties here in Italy, but they never seemed to make the news back home. This settled it. Victoria made her decision. "When you're finished with your meeting," she said slowly, "just let yourself in. The door will be unlocked."

She smiled. Johnny seemed to relax a bit, and she gave him a quick kiss and left him to say her goodnights before returning to her suite.

When Johnny came through the door some hours later, he didn't know what to expect. His world had just been flipped on its head. All night he had been wondering how to broach the subject with Victoria. He felt a real, strong connection with her; but in a week, she would be heading back to New York. Would this just be a fling? Was there something more? And now this—a joint operation to hit one of the biggest black-market operations in Italy. The people involved were dangerous and well-armed. It was going to be serious.

He was pleasantly shocked as he entered the suite. There on the couch was Victoria, sitting with her legs under her, wearing a see-through black teddy and reading a magazine. Johnny put down his suitcase, admiring the view.

"Do you like?"

"Very much. But I, ah—I was hoping to talk."

Before Johnny could say anything else, Victoria stood up. That's when Johnny noticed that she was bottomless, and all the words left his open mouth.

She walked up to him and put a finger to his lips. "We'll talk later," she said; then she got up on her toes and kissed him like he had never been kissed before. "Take me to bed."

Effortlessly, Johnny picked her up and laid her in the bed that she had found impossible to sleep in for three nights.

It was approaching midnight. Outside, the snow had begun to fall again. Both Johnny and Victoria were staring off into the darkness.

She heard Johnny swallow hard. "Will I ever see you again?"

"I would like that very much," she said.

"How do we make this work?"

"We'll figure a way."

"There's gonna be an ocean between us."

"Was that a problem for your ex-wife?"

"Yes"

"Did she have a problem with what you did?"

"Definitely."

"I don't scare easy."

"I can tell," he said, and she could almost hear his smile in the dark.

"I have to get back to New York and figure out what to do with the rest of my life."

"I figured."

"You know I'm rich."

"I don't care."

"I know *you* don't," she sighed. "But I need to be smart about this. I need to feel like I'm contributing to society. I can't just spend money foolishly. It's just not me."

"I understand."

"Do you?"

"I think I do," he said, rolling on his side to face her. "You need to know where you're going for a change. You've been going with the flow, and keep getting knocked down with your teeth kicked in. You're tired of it."

And there it was, in a nice, neat little package: Victoria Shannon's most secret fear—allowing others to dictate her path, not truly feeling in control. With both Joel and Sebastian, there had been an expectation that her man would take care of her.

But she did not want to be taken care of. She wanted to be *loved*—loved as a woman, not worshipped upon a pedestal or admired as an ornament. At her core, she believed Johnny understood that.

There were no more words. Sitting up, she took off the teddy and climbed on top of Johnny, one last time for who knew how long.

A half-hour later, exhausted, the couple fell asleep in each other's arms as the storm continued outside.

25

CORTINA, ITALY—MIRAMONTE HOTEL

MONDAY, JANUARY 10, 1955
5:00 AM

The alarm went off at 0500. Breakfast was to be at 0600, with a departure time of 0700. Johnny went to shower, and Victoria decided to join him. *One more time for good luck,* she thought; at least if she cried, the water would hide her tears.

They took their time dressing, trying to hold on to every moment. Johnny was in his winter military outfit—army-green wool trousers and shirt with captain's bars on the lapels. The trousers were bloused in his highly polished russet jump boots. His bomber jacket was draped over a chair with his overseas cap on top.

She had never seen Johnny, who always so comfortable in his own skin, betray even a hint of anxiety—not even at the prospect of confronting Basil—but his smile was nervous. Finally, they stood looking at each other. It was quarter to six.

"Johnny, you will be careful, won't you?"

"Always," he said. "Please don't worry." He buckled on a holstered .45, attached to a khaki web cartridge belt. Victoria had grown up with guns around the house—par for the course, when your father's a cop—so she was unfazed.

"What about your skis and climbing equipment?"

"Mario said we could leave it all in the ski shack for the time being. Jo-Jo will pick it up later."

All at once, Johnny's stomach gave a little growl. "Somebody's hungry," said Victoria. Johnny held up his hands helplessly. Victoria herself could hardly think of food; her insides were in knots. "Come on, Mr. Hollow Legs," she said, trying to sound carefree. "Let's go see if we can placate your gastric complaints."

Several enlisted men were already eating breakfast in the dining room as they entered. They took a table off in the corner by a window. The previous night's snowstorm had blown through quickly, depositing several inches of fresh snow. The dawn was bright and clear, with more cold air behind a high-pressure system.

At 0625 the soldiers left, and at 0630 a second wave of enlisted men entered. The dining room would be opened to paying guests at 0700; the hotel was more than happy to accommodate the army, but wished to keep them separate from the guests. The general and his staff arrived at 0635. Everyone, including Victoria, came to attention, earning her a smile from General Thompson. “Carry on,” he bellowed. Austin Hill, Sam Rodgers, and William Jefferson went over to a separate table as the general headed over toward Johnny and Victoria. “May I join you?”

“Of course, General, please,” Victoria smiled. She had been pushing the fried eggs around on her plate for the last ten minutes.

“You two sleep well?”

The couple sheepishly shook their heads yes.

“Liars,” the general smiled. “I’m not that old.”

Victoria smiled. She was developing a fondness for the general. James had told her that the old man took an interest in every last soldier under his command, some of whom had been with him since D-Day, even since before the war. She could well believe it.

“Are you familiar with the buffalo soldiers, Johnny?” the general asked. Victoria was caught off-guard; prior to this, the general had always referred to Johnny as “Captain Gillespie.”

“Yes, sir, I am.”

“And you, Victoria?”

“No, General, I’m afraid not.”

“The buffalo soldiers were several calvary regiments formed after the end of the Civil War,” he said. “Made up mostly of Negroes, many of them freedmen, and some American Indians. Their mission was to combat the Indian hostilities in the Southwest and Great Plains, and pave the way for the Westward Expansion. They were instrumental in winning the Indian Wars from 1866 to the early 1890s.”

He smiled. "My grandfather, Sampson Thompson—Sam, they called him—was a buffalo soldier. After the Indian campaigns, he went on to fight with Teddy Roosevelt in the Spanish-American War. Charged up San Juan Hill in 1898. He retired, top soldier—a sergeant major—in 1900." The pride was evident in his voice.

"After retiring from the army, he actually went to work for the Colonel—that's what he called Roosevelt, till his dying day, even after he became president of the United States. The Colonel was very influential in mentoring my father. In fact, he helped him get into Columbia School of Law in 1901, at the age of forty-nine. Quite a second act. He finally passed in 1922, at the age of seventy."

"Sounds like a remarkable man," Johnny said.

"He was a man who loved the West," the general said. "Both my grandfather and the Colonel always said they had never seen anything as majestic as the Grand Tetons. Someday I hope to visit that corner of the world. Perhaps I'll take extended leave next year when my daughter gets married to Lieutenant Jefferson."

"Let me know, General, and I'll have the family turn out the red carpet for you."

"Thank you, Johnny."

Victoria smiled; it was the same line Johnny had given Basil. Had it only been thirty-six hours ago?

"Did you ever meet President Roosevelt?" Victoria asked.

"I did," said General Thompson. "Just prior to his death in 1919. I was nine years old when my father and grandfather took me to visit. It was a very emotional meeting for all of them, considering how much respect they had for each other. And you, Johnny—did you ever run across any veterans of the buffalo soldiers in Wyoming?"

"Yes sir, I have," Johnny grinned. "In fact, there was one I knew quite well—old Amos Weatherby. He was a sergeant with the Ninth Calvary during the Johnson County War, back in 1892." He turned to Victoria to explain. "The Johnson County War was a conflict between small farmers and wealthy ranchers trying to drive them off their land. The ranchers brought in hired guns; the farmers appealed to the law, and there were years of bloody standoffs between the gunfighters and a local sheriff's posse. Long story short, the Ninth was sent up to keep the peace. They set up shop at Camp Betten in Suggs, Wyoming, and remained there after the war. Amos retired from the army the next year, after twenty years of service. He came to work for my granddaddy on the family ranch. He stayed with us until he died in 1940. He was eighty." Johnny's voice became unsteady. "He gave me my first riding lesson when I was a kid."

"Was your family one of these rich ranchers you were talking about?" Victoria asked.

"If we were, it's news to me," he smiled. "Seems like the ranch has always been a step or two ahead of foreclosure. We're an independent-minded bunch."

Victoria realized the general would have liked to ask more questions of Johnny, but it was approaching 0700.

"Johnny," the general suggested, "Why don't you go and store your gear in the convoy now, so you can come back and say goodbye to Victoria properly."

Johnny rose and put on his bomber jacket and overseas cap; giving Victoria a peck on the cheek, he grabbed his bags and headed for the door. Watching him go, Victoria let out a long, lingering sigh.

"How are you holding up, my dear?"

"It ain't easy, General."

"I understand," said the general, rising to his feet. "I'll keep an eye on him. On all of them. And I'll keep you posted if I can."

Suddenly Victoria realized the immense scale of this gentle giant's responsibilities, sending all these young men into harm's way. She threw her arms around him and buried her face in his chest as if she were a child and he was an overgrown teddy bear. "Thank you," she said, half-sobbing. "And I'll pray for you. All of you."

"Thank you," the general said. Belatedly, Victoria realized she was making a scene, and the enlisted men in the dining room were at pains to ignore the encounter. She released the general. "My, it's 0655," he said, discreetly straightening his jacket. "Can't have the general being late, now can we?"

They walked together to the lobby. Out front, Victoria could see the convoy: the lead vehicle was an army Jeep with two soldiers in the front with a third in the back manning a machine gun, followed by two staff cars with drivers, a half-ton pickup followed by two ambulances, and another half-ton pickup, with another armed jeep taking up the rear. Whatever the cargo was, it was special—and highly secure.

"This is as far as you can go, Victoria" the general smiled. "Army business. But I'll send your soldier to you to say goodbye properly. Please, keep in touch—and say hello to James for me." He handed Victoria a card with his home address on the back as he headed toward his command.

"Colonel," the general bellowed as he stepped outside. "Is everything ready?"

"Yes, sir," Colonel Hill acknowledged.

"Good. Captain Gillespie, it is 0658. You have exactly two minutes to say goodbye to your young lady friend, and she deserves every second of your undivided attention—away from any editorial comments from this peanut gallery." This last earned smiles, chuckles, and eye rolls from the assembled men.

"Thank you, General."

Johnny jogged toward the lobby. Victoria went a little weak in the knees when he came in; he looked so dashing in his uniform. *When the bugle sounds,* she thought, *there will always be those that answer the call.*

She walked up and embraced him, a lump in her throat. "Be careful."

Johnny nodded, not trusting his voice. He held her chin in his hand, gazing into her face.

"The general said he'll try and keep me posted." She struggled to hold back the tears, with only partial success.

He nodded again, and finally kissed her—a long, gentle kiss. "Goodbye," he said at last, then turned and headed back to the convoy. It was 0700.

Victoria watched from the lobby as the convoy departed, dabbing her eyes with a handkerchief. Only when the sounds of the motors had faded in the distance did she turn to head back through the lobby, only to find Ernesto standing there with a fatherly smile on his face. "It's a beautiful day for skiing," he said. "Plenty of fresh powder. Did you have breakfast?"

"Yes," she said, taking his arm, "but as a wise man once told me, there's always room for a cup of coffee."

26

CORTINA, ITALY—MIRAMONTE HOTEL

MONDAY, JANUARY 10, 1955
3:30 PM

As promised, the day of skiing was wonderful. It was bright and sunny, and the several inches of new snow made the skiing both more challenging and more enjoyable. Though she had started the morning consumed with anxiety over Johnny and the rest of the guys, the physicality of it—shifting her weight, working with gravity, using her arms and legs—centered her in her body and helped to quiet her racing thoughts. Between the lack of sleep and the exertion of skiing, Victoria was exhausted by three o'clock.

After her lesson, Victoria took her biscotti and cappuccino into the bar. When Carlo saw her, he came out from behind the counter. "Signorina Marjorie left you a message," he said, handing her a folded piece of paper with a phone number written on it. "She asked for you to call her when you are finished skiing."

"Thank you, Carlo," she said. "May I use the phone in the bar?"

"Please."

After she connected with the Montana Hotel, Marjorie answered on the second ring. "Hello?"

"Marjorie? It's Victoria. You asked me to ring you when I finished?"

"Yes, Victoria, thank you for calling. Tonight's the last night for the girls and me," she said. "We leave tomorrow morning, so we thought we'd make a night of it. The three of us would love to take you out to dinner, if you're willing."

Victoria could not help but be suspicious. Was this just a thank-you gesture for what she did for Beatrix? Did they want to keep in touch? Or were they perhaps looking for dirt on Beatrix and Basil? *Only one way to find out*, she thought. "Sure, I'm game."

"Smashing! We have reservations at the Ristorante Ra Stua. Eight o'clock?"

"Sure. I'll see you at eight."

"Wonderful. See you then, *ciao*."

"*Ciao*."

It was four o'clock. There was just enough time to take a quick nap, shower, wash her hair, get dressed to the nines, and to be in town by eight.

Victoria entered the Ra Stua at eight o'clock sharp, wearing a black cocktail dress with a gold belt underneath the mink coat that Sebastian had bought her, a lifetime ago. It was bitterly cold outside, and Mario had insisted that Pepe drive her to the restaurant in the hotel's brand-new Dodge station wagon. Victoria was grateful for the old man's thoughtfulness. She was beginning to feel like one of the family at the hotel. It would be so nice, she thought, if these relationships could only last.

The girls were already seated when Victoria entered the dining room. All were smartly dressed. No doubt they'd had a bit more adventure over the last few days than they'd bargained for, she thought; they all had.

After Victoria was seated, Marjorie assumed command as Gigi had. "Right-o ladies," she said. "Before we get started—waiter, four glasses of Johnnie Walker Black, please."

When the scotch was delivered, Marjorie toasted: "To live, and fight another day."

Victoria, Portia, and Stephanie echoed the toast.

Swallowing the scotch, Victoria wondered whether the other three were feeling the gravity of the situation the guys were facing. Perhaps they were already over them, and this was just theatrics.

"I suppose it wasn't easy saying goodbye to Johnny this morning?" Stephanie asked.

"It was rough," Victoria admitted.

"Marjorie and I got a little weepy as well," Stephanie continued. "But Portia was an absolute horror to poor Jo-Jo! Pushing him away and all. 'Go ahead and get yourself killed,' she said—"

"Stephanie, that's enough," said Victoria. Portia sat silent with eyes downcast, looking miserable. "Portia, is it true?"

She nodded feebly, not raising her eyes. "I know I was simply horrible to him. He didn't deserve it. I wish I could take it all back." Victoria saw that her eyes were red, no doubt from crying. "He was so kind and gentle with me—not at all like Cedric."

"Cedric?"

"Cedric St. John Smythe—sorry, *Sir* Cedric St. John Smythe to us common folk, recently knighted for services to the Crown—is Portia's fiancé," said Marjorie. Victoria could see the disapproval in her face. "His family has been in the military for centuries—grandfather a retired major-general, father killed at Dunkirk, mother was killed by a V-2 rocket in 1944. His grandparents raised him, and he is—if I may be blunt—a right horror."

Victoria's eyes asked for more.

"He gambles, " said Stephanie. "And when his monthly allowance runs out, he goes to Portia's family for more." With a wicked smile, she lowered he voice. "He has a mistress. Carlotta Romero. She's an entertainer at Ciro's, a famous nightclub in London." She sipped her drink. "We all have our crosses to bear, I suppose. Be the dutiful pretty little wife, bear children, keep the house, manage the servants, appear at all the right events ..." She giggled. It was not an attractive sound. "Be happy for what you have, and all that rot."

Victoria shook her head. "Why, Portia?"

"Mother desperately wants us to be gentry," she said. "We're not badly off, mind you, but nowhere in that league. Cedric's family has money, connections, country houses. He's a catch, Mother says. She keeps assuring me that all of it—the gambling, the women—it will all change once we're married."

"Do you believe it?"

"No," Portia said, fresh tears welling up in her eyes. "No, I don't. Please, excuse me." Clutching her bag, she rose from the table. Marjorie also excused herself, following Portia to the powder room.

Victoria turned on Stephanie. "What is your *problem*?"

She seemed shocked. "Whatever do you mean?"

"Don't fuck with me, Miss Innocent. Where do you get off, talking to her like that?"

"*Really*, Victoria," Stephanie was flustered now. "You scarcely know Portia. What's it to you?"

"I know she's supposed to be your friend," Victoria hissed. "And *you* know she's torn up about losing Jo-Jo, about marrying this Cedric—how can you be so cruel to her about it?"

"Well, it's not as if she has a choice in the matter," said Stephanie fiercely. "We haven't all got the luxury of waiting for true love, you know. We're all in the same boat—Marjorie, Portia, Beatrix, me—we're new money. Our fathers are men of business." She spoke the phrase as if it were a curse word. "That kind of money will never be *respectable.* It's not like in America. Without titles or land, there are doors that will be forever closed, no matter how much money you've got. And those are the kind of connections you need, to rise in this world."

"And the only way to make those connections—"

"—is to marry up," Stephanie finished. "Our families have sacrificed for us, you know—the best schools, the best clubs, holidays in the best places, fashion, hair, make-up—all so we can land a respectable husband. We can't all be brave like you, Victoria—to spit in the eye of your fiancé because you thought there was 'nothing there.' However, much we may wish to do the same, the fortunes of our families are riding on us. "

That knocked Victoria down a peg. Who was she to judge, with what she had just been through? The Bossard family, marrying off their son to some shipbuilding heiress while preventing an interloper from throwing the proverbial monkey wrench into the works—it was the mirror image of Portia's dilemma.

"I appreciate the pressure you're under, Stephanie, I really do," Victoria said. "But it's not fair to play games with anyone's heart. Portia is hurting right now. She found somebody who made her happy, even for a little while—someone who's kind, and funny, and treats her well—and now she's lost him, maybe forever." She became aware that she was raising her voice, and decided she didn't care. "Now, you may think that's foolish, or childish, or unrealistic. But the fact is, her heart is broken, and she needs her friends to rally around her. You telling her to lie back and think of England isn't helping one bit."

Stephanie rolled her eyes. "For heaven's sake, it was just a fling!"

"Think of who you're talking about," Victoria said. "I believe those four are the finest men I know. Not only are they charming, not only did they treat you all like queens—you've seen the passion they have for what they do, the loyalty they have to each other. And now they're going into God knows what kind of harm's way. They deserve to know the truth. I mean, Johnny didn't know Beatrix had a fiancé until Basil was knocking on her door three days ago."

Stephanie wavered; for a moment, she could not meet Victoria's eye.

Slowly, Victoria said, "How did you leave it with you and Tony? What did you tell him?"

"He asked if I had a fiancé," she said. "I told him no."

"Is that the truth?"

Stephanie was suddenly sheepish. "Technically."

"Technically?"

"I'm to be engaged to Roderick Waverly next month. He's a banker who was very helpful in rebuilding not only England but France and Germany after the war." She dropped her eyes. "But the engagement's not official yet. I only told Tony I was dating someone."

"Do you think that's fair to Roderick?"

"Honestly, I don't think he even cares."

Again, Victoria was caught short. This could have been her life with Sebastian; married to someone who did not care whether she was having affairs or not, each leading their own life, with a life of luxury and leisure being the price for that discretion. Not for the first time, she thought she had dodged a bullet.

"What's Marjorie's story?"

"A bit different. She's engaged to a retired colonel, a widower, who spent his entire military career in India. Sir Edward Toliver. He's forty-five." Stephanie had the glee of a born gossip. "He knows all about Marjorie's affairs, and doesn't mind one bit. It seems that he and Marjorie both like men."

As with Beatrix, Victoria's anger now turned to sympathy. She knew of several marriages of convenience, where prominent men who would marry a woman just to hide their homosexuality and advance their careers.

"Marjorie says he's nice enough. Pleasant company, doesn't expect her to look after the house, won't put a leash on her ambitions. She's seriously considering applying to medical school next year."

"Good for her."

"In a way, I think she's luckiest of all of us," said Stephanie. "Even if her husband-to-be is a—you know."

Just then Marjorie and Portia returned from the ladies' room. Portia seemed much more composed. "Sorry for my behavior, everyone. Let's see if we can enjoy the evening."

Victoria cleared her throat and shot a significant look at Stephanie.

"I'm sorry for being so terribly catty before, Portia," Stephanie said, eyes downcast. "It was quite unfair of me."

Portia looked surprised, but not displeased. "Thank you, Stephanie."

Marjorie leaned in toward Victoria. "I believe you're a good influence on that girl," she whispered.

"Victoria," said Portia, "if you would—since you will be here for several more days, would you mind if I left this note for Jo-Jo with you? I do hope he'll forgive me for the way I left things with him."

"I'd be happy to," said Victoria, smiling. "Shall we order now? I'm starving."

After they placed their orders, the conversation turned to Beatrix and Basil. Quite of the blue, Portia—who appeared to have known Beatrix the longest—asked, "Do you think Beatrix might be pregnant? In your medical opinion, I mean. As a nurse."

"Why do you think that?" Victoria asked, not wanting to expose too much.

"She seems as if she's put on a bit of weight lately," Portia mused. "She claimed she was eating more because of nerves. But if anything, she seemed to be eating less."

Victoria put her hands up helplessly. "I suppose it's a possibility," she lied, "but without testing …" She trailed off. Then, changing the subject, she said, "Tell me about this Liam O'Donnell."

"Oh, he is a handsome rogue," Marjorie said.

"A little bit broader in the shoulders than your Johnny, slightly shorter," Stephanie added.

My Johnny, Victoria thought. "Anything else?"

"Thick, black wavy hair. A stubborn curl that hangs down over his forehead. Deep blue eyes, blue like glass, even more blue than your Johnny's," Portia added. "And he's terribly clever. He was attending Queen's University in Belfast, studying to be a mechanical engineer."

"What happened? How did he end up driving a limousine?"

"His parents owned a butcher shop. His father was involved in local politics—there was talk of him standing for election for city council—and he was an outspoken critic of the IRA," Portia said. "Two years ago, the shop was bombed. They were killed, both of them, and Liam and his sister were left destitute. They went to England for their own safety. Liam's plan was to work and save money to finish his engineering degree, then get a job as an engineer. The chauffeur's job paid rather well, so he was hoping to save money quickly. At least, that was the plan."

"Then he met Beatrix," Marjorie broke in. "They couldn't keep their hands off each other." A quirky smile crossed her face. "Basil wasn't exaggerating. It was like watching the fall rut."

"Jealous?" Victoria smirked, winning her a two-finger salute from Marjorie. The table to erupted in laughter, earning them some condemning looks from the other patrons.

Throughout dinner, they talked about their plans. Portia's wedding to be in two years, when Cedric turned twenty-eight and came into his full inheritance. Stephanie was trying to figure out what type of engagement party she (and more importantly Roderick) would like; and Marjorie was beginning to compile a list of medical schools she would consider attending. Listening to them chatter about their future plans either with longing or dread, Victoria wrestled with her own thoughts as to what might become of her—and *her Johnny*. Multiple people now had used that phrase in reference to Captain John Merriwether Gillespie. What did they know that she didn't? Did they see some future that was still hidden from her?

All three women gave Victoria their addresses, hoping she would write to them from New York, each promising to update her on the saga of Beatrix, Basil, and Liam. To herself, Victoria thought, *If you only knew what I know! But—loose lips sink ships.* Still, she promised to keep in touch.

After Marjorie paid the bill, the Englishwomen donned the coats and returned to the Montana. Victoria called the hotel for her ride. Pepe said he could be there in a half-hour. Victoria told him to take his time; she would have a nightcap at the bar.

She ordered a caffè Italiano. Before she could take her first sip, a man's voice interrupted her. "Excuse me. but I heard you speaking English." The voice was heavily accented. Victoria turned to see a very handsome gentleman, five-eight or a little taller, with wavy black hair and deep brown eyes. He was fashionably dressed: camelhair coat with blue wool trousers and oxblood-colored loafers, pink shirt, and a blue patterned tie.

"I so much would like to perfect my English," he said. "I would very much like to buy you dinner in exchange for conversation in English?"

"Sorry, I've already eaten," Victoria said. Something felt wrong about this. She felt she was being assessed for her net worth.

"Maybe tomorrow night, then?"

"I don't know," she said. "I'm kind of the homebody type. The only reason I came out tonight is because my friends are leaving for England tomorrow, and today, we all said goodbye to our boyfriends who are in the military. Usually, I'm exhausted after skiing all day." The words came out in a New York City rush. *Perfect your English on that, pal*, she thought.

"Please," he smiled. "My name is Umberto Racine. I am a publisher from Roma, and I'm just taking, as you Americans say, a break to relax here in the mountains. It is so beautiful, yes? I assure you my intentions are honorable."

I bet they are, Victoria thought. Umberto kept talking as Victoria sipped her coffee, occasionally pausing to refuse an invitation to dinner, for coffee, for drinks. She was nearly finished when Pepe walked in and eyed Umberto suspiciously.

"What are you hanging around for?" Umberto scolded Pepe in Italian. "Get lost, kid. She's too much of a woman for you."

"I'm the signorina's personal driver," Pepe fired back. "I've been instructed to collect the signorina and take her back to her hotel."

Umberto pulled 200 lira from his pocket. "Tell you what, kid—why don't you take this and come back in a half-hour."

Pepe was irritated. He balled his fist and waved it at Umberto. "I'll tell *you* what, Mister—why don't you take *this,* and you can—"

"*Basta!*" Victoria said. Then she rounded on Umberto and said, in perfect Italian, "I'm leaving with Pepe. Now, and not in a half-hour. I've had enough socialization for one night, thank you." With that, she handed the bartender twenty lira for a five-lira drink and told him to keep the change. She allowed Pepe to escort her out of bar to the hat-check area. As Pepe helped Victoria on with her coat, he kept shooting daggers at Umberto. Soon she was bundled in her mink, and they walked out and drove off into the night.

In the bar at the Ristorante Ra Stua, Umberto Racine sipped his grappa, feeling the liquor burn down his throat and into his empty belly. He could hardly believe his luck. The rumors had been true: an *Americana* staying at the Miramonte, rich, and with loose morals—two men in the same week! This was perfect for Umberto. *So long as she's not like the last one*, he thought.

Three weeks ago, Umberto met Barbara Anderson—Babs, she liked to be called, a name he despised—forty years old and recently divorced. Overweight after two children, loud, obnoxious, and stupid. Babs's two boys were in college now, and were closer to their father. It was decided that they would spend Christmas with their father in Vermont, skiing. And Babs—after years as a glorified maid and nanny to the three of them—was left with no plans for the holidays, only a large sum of money and a vague desire to "find herself" in Rome.

Umberto tolerated listening to Babs as she droned on about the sacrifices she made, how she'd dropped out of college when she became pregnant for the first time, about the career she could have had. Her father, who was extremely rich, paid for her divorce lawyer. Having won a handsome settlement, she was now taking this time to make up for all she had lost.

Umberto was part of this grand scheme to regain that time lost: the exotic foreign lover, young and passionate, over which Babs would exercise control—not vice-versa.

It was an arrangement that satisfied both of them, for a time. Unfortunately, Umberto got a little too greedy. When Babs's favorite diamond brooch went missing, she realized several other pieces of expensive jewelry were gone. Rome was becoming too hot for Umberto; it was time for a colder climate. Fortunately, his old friend Marco, another gigolo who lived outside of Cortina, was letting him stay on a couch in his cold-water flat for twenty lira a night.

Things had not gone well with the Americana tonight. But Umberto knew her face, now, and knew where she was staying. There would be other opportunities, and he would make the most of them. This was a big score; he could feel it. But it would take time, patience, and planning. He only hoped his money held out.

27

CORTINA, ITALY—MIRAMONTE HOTEL

WEDNESDAY, JANUARY 12, 1955
3:30 PM

The weather was not as cold as it had been, so Victoria took her biscotti and cappuccino outside to the balcony. The sun was still high; the days were growing noticeably longer.

Once again Carlo came out to greet her with a message, this time from Gigi; he was going to be in Cortina tonight, arriving around 6:30, and would like to have dinner with her if possible. Victoria could not help but wonder how much Gigi could reveal about their upcoming mission. Not that she cared about the details, except inasmuch as they weighed on the safety of Johnny and the others—but especially her Johnny.

Her Johnny. Victoria had spent the lonely night reflecting on that phrase. Was there something truly there, or was it just a lustful infatuation with this tall Army Ranger from Wyoming? No: not infatuation. Johnny *knew* her. He had intuited her deepest fear after knowing her for less than week—and she was beginning to understand his. It appeared that his former wife could not put up with the separation or the dangerous nature of his work. To Johnny, it was important that he be accepted for what he was—and that was a soldier, through and through. More than anything, she thought, Johnny was afraid of empty promises. He had been let down before; he needed—he deserved—someone who would give her heart and mean it. Someone who would keep her word to love him just as he was.

Was Victoria up to it? Was it even what she wanted? Only time would tell. She knew only that if the relationship were to succeed, honesty would have to be its backbone. Both had been hurt by dishonesty in the past. Moving forward, there could be no secrets from each other.

It was four o'clock. She had time for a quick nap before she had to get ready for Gigi.

Gigi entered the bar at a quarter to seven to find Victoria at the bar, nursing a scotch. She was wearing a black turtleneck with a gray pencil skirt. Victoria saw Gigi enter; he was not alone. With him was serious-looking soldier, older than Gigi but clearly his subordinate. The stranger had steely grey hair, closely cropped, with broad shoulders and a barrel chest, supported by tree trunks for legs—the type of body built for pushing and hauling tremendous weights up and down mountain ranges.

"Victoria, my dear!" Gigi greeted her warmly as she stood to meet him. "This is my *sergente maggiore*, my sergeant major, Mateo Bianchi."

"Bianchi?" She smiled. "He's not native to Cortina, is he?"

"Oh yes," Gigi grinned. "He's Ernesto's cousin. Mateo speaks very little English, however." Gigi stated switching to Italian, "*Questo qua la findazata de Cowboy,* Victoria Shannon."

"*De Cowboy? En be! Bona sera, signorina Shannon.*"

"*Bona sera, Sergente Maggiore Bianchi.*"

"I'm taking a room here at the hotel. Mateo is going to visit with Ernesto and their aunt—he'll spend the night there. He'll pick me up at seven tomorrow morning."

"*Bona sera*, Mateo."

"*Bona sera, colonella. Bona sera, signorina Shannon.*" Mateo turned and existed the bar.

"*Ciao,* Mateo," Victoria called, then turned to Gigi with a smile. "Drink, *colonella*? Our reservation is for 7:15."

Carlo brought over a scotch for Gigi and topped off Victoria's. "Shall we?" she asked.

"Most certainly." They toasted: "To live, and fight another day."

After the scotches were refilled, Gigi commented, "You're becoming one of the boys, aren't you?"

"Sure am," she said brightly. "Johnny said I passed the physical."

Gigi's scotch nearly wound up all over Victoria; it took several moments for him to compose himself. "I'm sorry, Gigi," she said. "I say stupid things when I'm nervous. Honestly—how is he doing?"

"Well, several higher-ups from both armies are noticing the capabilities of your Johnny. By the way, General Thompson sends his regards, and has authorized me to say that everything is proceeding nicely."

There it was again: *her Johnny*. "How's everyone else doing?"

"Everyone else is well," Gigi reassured her.

"And you? Why you here?"

"Administrative duties, unfortunately," Gigi said. "You'll forgive me if I can't say anything that could put the mission in jeopardy."

Victoria understood, so she changed subjects. "On Monday night, I had dinner with the girls."

"Do tell?"

"I have a letter from Portia for Jo-Jo. Apparently, she wants to apologize for the way she treated him Monday morning."

"Yes, she was quite dreadful to him that morning—telling him she hoped he'd get himself killed, all that sort of talk." He sighed. "You see it, on occasion. Lovers—even family—they can't bear the thought of losing a soldier in combat, so they push him away. All you can do is try not to take it personally. Jo-Jo tried to take it in stride, but you could see it bothered him."

"If you ask me, I think Portia might be in love with the major."

"Really?" Gigi raised an eyebrow. "Care to elaborate?"

"She's engaged to some upper-crust creep back home who treats her like chattel, all because mummy dearest believes it's the closest she'll every get to being gentry herself."

"An age-old problem for merry old England, I'm afraid. Who's the offender?"

"Cedric St. John Smythe."

"I know his grandfather, General Percy St. John Smythe. He was instrumental in getting the whole Desert Rats operation up and going in North Africa. Apparently, the poor lad lost both his parents—something about a rocket during the Blitz, wasn't it?"

"Correct—but it doesn't excuse him from acting like a friggin' asshole to Portia and her family."

"That doesn't explain why she might be in love with Jo-Jo, though," he mused. "Have you any thoughts?"

"Only the obvious," she said. "Jo-Jo is charming, funny, and sensitive. He treats her like a woman, not a prized heifer."

"Anything else?"

"Plenty. But it's 7:15—I'll tell you over dinner."

Dinner was a lamb shank and risotto served with a Barollo. It was during the entrée that Victoria told Gigi about Marjorie and Stephanie. Gigi took it in stride; he already knew that Marjorie was in a relationship of convenience, but hadn't realized that Tony's Stephanie was so far along in her relationship.

"It's not unusual for English women to stray," he said. "Most English men are still saddled with the Puritan influence. Terrible lovers—no imagination whatsoever. Then again, it could be a hangover from the Victorians. All those ostentatious displays of prudishness, and obsessed with sex underneath it all. Doctor Freud would have a field day." Seeing Victoria's smile, he wagged his finger at her. "I've lived among these creatures, my dear, don't forget. An Englishman who even knows how to *talk* to a woman—why, you'd have better luck finding a unicorn in Leicester Square. If they're not attracted to men, they feel it's their God-given right to be philanderers. Most don't care what their wives are doing—what's good for the goose is good for the gander. Or vice-versa, I suppose."

Victoria could not tell if Gigi was sincere or just trying to put on a brave face. Was he saying this because it was true, or did he have stronger feelings for Marjorie than he cared to admit? Was Tony struggling with the same thoughts toward Stephanie?

The dessert of cannoli and espresso was finished, and it was going on nine o'clock. "I've got to get to bed," she said. "Five o'clock comes around pretty early in the morning."

Gigi's eyes asked the question for him.

"Carmella and I go to morning mass at six. Pepe drives us. We started going yesterday morning., to pray for you bunch of brigands—to keep you safe when you go into harm's way."

"Really?"

"Yes, really. Care to join us?"

"Me? My dear, I've spent entirely too much time in England. Why, I'm practically high church Anglican by this point! And that's leaving aside the issue of my questionable morals. The pews might fall in on me."

"That's okay. I had the same fear."

"And?"

"I stole a line from *The African Queen.*"

"Eh?"

"I asked the Lord not to judge us on our weakness, but for our love for each other."

Gigi laughed and shook his head. "Nurse Shannon, you never cease to amaze me. There appears to be no angle you have not considered. I'll think about church. For now, though, allow me to escort you to your suite."

"Thank you, *colonella,*" she said, taking his arm.

As they passed the lobby, Umberto Racine watched from the bar. This was going to be more difficult than he thought. His money was dwindling; and how could he compete with an Alpino officer? Was it even worth it?

He had little choice, he thought. Prospects were fewer here in Cortina than in Rome. Besides, all he needed was one good night with her. The mink coat alone could be worth 10,000 lira. A crushed sleeping tablet in her drink after some lovemaking, a couple of pieces of jewelry, and he would be off to Milan, where he could fence the items quickly. The trick was how and when to get her alone.

The next morning as Carmella and Victoria attended church, they were flanked by Gigi, Ernesto, Mateo, and Pepe. *Great,* Victoria, thought as she made the sign of the cross, *I've started a cult.*

28

SIX KILOMETERS SOUTH OF INNSBRUCK, AUSTRIA

THURSDAY, JANUARY 13, 1955
2:30 PM

Aldo and Wolfgang were sitting in a mountain cave over the Austrian border. The cave was lit by lanterns; there were two bed palettes, and a decent supply of nonperishable food. It was one of Aldo's regular hideouts for his smuggling operation.

The two of them had gotten to the cave late Wednesday night. It had taken four days to make the trip from the little cabin where Wolfgang had taken Aldo into his confidence. As promised, Aldo carried all the equipment; all Wolfgang had to do was to carry himself on his skis. They took frequent breaks to make sure that Wolfgang stayed well-hydrated, leaving at first light and not stopping until they reached the next of the mountain huts along their route. In all that time, they had seen no other travelers.

Upon reaching the cave, Aldo had left Wolfgang alone to rest and continued on to the roadside to arrange the rendezvous. For his own safety, Aldo was not to meet Wolfgang's handlers directly. Fidelio had arranged for Aldo's usual smuggling client, Franz Beerbauer, to take charge of Wolfgang. A third party would then transport Wolfgang from Franz's warehouse in Innsbruck to his superiors. Aldo would thus use his usual signal system—leaving a sign by the route marker on the road out of Innsbruck to alert Franz that he was here for a delivery. Franz would check the spot twice a day, at eight in the morning and three in the afternoon, for five days running, beginning with the estimated delivery date; the rendezvous would occur at the next check time after the sign was spotted.

When Aldo returned that night, Wolfgang had already begun preparing their supper, opening several cans of Campbell's concentrated soup. Aldo brought out some dried salami and cheese that he had stashed in the cave, and they ate with a subdued sense of satisfaction.

"The sign is up," Aldo told Wolfgang. "Franz will see it in the morning."

Wolfgang nodded over his steaming mug of soup. "Your part in this is nearly finished, then."

"You should rest," said Aldo. "At least you can sleep late tomorrow. The handover won't take place until afternoon."

"I don't know that I'll be able to sleep at all," Wolfgang admitted. "I'm a bundle of nerves."

"You've been travelling hard for days," Aldo said. "Your body will remember how."

And indeed, Wolfgang slept very well that night in the cave. When he woke the next morning, he was alone. The sun was already climbing up the sky. He checked his watch; it was just past eight o'clock. His handlers would have seen the signal by now.

He had just finished dressing in his winter gear when Aldo reappeared at the mouth of the cave. "I thought you might be getting tired of soup," he said. "There's a farmhouse down the road. They know me there." He opened his bundle to reveal a loaf of fresh bread and a handful of fresh eggs, wrapped in crumpled newspaper.

"Aldo, you are miraculous," Wolfgang said.

"That's not all," said Aldo. From an inside pocket, he brought out a small paper bag. He shook it; it rattled softly, as if filled with sand. "Espresso," he said.

After breakfast, they prepared for the meeting. Because this was not one of Aldo's regularly scheduled runs, he did not expect to be carrying any cargo on his way back. He loaded his own gear on the sled and replenished his food supplies from the canned goods in the cave.

The hour of departure was drawing nigh. "How long will it take you to get back?" Wolfgang asked.

"If the weather stays clear, three days. Perhaps four."

"I've slowed you down terribly."

"One always travels more slowly with cargo." Aldo shrugged. "We'll leave in fifteen minutes for the rendezvous point, and then your colleagues can take responsibility for you—after they pay me."

"I don't know how to thank you for saving my life."

"I know you mean that, Wolfgang. And I appreciate your sincerity. This is a business arrangement—but, in my soul, I could not let you die." Aldo gave him a sad smile. "I could not let anyone perish when I'm responsible for them."

Wolfgang also smiled. "Do we have time for some coffee before we leave?"

Aldo quite suddenly looked serious. "There's always time for coffee."

When Aldo and Wolfgang had reached the rendezvous spot, it was immediately apparent that something was wrong. There was another man standing in Franz Beerbauer's place, a man Aldo did not recognize, broad and pale, with pale blue eyes behind steel-rimmed spectacles.

"Hello, Wolfgang," the stranger called. He spoke German with an accent that Aldo could not place. "It's been almost twelve years. How are you, my friend?" His smile could not have looked more false if it had been painted on.

"You know this man?" Aldo asked. Wolfgang only nodded; he looked slightly sick.

"Where's Franz?" Aldo called.

The pale stranger shrugged. "Franz agreed to send me because Wolfgang and I know each other so well. From the war." His spectacles glinted in the afternoon light.

"This is not the normal arrangement."

"These are not normal times," said the stranger. "Wolfgang is precious cargo. He's not a case of whiskey or a carton of cigarettes. The stakes are higher."

Aldo could see that Wolfgang was becoming agitated. Whatever he had expected, this was not it. "How did you know I was coming?"

"We know everything, Wolfgang. It is our job to know." The stranger's smile moved over his face like an oil slick spreading on water. "Did you think just because the war ended, we would stop? Come, now. You know us better than that."

"What about my family? Will they be safe?"

"That all depends on you, Wolfgang," said the pale stranger. "You, and how cooperative you are."

As Wolfgang and the stranger spoke, Aldo saw for the first time that the snow around the rendezvous spot had been disturbed. He walked a few steps away from the others, and caught sight of a shallow ravine. Drawing closer, he saw a dark shape lying at the bottom. A human body. Franz Beerbauer's body.

Aldo's back was turned to Wolfgang and the stranger. He reached beneath his jacket and quietly removed the small throwing axe that he kept in his belt.

Suddenly Aldo heard Wolfgang shout: "No, Yuri! Don't!" A shot rang out.

Aldo spun with the axe in his right hand. He barely had time to register the stranger—Yuri—releasing Wolfgang from his grip, leaving him to crumple to the snow, bleeding. Yuri turned toward Aldo and raised the pistol again, but the axe had already left Aldo's hand. It seemed to Aldo that the gunshot made no sound. There was only the pounding of his own heart, the muzzle flash—then Aldo's axe was buried in Yuri's forehead and Aldo's right flank felt like it was on fire.

Gritting his teeth against the pain, Aldo opened his jacket to examine the wound. The bullet had not struck any internal organs—all his layers of clothing had slowed it enough for that—but it had not passed through; the slug was embedded in the muscle of his side, deep in the external oblique near the latissimus dorsi.

Pressing his hand against the wound, Aldo made his way over to Wolfgang. He had managed to rise to his knees; he coughed, and blood spilled down his chin in a fine trickle. "I'm sorry, Aldo," he said, struggling against the pain. "I had no idea." He saw the blood on Aldo's jacket. "You're wounded!"

"It's not serious," said Aldo, though in truth it hurt like hell. "Lie still. Don't try to walk."

"I haven't much time," Wolfgang said. "I need to tell you, Aldo. I need to tell someone. It's their only chance."

There was a fallen tree nearby. Aldo sat Wolfgang up against it, keeping him upright so the blood would not pool in his lungs. "All right," he said. "What is it, Wolfgang?"

"I told you I was at Stalingrad," Wolfgang said.

"Yes, in the siege."

Wolfgang shook his head. "I was there before the siege began," he said. "In the summertime. It was secret mission. Three of us were smuggled into the city, all of us demolitions men. We were saboteurs. We were to attack infrastructure targets—water mains, power plants, telephone lines, train tracks. Our chances of doing any real damage were slim, but that wasn't the point. We were to create as much chaos as possible—leave the city weakened and overstretched, so that when the army of the Reich rolled in August, Stalingrad would fall into our hands like overripe fruit."

"It didn't work out?"

"We were captured. We thought they were Red Army. Turned out they were ours—but really not ours at all."

"You're not making any sense."

"Double agents," said Wolfgang. "The Reich had recruited men inside the Red Army to work secretly against the Soviets. This was who had captured us. They knew all about our mission, knew where we would be. But they were not truly servants of the Reich. Double agents. In reality, they were working for another organization—an organization that went beyond national borders. They had ties to powerful families throughout Europe, but acted independent of these families with criminal intent. They were happy to play the Reich and Soviets against one another for their own ends. They would remain in power whoever was victorious in the war. They are playing the same game now, using the NATO allies and the Warsaw Pact."

"A criminal conspiracy?"

Wolfgang tried to shrug, which caused him have a spasm of coughing, producing more blood. "*Conspiracy* is too small a word," he said when he recovered. "They are power, Aldo. Power beyond politics. Power that cares nothing for human life.

"Yuri was the leader of a cell within this organization. He offered us a choice: Join them, or die. There were three of us—Thomas, Ehrich, and me. Thomas chose death. They put a bullet in his brain. He was three feet away from me when they shot him. I couldn't stop screaming." He took a long, raspy breath. His face had gone the color of putty. "I was twenty-two, Aldo. I was so scared to die. I joined them. Me and Ehrich both. I betrayed the Reich. I betrayed everybody.

"They took us in. While the army of the Reich exhausted itself trying to take the city, we were safe inside. They kept us hidden and fed and taught us what we would need to know to serve this cabal we would be working for. Yuri told us that they had agents everywhere, all across Europe, among the Allies and the Axis. They would work with whatever governments were in power, tipping the scale this way and that, to maintain their own control over Europe—and soon the world." He shook his head. "I thought it was all nonsense. I thought Yuri must be delusional. I only wanted to live through the winter and get back to Germany. I thought that would be the end of it."

"What about the rest of it?" asked Aldo. "This New Reich in South America?"

"All true," said Wolfgang. "They released us in February, and we joined in the retreat back to Berlin. There were so many dead, so many dying, that nobody even noticed us. Ehrich and I told our superiors in the SS that when our mission inside the city had failed, we had joined up with the besieging army. They believed us without question. Didn't even check. They complimented us on surviving, gave us both medals, and then they reassigned us."

"But why was Yuri here? Why now?"

"The cabal must have infiltrated the New Reich organization," Wolfgang said. His voice was growing weaker. "They have agents everywhere, Yuri said. Every government, every revolutionary movement, every subversive group. I didn't believe it, then." He looked at Aldo. His eyes were growing dim. "They killed your friend Franz, I think."

"I know," said Aldo. "I found his body in the ravine. But why did Yuri bring you all this way to kill you?"

Wolfgang tried to laugh, but it turned into a cough. "You don't understand," he said. "That first bullet was meant for you. They can't afford loose ends. I tried to stop him."

Aldo was silent.

"I'm sorry," Wolfgang whispered. "I'm sorry about so many things. They had plans for me. What, I don't know. But those plans will no longer involve me. Thank God."

Wincing with pain, he took off his gloves and removed his wedding ring. He held it out toward Aldo. "Take the rest of the sovereigns sewn into my pack. There are nine more, about 5,000 dollars' worth. You will also find a letter for my wife, in Paraguay. The address is already on the envelope. There are instructions for her safety." His hand clasped Aldo's. "They will come for her. They must not find her, or our daughters. The letter, Aldo. She must get the letter."

"I promise," said Aldo.

Wolfgang sank back. "That's enough to satisfy any man," he said, and closed his eyes.

"Wolfgang?" Aldo said. "Wolfgang, can you hear me?"

"You have brought me so far, my friend," Wolfgang whispered faintly. His eyes did not open. "But I must go the rest of the way alone."

He lapsed into unconsciousness. Aldo stayed by Wolfgang's side until his breathing stopped. It did not take long.

It was beginning to snow.

Aldo's first order of business was to hide the bodies. He wished he could have at least given Wolfgang a decent burial, but survival was of the utmost importance at the moment. He dragged Wolfgang's body down the ravine, leaving a crimson trail in the snow, and laid him next to Franz. Then he dealt with Yuri, first tugging the axe from his forehead, and returning it to his belt. Rifling through Yuri's pockets, he found at least 1,000 schillings in various bills, plus an expensive watch, his gun—an Astra 600—and a ruby ring. Then he dragged Yuri's body down to the other two. Almost as an afterthought, he checked Franz's pockets and found twenty ounces of gold bullion—the promised amount, and then some. He took it and stowed it in his pack. He'd kept up his end of the bargain, after all.

Using his hands, he buried all three bodies in the snow. By the time he was finished it was snowing heavily. It smelled as if they were in for another blizzard. For once, he was thankful. Not only would it cover the bodies, but all the tracks; with luck, nobody would follow him—and no one would find the bodies until the spring thaw.

It was twilight before Aldo made it back to the cave. The exertions of dragging two bodies had reopened his wound. By applying pressure, he had been able to stem the flow of blood; but the bullet was still in his flank. There was a medical kit stashed in his hideout. He lit every lantern and started a large fire. For the work ahead, he would need light.

He stripped to the waist and, using a mirror, began to probe the wound. It appeared that the bullet was only a few centimeters under the skin; its impact had been slowed by the cushioning of the thick heavy jacket, sweater, quilted shirt, and woolen undershirt.

He poured out some alcohol into a pan and laid a set of forceps in the pan to soak. There was a worn leather strap in the medical kit; taking it in his teeth, he took the forceps and reached into the wound for the bullet. The pain was excruciating; beads of sweat sprang up all over his body, though the cave was chilly despite the fire. The angle was awkward; even with the mirror, he could see the wound site only out the corner of his eye.

After several attempts, he made contact. He bit down on the strap and pulled slowly until the forceps came free. He sat there panting for a moment. The bullet appeared to be intact. Once his breath returned, he cleaned the wound as best he could with peroxide, packed it with gauze soaked in alcohol, and bound himself with bandages. Looking through the medical kit, he found what he was looking for: a syringe and an ampoule of morphine. He measured the dosage carefully and injected it into his left quadriceps.

After about half an hour, Aldo was pain-free, and though stiff and sore was able to dress himself. He needed to eat and drink, he knew, to keep his strength up. There were eggs and a few slices of bread left over from the morning. He fried the eggs with some salami and put on a pot of water to boil. There were envelopes of instant hot chocolate; something sweet, to stabilize his blood sugar and help him think, as well as helping with hydration.

Once the hot chocolate was poured, Aldo sat down and contemplated what had just happened. The story that Wolfgang had told him seemed unbelievable; but who would waste his last breaths in such a lie?

He took a sip, grateful for the warmth. He began to think about his own safety. Between the gold sovereigns, the bullion, and the money squirreled away in his cabin outside Bolzano, Aldo could probably lose himself in a major city—Rome, or Venice. Maybe he would even return to Paris. But he could not undertake such a scheme alone. It would take planning. He needed someone he could talk to. Someone he could trust.

He nodded to himself. In the morning, he would head back toward Bolzano. He knew a man on the Italian side—a physician he knew from the old days, who could patch him up. A man who was sympathetic to the cause. Aldo's cause.

When Aldo was a student at the University of Paris, toward the end of the war, he had been still naïve enough to believe that he could remain a political atheist and pursue an academic career. That all changed in the beginning of August, 1944. Before that, he had believed that if he left his neighbors alone, they would leave him alone. Unfortunately, that was not the case. After that day, he went from tolerating the Nazis to helping them, and despising the partisans and their allies. With this new turn of events—with what had now learned—he needed a new plan of action.

Walking to the entrance of the cave, Aldo was happy to see the snow coming down so heavily. He threw another log on the fire and went back inside to sleep. He had a long day of skiing ahead of him tomorrow.

29

AVIANO AIR BASE

FRIDAY, JANUARY 14, 1955
8:30 AM

Johnny sat outside a conference room in one of the administration buildings at Aviano Air Force Base, replaying the week's events in his mind. On Monday, Johnny was introduced to his unit—forty men, all volunteers, who had at a minimum undergone airborne training. The mission had almost been scrapped, because the previous CO of the unit—one Captain David Alexander—was found to be on the take, and it was feared that the black marketeers had already been alerted. Alexander, Johnny was told, had a fondness for underage girls, and the Italians kept him supplied. They'd only found him out because his second-in-command had himself been caught pants-down with some street hustler, and had ratted out Alexander to

CID to save his own skin. This lieutenant was already back in the States, another civilian with a dishonorable discharge in hand, instead of busting rocks in Leavenworth.

Even though the war had ended ten years ago, the Italian black market was not only flourishing but branching out into new areas, evolving into a full-blown criminal power. Along with weapons, cigarettes, alcohol, and medical supplies, they were beginning to branch out into drugs and human trafficking. There was also a push into politics through corruption and persuasion—including the lethal kind. These syndicates were now equipped not only with stolen Allied weapons, but weapons salvaged from both the Nazis and the Soviets. The Italian government had appealed to the army for help through diplomatic channels because it was afraid of leaks within local law enforcement; but it was evident from the Captain Alexander incident that the tendrils of the black market extended even into the militaries of both countries. It was hoped that this new squad, under new leadership, would break the power of this criminal empire where others had failed.

Without an experienced CO, the mission had been slated for the chopping block. As fate would have it, General Thompson had run into Johnny, remembering he was the runner-up for the position—a fact of which Johnny himself had been unaware. Luckily, Captain Alexander was not well-liked among the volunteers; they viewed his replacement as a welcome sign.

On the way to Aviano, Johnny had also learned that the highly guarded "packages" carried by the convoy were four

Soviet spies, caught working at various levels of NATO intelligence in Rome; the CIA had gotten an anonymous tip on their identities from a source in Vienna.

Most of his days with the unit so far had been spent at the firing range, where Johnny was having some concerns. The mission was to advance on a farmhouse, clear the rooms, arrest everyone there, and confiscate the contraband. All the soldiers were equipped with M1 Garands—an excellent field rifle, but of limited use for close-quarter combat. Fortunately, in the armory Johnny was able to find M2 carbines with folding stocks, which were lighter and smaller and would work better in close quarters. A few of the volunteers favored the Thompson submachine gun, while three in particular were partial to the M3 submachine gun, nicknamed the "grease gun" because of its visual resemblance to the mechanics' tool for injecting grease into automotive joints. There were also several M3 carbines equipped with infrared scopes. He assigned two to his sharpshooters, Dulvaney and Malone; they would be the company's snipers.

Also in the armory, Johnny found ten silenced Sten guns, which had been used extensively by British paratroopers and SAS in the second World War. The Sten gun was a submachine gun with its magazine extending from the side. Though of a simple design and inexpensive to make, the gun was highly effective; the suppressors were another selling point, given the importance of stealth to the mission. The base's armorer, First Sergeant Fred Baker, had extensively refurbished the Sten guns, eliminating several of their characteristic malfunctions—especially their tendency to fire when the bolt was opened and bumped—making the guns perfect for covert work. Johnny took one for himself and assigned the others to the better shots in the group.

That first afternoon, Johnny had the men working not only on practice fire but on rapidly transitioning from rifle to sidearm. Johnny believed that all the men in the unit should be equipped with a sidearm; having an additional weapon available could be a lifesaver if a magazine switch was not an option.

The whole unit was impressed with the Sten guns. The baffling of the suppressors added weight to the barrel of the gun, which improved their accuracy. Colonel Morton, who was overseeing the training, took note of this and, thinking it prudent for the whole team to be trained on Sten guns, put in a call to General Thompson.

On Monday night, the company had worked on night operations and communicating while moving silently, returning to barracks at four in the morning. Fortunately, the company had their own barracks, situated away from other operations. They were up at ten, had an early lunch, and were briefed on the farmhouse by both US intelligence and Italian authorities. There was a certain level of endemic corruption within Italian law enforcement, and because most of the items sold by the black marketeers were stolen American property—including medical supplies, guns, and ammunition—the operation had been turned over to the US military. The Alpini would work as backup, so as to minimize any conflicts that might occur between soldiers and marketeers.

On Tuesday afternoon, after more firearms training, the unit was broken up into teams. Johnny assigned a total of four men to make up two sniper teams, then four nine-man squads further broken down to two teams in each squad, each led by a sergeant. Master Sergeant Caleb McIntosh, a fifteen-year veteran, oversaw Squads 1 and 2, while Squads 3 and 4 fell under direction of Chief Warrant Officer Danny Porter. The latter also served as acting second-in-command, since the brass could not find an adequate replacement at such short notice.

Fortunately, there was a last-minute volunteer: Sammy Chin, a twenty-year-old corporal from San Francisco, an orphan brought over from China by Catholic missionaries at the end of the war. Sammy had been a ham radio operator since the age of twelve, and was a wizard when it came to electronics. As the unit's radio operator, Sammy was able to set up communications among all ten teams, equipping one member in each team—including the spotters in the sniper teams—with a walkie-talkie. Once radio silence was broken, Johnny would be able to communicate with each team.

Wednesday night's mission went off like clockwork, without casualties. They swooped in just after dusk. The Italians in the farmhouse, realizing quickly that they were outmatched and outgunned, surrendered without firing a shot. It was not until the intelligence people got in there that the enormity of the situation became clear: the Italian syndicates were assisting both German neo-Nazi factions and Soviet subversives in their European operations.

For the Germans, it was Odessa in reverse. At the end of the war, many of the Nazi command fled to South America via Switzerland. Odessa was one of several organizations that helped Nazis escape Europe at the end of the war, resettling them in Argentina, Paraguay, and Uruguay. Now, ten years later, former Nazis and their relatives were trying to reinsert themselves into European politics. The Soviets, on the other hand, were using northern Italy as a staging area—not only for introducing insurgents into Western Europe, but as a pipeline for intelligence and counterintelligence operatives. The Italian syndicates catered to both factions; money has no political affiliation.

Two of the black marketeers, overawed by the power and efficiency of the American assault, were willing to give accurate details of both operations. Both the German and Soviet groups had been gathering armed paramilitary forces in separate isolated compounds deep in the countryside. The informants had no reliable numbers as to troop strength, but each facility was well-armed. Both groups were highly trained and dedicated to their causes; unlike the Italians, who were petty criminals at heart—tough against the locals, but their weapons were mostly for show—these were soldiers, willing to die for their beliefs. The decision was clear; these incursions had to be neutralized immediately, before either the Nazis or the Soviets realized that they had been compromised.

As field commander, Johnny had to make a snap decision. The Nazi compound was the closer of the two; it would be the first target. Last-minute intelligence put the troop strength there at no more than twenty, but according to the informants they were all ex-military and well-armed. For the safety of the NATO troops, the mission was declared a covert military operation, and not a police or law enforcement issue.

Twenty of the MPs from General Thompson's detachment—lifers, mostly, many of whom had seen extensive action in the last war—volunteered to join the assault on both the Nazi and Soviet facilities. They would act as backup, sweeping the compounds for holdouts and strays after the active fighting was done. First of the volunteers was Master Sergeant Izzy Robinson. There was some consternation, given that one of the forty-man squad was a fresh-faced corporal from New York City, born Isadore Abraham Cohen, who was also known as Izzy. Their new designations were Izzy One and Izzy Two, in order of seniority.

The assault on the Nazi compound was swift and brutal. The order was shoot to kill, and the Germans were caught completely by surprise. Dulvaney and Malone took out the sentries from cover before they had the chance to raise an alarm. Most of the rest were already in barracks, with only their sidearms. They took an aggressive posture, but were badly outgunned; most never even got off a shot before being cut down. Only three of the Nazis—all high-ranking officers—survived long enough to surrender, and were taken away by the CID and MPs from General Thompson's unit. The mission was completed by 2200 hours without NATO casualties.

They rolled into the Soviet encampment in heavy snow, not long after midnight. Intelligence put the enemy strength at approximately sixty, heavily armed, with a number of PMK machine guns.

Whether the Russians had somehow gotten wind of their arrival or were simply light sleepers, they put up considerably more fight than the Germans. The assault force was able to take up defensive positions in the compound due to the heavy snowfall and the use of the suppressed Sten guns.

Once the alarm was sounded, though, the Russians fought fiercely. They deployed one of the PMKs, pinning the NATO troops down for several tense minutes before Dulvaney got a bead on the operator. When Johnny's men stormed the compound, they scattered, leaving the NATO troops to go room-to-room in a series of running gun battles and hand-to-hand encounters.

In the end, though, it was a rout. Only two of the Soviets surrendered. Forty were killed outright; ten were gravely wounded and were not expected to make it through the night. Most distressingly, for Johnny, eight took their own lives rather than be captured: five by pistol, two by knife, and one who seemed to have a poison pill in a false tooth.

The victory was not without its costs on the NATO side. There were ten casualties in all—two fatalities, two serious wounds, and six with non-life-threatening wounds.

By 0400, the snow was tapering off. Eight Sikorsky CH-34 helicopters approached the now-secured compound, evacuating first the critically wounded and the NATO dead, then those less seriously injured. By 0500 a relief company made of CID troops and officers from the Defense Intelligence Agency relieved Johnny's command, including Porter and McIntosh. Izzy One and the rest of the MPs would wait with the relief command, and take care of the Soviet bodies. The Soviet prisoners had already been evacuated to some classified destination.

Johnny and his team touched down at Aviano Air Base at 0600. He was utterly spent, and wanted nothing but to sleep; but there were debriefings ahead. He showered, shaved, and changed into his dress uniform before having breakfast.

And now he was here, at 0830, waiting outside the conference room, hoping the coffee and toast would be enough to keep him awake. After four nights of working in the cold, with little sleep and sporadic food, Johnny was not only exhausted but apprehensive about what was to come next. He was contemplating what the meeting had in store for him when a sergeant major came out of the conference room.

"Captain Gillespie? They're ready for you, sir."

Johnny entered, came to attention, and saluted. Around the conference table were General Thompson, Colonel Hill, Colonel Morton, Captain Samuel Rodgers, and Lt. Jefferson. Off to the side were three men in civilian dress. The sergeant major and a number of other non-coms were arranging files and taking notes. Johnny noted a sideboard with refreshments along on wall.

"At ease, Captain Gillespie," General Thompson said. "You know everyone here, with the exception these gentleman over there. Special Agent Howard Green of the FBI, Major David Oglethorpe with the DIA, and Curtis Stetner with the State Department." Agent Green and Major Oglethorpe both wore black suits with nondescript ties. Oglethorpe's ramrod posture and close-cropped hair, red going to gray, marked him as military as he lit a new cigarette with the remnant of the previous. Green had a hawklike face with sharp black eyes. Stetner was wearing a three-piece suit, a blue pinstripe number, and a red-and-gold tie. There was nothing flashy to his look, but everything was obviously expensive, probably handmade. His shoes probably cost more than Johnny made in a year.

The introductions made, General Thompson said, "Congratulations on a successful mission, Captain. We asked a lot of you, stepping in for Captain Alexander at short notice. Given what we have discovered this week, it is fortunate indeed that we were able to carry on with the mission. Had we canceled, who knows what would have happened with these rogue elements? I don't think we should downplay the gravity of this. By catching the Italians by surprise, we have nipped a grave threat in the bud. And for that, we owe you our thanks."

The general led the room in a round of applause. Johnny accepted the congratulations humbly, but he could not help thinking of the casualties. Sergeant Max Peters was an eighteen-year veteran, an orphan, a loner with no family, who had joined up at seventeen; he had planned to retire after twenty years and return to Michigan. He was killed outright, caught by a bullet when his squad made an assault on the Soviet barn. Corporal Bobby McGraw was nineteen years old. He planned to make a career out of the army, and was looking to marry his sweetheart back home in Hershey, Pennsylvania, once he made sergeant. He had taken a bullet in the upper leg and bled to death; because of the covert nature of their mission, there had been no medics. Even now, Privates José Lopez and Hal Anderson were fighting for their lives in the OR. After his four-year commitment, José had been planning to go back home to Mesa, Arizona. Thanks to the GI Bill, he had prospects of being the first in his family to go to college; he had taken a submachine gun burst in the left shoulder. Hal was from Cleveland, Ohio, and he, too, was considering college after his hitch. He had been knifed in the belly as he grappled with one of the Soviets, finally getting his sidearm clear and dispatching the Russian with several slugs from his .45.

The other six injuries were not serious but required attention. Izzy Two had taken some shrapnel in his right thigh; Mulvaney had twisted his ankle leaving his hide when he rejoined the unit after the shooting had stopped; his spotter, Brooks, had also fallen, fracturing his wrist. Privates Saunders and Beverly had lacerations to their arms from when one of the Soviets charged them with a knife; they both fired on him at the same time, and neither was quite sure who'd gotten the kill shot. Corporal Vinnie Salerno had a couple of broken ribs. One of the Russians had jumped him in a stairwell, and both had tumbled down the steps; the Russian got the worse of it, with a broken neck.

Johnny was roused from his thoughts by the voice of Curtis Stetner. "That was excellent work, Captain. We've already interviewed both Sergeant Macintosh and Chief Warrant Officer Porter. They had nothing but praise for the way you took charge and organized the unit into an efficient fighting force. Trust me when I say I know what's it's like to lose men in action. But considering what you were up against, and at short notice to boot, the casualties could have been far, far worse."

"Thank you, sir," Johnny said. And then, more to himself: "It still isn't easy."

"I understand," Stetner continued. "But if I may change the subject for moment—how'd you like using the Sten gun?"

Johnny looked at Stetner, slightly surprised. "They were a real help with the Soviet mission," he said. "We were able to take out most of the guards without raising the alarm, thanks to the suppressors. Damn accurate, too."

"Don't I know it!" said Stetner with a smile. "I traded in my M2 for a Sten gun when I ran the Jedburgh units in Northern Italy. Fortunately, I knew enough to have an armorer take the kinks outta mine before I went into the field."

That got Johnny's attention. "You were with the Jedburghs?" he said, sounding a little bit more excited than he would have liked. The Jedburghs had a reputation as one of the toughest commando units of the second World War. Devised by the US Office of Strategic Services—the predecessor to the CIA—they were an international force of American, British, French, Dutch, and Belgian operatives who were sent behind enemy lines in Europe in preparation for the Allied invasion.

"Damn straight," Stetner smiled. "I even worked with your three *paisans* on occasion. They proved extremely helpful—especially that big son-of-a-bitch Tony Pagnozzi, even if he's a Giants fan." He chuckled at Johnny's confusion. "I'm from Philly, son. That's Eagles country. By the way, heard you're gonna be General Thompson's new strong safety. Good for you, son. Make the army proud."

Several thoughts went through Johnny's mind. He was taken aback that the general was apparently talking up his gridiron skills sight unseen; but more than that, he had a sudden suspicion that Curtis Stetner was not in fact State Department, but more likely CIA. When the OSS was dissolved and the hot war gave way to the cold, it was deemed that the United States needed a coordinating intelligence agency to help it navigate the second half of the twentieth century. Many former operatives of the OSS had ended up with the Company.

"Tell me, Captain," Stetner continued. "What made you employ sniper units?"

"Well, sir, we knew we needed eyes up high. Putting one unit at the northeast corner of the compound and the other at southwest gave us the best view. With Sammy Chin's radio technology, we had full communication.

Once the shooting started, none of our positions were outflanked—even though the Soviets tried. The snipers and their spotters were the eyes for the whole unit."

"The snipers registered twenty-two kills between the two operations," Colonel Morton commented, "and provided a great tactical advantage for the unit. It certainly gave both the Soviets and the Nazis something else to think about. Very impressive, especially with only three days of training."

Colonel Hill was the next to speak. "Captain Gillespie, if you were to take command of this unit on a permanent basis, what do you think you'd need"

Without a moment of hesitation, Johnny said. "I think the first thing is more specialized personnel. At least two more snipers, with more advanced weapons. A couple of more radio operators." He was counting on his fingers. "And we need medics on the ground, at least four—medics who are willing to carry and use weapons. Weapon-wise, outside of better sniper rifles, I am sold on these modified Sten guns. I believe they should be standard issue for every man in the unit, silencer-equipped—along with a primary weapon of their choice. Tailor the equipment to the strengths of the man. Also, we need to consider clothing. We need to decrease the amount of bulk the soldiers carry so they can maneuver more quietly without freezing to death. I have some ideas there, also."

There was stunned silence for a moment. Finally, General Thompson cleared his throat. "It appears, Captain Gillespie, that you've given this a great deal of thought?"

"Yes, sir, I did. It was a long flight back here to Aviano."

Major Oglethorpe spoke for the first time. "And why should such a thing even be on your mind, Captain?" Johnny hesitated for a moment, unsure how to answer. Oglethorpe pressed him. "By which I mean, for what mission would such a permanent unit be required?"

Johnny collected his thoughts. "It appears to me, sir, that whether we like it or not, we find ourselves in the middle of a clandestine war over control of Europe. And if we want to keep Europe free of totalitarian rule, either from the Soviets or some resurgent fascist movement, we need to step up to the plate."

Again, there was silence. The ranking officers and the civilian VIPs exchanged meaningful looks.

"Thank you, Captain Gillespie," General Thompson said. "That will be all for now. Sergeant Major, please escort Captain Gillespie to the officers' club. I'll join him shortly."

Johnny saluted and exited the conference room.

The sergeant major—Cecil McKenzie was his name—noted the dejected look on Johnny's face as they walked. "Damned successful mission, Captain," he said.

"Really?" said Johnny. "Then why do I get the impression that their major concern was that I not let the door hit me in the ass on the way out?"

McKenzie laughed. "You put them on their heels, that's why," he said. "Your predecessor had a completely different take on the situation."

"How so?"

"Captain Alexander was doubtful even as to the existence of neo-Nazis," said McKenzie. "And he certainly wouldn't admit that there was any Soviet incursion into Italy. He insisted that our black market problem was all just local boys—Mafia making trouble." He lowered his voice. "Scuttlebutt has it that the good captain is being questioned by some of Mr. Stetner's associates right now, and will be turned over to Special Agent Green when they're finished."

That confirmed Johnny's suspicions about Curtis Stetner; he was definitely CIA.

"Stetner and Green play real nice together in the sandbox, thanks to the general's persuasion."

"The general's quite a guy, isn't he?"

"Damn straight," said McKenzie with a smile. "I've been with him since he took over CID in Rome back in '45. I was a first sergeant back then. I threw him one hell of a bachelor party back in '47, howled at the moon with him the night his daughter Lizzette was born in '48." He turned somber for a moment. "And I sat up all night with him when we found out about his son Oliver being killed in Korea, just three years ago."

Johnny nodded silently. It was a rare officer who would share his life, in all its joys and sorrow, with the men under his command.

"Well, here we are, Captain," said McKenzie, extending his hand. "It's been a pleasure meeting you. Good luck, and again—congratulations on a job well done."

"Thank you, Sergeant Major," Johnny said. "I hope to meet you again."

But privately, he doubted he would.

Johnny was nursing another cup of coffee when General Thompson entered the club. All six officers in the club came to attention. "At ease," bellowed the general as he walked over to Johnny. "Sorry, Captain. It took us a little longer than I expected to conclude our meeting."

General Thompson removed his hat and overcoat and handed them to a sergeant who seemed to appear from thin air. "Thank you, Sergeant. I will be opening the bar for Captain Gillespie and myself."

The colored drained from the sergeant's face. "Yes, sir. I'll go find a bartender."

"I'll be tending the bar myself," said the general. "No need to get anyone else involved. If there are any questions, they can be directed to me. Care to join me, Captain?"

The general's tone was clear: This was to be a private meeting between the two of them: non-essential personnel not invited.

"Yes, sir," the sergeant confirmed, seeming to fade from sight.

The general took off his jacket and rolled up his sleeves. As he stepped behind the bar, he loosened his tie. "'What'll it be, Captain?"

Johnny hesitated, realizing it was ten-thirty in the morning.

"Come now, Johnny," the general smiled. "It's five o'clock somewhere."

All Johnny could think was *It must be pretty fucking bad if they're offering you booze at ten in the morning.* "Scotch, thank you."

"Scotch it is. Ah! Here we go. Johnnie Walker Black. Perfect."

General Thompson poured at least three fingers worth in each glass. "Well done, Captain," he said, clicking his glass against Johnny's. "Don't look so confused, son. You stepped in at the last second and set off a cascade of events that has helped not only the United States but its NATO allies in more ways than one."

"Well, that's kind of you to say, General," said Johnny. "But some of those birds didn't seem all that impressed with my report."

The general made a scoffing sound. "Some folks, as they move up the ranks, lose their taste for truth plainly spoken."

"I reckon it's a little late for me to be learning diplomacy," Johnny said. "And I haven't the inclination to begin with."

"You are a diamond in the rough, Johnny," said the general. "I tell you that candidly. But the men in that room know enough to recognize you as a diamond, for all that."

The skeptical look would not leave Johnny's face.

"Unlike your predecessor, you apparently see the big picture," continued General Thompson. "Captain Alexander was under the belief that all we were facing was a highly organized black market. Mr. Stetner, on the contrary, is of the opinion that both the Nazis and Soviets are educating the black marketeers—that's why they've had so much success. He's also speculating that Alexander was aware of the foreign involvement. He expects to confirm that very soon." He grinned. "I'd hate to be Alexander right now."

Johnny suddenly wondered if Captain Alexander was sequestered somewhere on the base. "What's Alexander's story, anyhow?"

"Captain Alexander was a graduate of the Wentworth Military Academy in Missouri, and was fast-tracked in the army due to family influence. He joined up in 1947. He comes from a family of industrialists who had sizeable government contracts during both the second World War and the Korean conflict. As you can imagine, his family has significant ties in congress." He looked grave. "President Eisenhower has spoken to me privately of his fears that the United States will develop an unhealthy relationship between the military and industrial sectors, such that the Congress would become an arm of big business, starting wars of choice around the world all for the sake of profit, at the risk of its own national security. That is the state of affairs that would benefit Captain Alexander and his family. If Alexander hadn't been caught, he would no doubt have ended up at the Pentagon, forging just that sort of unholy alliance."

Johnny looked at the general in disbelief. In this new cold war, he realized, the enemy would be multi-faceted, with parties motivated more by self-interest than national glory.

"And this brings me to my next point, Captain Gillespie. Knowing what you know now, how do you see yourself fitting in to this whole operation?"

Johnny took a healthy swig of scotch, collecting his thoughts. After this morning's chilly reception, he still half-expected to be shown the door; so he saw no harm in speaking his mind freely. "First of all, the kind of unit I'm imagining would need a close relationship with all the intelligence agencies involved."

"That would be DIA, FBI, and elements of the State Department—otherwise known as the CIA," mused the general. "Interestingly enough, David Alexander believed that he should oversee both the military and intelligence aspects of the unit—which, given what we know now, is not surprising. Do you have any such aspirations?"

"No, sir," said Johnny. "I believe there should be a nucleus of command between both operations and intelligence. We need checks and balances to minimize compromises like what we just experienced. We can't have elements of either intelligence or operations going rogue."

"Excellent," boomed the general. "Take the next seventy-two hours to put together your ideas—not a formal proposal, not yet, but just your thoughts—on how you would like to see your unit operate."

"*My* unit, sir?"

"It's yours if you want it," said the general. "Or do I presume too much?"

"No, sir," said Johnny, a slow smile spreading over his face. "You're not presuming at all. I was looking to see how I could fit in, realizing that we're in the middle of a power struggle with the Soviets." He shook his head. "To tell you the truth, though, I thought we'd seen the last of the Nazis."

"The Nazi high command realized by the end of 1943 that the war was lost," General Thompson said. "Hitler had become overambitious. His own generals knew it. So, they set up cells in the Americas, along with enclaves in the Middle and Far East." He shook his head. "We've got plenty of rumors, but before last night, no actionable intelligence. There's even some speculation that both the Soviets and Nazis have double agents, each working for the other. No matter what, it all boils down to those that want to control the world versus those who wish to live in a free society."

Johnny contemplated General Thompson's words. Authoritarianism wore many disguises and bore many names: Communism, fascism, even the divine right of kings. Free people all over the world were fighting not against any particular ideology, but against those who wished to deny them their right to self-determination.

"You know, General," said Johnny, "I believe my rheumatism is acting up. May I have another taste of the Johnnie Walker Black, please?"

There it was: the deal was sealed. "I do believe my rheumatism is playing up as well," General Thompson, smiling as he raised the bottle.

30

CORTINA, ITALY—MIRAMONTE HOTEL

FRIDAY, JANUARY 14, 1955
3:30 PM

General Thompson gave Johnny three days' leave, with orders to report to his headquarters in Vincenza by noon on Monday. He was told to enjoy himself in the meantime. The general left it up to Johnny how much he wanted to share with Victoria; considering what General Thompson had seen of Victoria—and knowing her brother—the risk of her being a Soviet spy was about as likely as Groucho Marx becoming a Shakespearean actor.

The concern for Johnny was what kind of reception he could expect from Victoria. Would it be like it had been when he left? Had she already moved on? Johnny tried to push that thought out of his mind: Gigi had reassured Johnny by telling him about Victoria's recent enthusiasm for church, which surprised Johnny more than he wished to admit. Did she really care that much? Would it last? Time would tell. Regardless, the two military officers set up a contingency plan if things deteriorated and there was need for a quick evacuation. Hope for the best, but prepare for the worst, as they say in the military.

Before Johnny left for Cortina, he stopped by the hospital to check on his men. Lopez and Anderson were both out of surgery and would make full recoveries. The rest of the casualties were in the process of being discharged, all of them hoping that the unit would not be disbanded by the time they were cleared to return to duty. Johnny assured them that was the case and ordered them to get better ASAP.

Colonel Morton assured Johnny that he and General Thompson would take care of letters for McGraw's family and fiancé. In addition, it appeared that Max Peters had listed St. Catherine's Orphanage as his beneficiary. Among his personal effects was a letter addressed to the current director of the orphanage, Mother Superior Joseph Michael. Though Max was a loner among his colleagues, he had only high regard for the nuns at the orphanage. Again, Colonel Morton assured Johnny that a letter would be sent to the orphanage.

Satisfied, Johnny wedged himself into Gigi's maroon 1952 Chevy Skyline Deluxe along with Tony and Jo-Jo, bound for the Miramonte Hotel.

It was a little after three o'clock. Victoria and Ernesto had finished their lesson and their ski equipment was put away. Ernesto had to go back to the house; his aunt had been baking all day, and she would need a hand cleaning up and putting the baked goods away. He told her he would meet her in the dining room the next morning at a quarter to eight.

Victoria had just walked into the bar to order her biscotti and cappuccino when she felt several pair of eyes on her; but the only ones that registered were those of Captain John Gillespie, US Army, smiling at her like she was the last woman on earth.

"Johnny!" Victoria shouted, a little more loudly than she wanted to, but she didn't care. She ran to him. The tears were flowing freely as she wrapped her arms around his neck and kissed him, not caring who was there. Johnny brushed the tears away, telling her everything was okay and that he could not even begin to tell her how much he missed her.

Eventually she looked over Johnny's shoulder, and there they were: the Three Musketeers, beaming like teenagers picking up their prom dates. Releasing Johnny, Victoria went over and hugged and kissed all three. They thanked her for all her prayers and well-wishes.

She then looked a Gigi. "Shall we, Colonel?"

"As you wish, Nurse Shannon." He signaled to Carlo, who brought over the Johnnie Walker Black.

The glasses were poured, and Carlo was allowed to join in the toast: "To live, and fight another day."

"Leave the bottle, Carlo," Tony said, as he and the other two Musketeers took seats at the bar, leaving Johnny standing with his arm around Victoria as if she might disappear if he let go.

"Gentlemen—and I use the term loosely," Victoria said, smiling. "If you'll excuse us, I need to discuss an urgent matter with the good captain here."

"Really?" Tony asked, mock innocence on his face. "What's that?"

"Oh, Tony darlin'," Victoria said, switching to her Irish brogue, "Captain Gillespie here needs to help me sort out me holy cards, if you know what I mean." And with a wink over her shoulder, they headed toward her suite.

"Lucky bastard," was all Gigi could say as he poured another libation for himself and his compatriots.

From his seat at the bar, Umberto Racine watched Victoria and her American army captain go up the stairs. He was seething; as they disappeared, so did his final plan for a score. Earlier today, word had come to him that the police were inquiring about him at his friend Marco's apartment. When he was finally able to talk to Marco, he was told that that Babs had high-level friends at the US Consulate, and she wanted not only her jewelry back—she wanted to see Umberto in jail. His plan was to check into the hotel, try to seduce Victoria, take the mink coat and some jewelry, rendezvous with Marco and fence the items in Milan, then go to Naples, where he had some friends who would hide him for several months.

Umberto was trying to figure out his next move when a voice from behind the bar said, "Did you really think you could compete with that?"

Turning around Umberto came face-to-face with a wiry older man with an immaculate little mustache and the gold-rimmed spectacles of a bank clerk. Umberto was annoyed. "Eh, and who are you?" he said, pouring on the arrogance.

"Mario Agnolini, general manager of this hotel."

"Do you treat all your guests with such disdain?"

"Only those who are wanted by the police for questioning."

"Who says the police want to question me?"

"They do."

"*Che cazzatta*!"

"You think it's bullshit?" Mario picked up the phone. "Would like me to put that to the test?"

The color drained from Umberto's face. He was cornered, without even a vehicle. The police could be here in a matter of minutes. Where could he run to, with a meter and half of snow on the ground? He attempted an ingratiating smile. "What would like me to do?"

"Go upstairs, pack your belongings, and get the hell out of my hotel. I do not want your kind around here. If you do it in fifteen minutes, I won't charge you for the room."

Umberto was dejected, but knew he had no recourse. He needed to hold on to what little financial resources he had. He paid his tab, left the bar, and went upstairs to pack.

When he came down to the lobby, he was met by not only Mario Agnolini but the three Alpini officers who were with the Americano army captain.

"These gentlemen are willing to give you a ride," Mario said.

"Eh?"

It was the colonel who spoke. "We're heading to Milan. You are welcome to ride with us. Or we'll drop you off at the train station. The choice is yours."

"And what if neither of those is my destination?"

"In that case," said the big major, "we can drop you off at the police station, and you can have a nice little chat with them."

"I haven't been to Milan for several years," Umberto said quickly, trying to put on an air of importance. "It would be nice to visit old friends there. Thank you, gentlemen. That is very noble of you."

The Alpini swarmed around him and moved forward as a unit, forcing him to match their pace or be trampled. They not-quite-manhandled him out of the hotel and into a maroon Chevy Skyline Deluxe; the smaller of the two majors sat up front with the colonel in the driver's seat, and the big major settled in the back with him. For once in his life, Umberto found it prudent to not get any big ideas.

Johnny and Victoria lay back on the bed, spent. They were still half-dressed; as soon as they closed the door to her suite, Johnny had lifted Victoria bodily and deposited her on the bed, pulling off her boots, ski pants, and panties. Their climax was simultaneous, violent, and spectacular. Days of anxiety, apprehension, and fear dissolved instantaneously.

"Johnny, I missed you more than I want to admit," Victoria said. She was crying again, and the tears were a joy. "I prayed every day for your safety. Yours, and all the rest."

"I thought of you every chance I could," Johnny said, afraid to say anything more for fear that he, too, would be reduced to tears.

Victoria rose and walked to the bathroom in her ski sweater and socks. When she came out, she stripped naked and said, "Okay soldier—a quick shower, then a nap. We'll see what to do about dinner later."

Johnny complied and began hanging up his uniform as Victoria went back in and turned on the shower. "Will the Three Musketeers be joining us?" she called from the bathroom.

"Nope. They're heading to Milan. Apparently, they know the owner of a modeling agency, and usually they have parties on Friday nights."

Victoria came out to make sure she heard Johnny correctly and was horrified at what she saw. Johnny had lost at least ten pounds; his ribs were much more visible, and she could see the striations of the muscles in his legs, arms, and pectorals.

"Johnny," Victoria gasped, "you're emaciated!"

Johnny looked in the mirror. He hadn't realized until now how right Victoria was. "Damn!" he whistled. "Guess I haven't been getting many spare calories. It was cold all the time, and we were mostly eating on the go. I look like a scarecrow."

"And you're scaring me," Victoria said. "I'll take care of this pronto." She marched herself naked over to the phone and asked to be connected to the kitchen.

Johnny had just enough Italian to understand that Victoria was ordering him a large plate of spaghetti aglio e olio, bread, and a bottle of Chianti, all to be delivered in a half hour.

"Okay, soldier," she said, hanging up the phone. "Now march that skinny ass of yours into that shower before all the hot water is gone. *Harch!*"

Johnny smiled. "Yes, ma'am," he said. When a woman like this gave an order like that, he knew better than to argue.

31

CORTINA, ITALY—MIRAMONTE HOTEL

SATURDAY, JANUARY 15, 1955
5:00 PM

The next evening, Johnny sat at the bar of the Miramonte Hotel, sipping a scotch and wondering what Victoria was up to. She had been secretive since returning from church this morning. The last twenty-four hours were a whirl in Johnny's head. His emotions when they met after several days apart were genuine—and so, it seemed, were hers. The way she had taken charge of putting his lost weight back on was touching. After the spaghetti aglio e olio and a nap, they had been able to sneak into to the dining room after hours for a pizza margherita and a beer. Afterward, they had talked until midnight—mostly about Johnny's week. He had broken down in tears over the loss of the men under his command; at first, he felt embarrassed, but Victoria's eyes did not show disappointment or disgust—only understanding. He fell asleep with his head on her chest.

When the alarm went off a five o'clock, he had been completely disoriented. They had slept in the same position for nearly five hours. Victoria extracted herself from his embrace, saying she needed to get ready for church. He had started to rise, offering to join her; but she ordered him back to bed. He did not protest, and slept until noon. Victoria had still been out skiing with Ernesto when he finally came down for lunch, freshly showered and shaved; they had not met again until three o'clock, when they shared cappuccino and biscotti.

Victoria had been pleased with Johnny's "recovery," and told him she had special plans for that evening's dinner. He asked for a hint, but she was not forthcoming. She proclaimed her suite off-limits until after 4:30; she would leave ahead of him, and they would not see each other again until Pepe drove him to a secret destination at 6:15.

"Is this a formal occasion?" he asked. "Should I dress up?"

"What you're wearing is fine," she said, "cowboy boots and all." Then, with a smile: "And that's the only hint you're getting!"

With that, she had kissed him and gone upstairs to get ready, while Johnny lingered over a second cappuccino and more biscotti.

He returned to the room at around 4:45 and, with an hour or so to kill, found himself at a bit of a loss to what to do with himself. Then an idea dawned on him. He did the math in his head. It was not yet lunchtime in New York City. Perfect. He would likely catch Kip in the office.

He placed an oversea call through the hotel switchboard—*Screw the expense,* he thought; *The Bossard family can afford it.* Soon, he was connected to his good friend Kip Van Styles, and after a twenty-minute conversation had formulated a plan that might help Victoria in the immediate future. Victoria had mentioned that she needed to be smart with her newfound wealth. Kip had helped Johnny significantly in that area, and Johnny knew he could do the same for Victoria—if she wanted it. The final decision would hers, he'd introduce Kip up as a potential resource. The conversation over, Johnny grabbed his bomber jacket, watch cap, and gloves, and headed back to the bar for a quick drink before his secret rendezvous.

It was only a ten-minute drive in the hotel's station wagon to what looked like a small house in the woods. In the fading twilight, it seemed especially picturesque, surrounded by pine trees and with smoke coming from the chimney and lights on inside.

"What the hell is this, Pepe?"

With a cat-who-ate-the-canary grin, Pepe said, "Captain, consider yourself one of the luckiest men in Italy right now—if not the world."

"C'mon, Pepe!"

"I will pick you and Signorina Shannon up at half past ten." Pepe came around and opened Johnny's door for him. "Enjoy your evening."

Johnny could tell that the path to the house had been cleared only recently. He racked his brain trying to figure out what Victoria was up to.

He lifted the heavy brass knocker and rapped at the door. From inside, Victoria's voice called, "Coming."

When the door swung open, he beamed. There stood Victoria in a black turtleneck sweater and black cigarette pants—and wearing an apron. Her sleeves were rolled up to her elbows and her hair was up in a messy bun, one lock hanging in her face. Her smile spoke of warmth and comfort. She kissed him, then said, "Here, let me take your coat and hat."

She closed the door behind them as Johnny took in the surroundings. To one side of the entry was a living room—small, but comfortable and nicely decorated. Soft jazz was playing on a record player, and a fire crackled in the fireplace. In the dining room opposite, the table was set for two, with fine china and candles. There was a bottle of wine on the table; after Victoria deposited Johnny's jacket on an easy chair next to the couch, she poured him a glass. It was a cabernet, rich and spicy.

Victoria motioned for him to follow her into the kitchen. "I just didn't feel like getting dressed up to go out to dinner tonight," she said. "I hope you don't mind?"

Mind? Johnny thought. *Beautiful, professional, passionate, empathetic, wealthy*—and *she wants to cook*! "I don't mind a bit," he said. "What's for dinner?"

"Steak with potatoes and spinach," she said. "It's what I grew up eating almost every Saturday night. Will that be all right?"

"Better than all right," he smiled. "How can I help?"

"You just sit there and keep me company, and that'll be help enough," she said, smiling like she was the happiest woman in the world.

He sipped his wine. "I feel like I should've at least brought dessert."

"Already handled, Cap. Homemade brownies." She pointed to the mixture already poured into a Pyrex pan, waiting to be baked.

Johnny looked around, noting for the first time how modern the kitchen was. "What is this place, anyway?" he asked. "It looks like a little old cabin from the outside, but all these appliances look brand-new. And that hi-fi in the living room is top of the line."

"Carmella found it for me," she said. "I'd been telling her I wanted to do something special for you. I felt like I hadn't cooked for ages. After church this morning, she told me about this place. There's a rich fellow in Milan—he owns one of the leather factories, I think—he keeps this as a summer house. Carmella keeps an eye on it for him in the off-season."

Johnny looked at her doubtfully. "Trespassing is certainly one way to spend and evening."

She swatted him playfully with a dishtowel. "It's all on the up-and-up," she laughed. "Carmella called the owner when we got back to the hotel, and he agreed to let me use it tonight. In fact, according to Carmella, he thought it was a fine idea, just to make sure everything still works."

"You arranged all this just since this morning?"

She grinned. "When I came in to change into to my ski clothes, you were still sound asleep. I wrote up a grocery list and gave Carmella a hundred dollars in cash. She hired someone to shovel the path, arranged for everything to be delivered, got the heating switched on, started the fire ..." Victoria trailed off. "She's quite an amazing woman."

Johnny wondered momentarily how a chambermaid might have the direct phone number for a wealthy Milanese industrialist. Then he remembered what Tony had told him about Carmella Vecchi—how she had helped so many partisans during the war. Doubtless there were people all over Italy who would grant any favor she requested. "I'm in her debt," he said. "And yours, too. I guess I'll have to do the dishes."

"Nope!" she said brightly. "Carmella said just to pile everything in the sink, and she'll have someone come in the morning and clean up. Apparently that C-note went a long way."

Dinner was exquisite. Victoria seared the steak in a cast-iron skillet before finishing it in the oven with a couple of cloves of garlic and rosemary, giving it a perfect crust with a tender rare center, just as they both liked it. The small red potatoes were quartered and baked with olive oil and parmesan cheese, and the spinach was sautéed with olive oil and garlic.

Johnny devoured a significant portion of his two-pound T-bone, using copious amounts of *pane cafone* to sop up the juice. When dinner was done, Johnny finalized it with an unconscious belch. He looked up in embarrassment.

Victoria looked at him with one eyebrow wickedly raised. "I'll take that as a compliment tonight, Captain," she said. "But if you ever do that in public with me, I will slap you into next Tuesday."

"Yes, ma'am," he said, grinning.

After dinner, Victoria popped the brownies in the oven and they both stacked the dishes, along with the pots and pans, in or near the sink.

As the brownies baked, they sat on the couch in the living room, watching the fire and talking: about skiing, about music, about growing up with crazy parents, about siblings whom they loved but who drove them to distraction—just talking. The conversation continued after the brownies were done and served with vanilla gelato and espresso.

Ten-thirty was approaching. Neither one wanted the evening to end. They knew it would not, of course—there would be things to "discuss" when they got back to the suite—but it was a strange and wonderful thing for them to sit in this little house. What might it be like, Johnny wondered, to have a little place like this—a place to call home, and someone to come back to at the end of the day? It wasn't the life he had chosen; but it might not be so bad, at that.

The conversation faltered. He looked at Victoria, wondering if she was thinking the same thing. She looked into his eyes for a long moment, then kissed him like she did the previous Sunday, when he had been transferred to General Thompson's command—as if kissing him could freeze this moment in time forever.

Then she turned away. "Pepe will be here in a few minutes," she said. "I suppose we ought to let him have the rest of those brownies." Victoria cut up the rest of the brownies into squares; silently, Johnny helped her wrap them up in wax paper.

Victoria and Johnny climbed the front bench seat with Pepe. It was freezing outside. As the headed back to the hotel Victoria explained to Pepe the best way to eat the brownies.

In the empty bar, Pepe had gathered Carlo and Toto. He unwrapped the package of brownies. "Signorina Shannon said they're for sharing," he said. "She said they're best with a glass of milk."

Carlo fetched a bottle of milk from the kitchen and poured them each a tumbler.

"*Dio mio*," Toto groaned in ecstasy. "That decides it. I'm going to go to America and marry me someone like Signorina Shannon! My God—she's beautiful, smart, rich, *and* she can cook."

"You stupid little bastard!" Carlo playfully slapped his friend upside his head. "You think all American girls are like Signorina Shannon? Think! You've seen some of the Americana *scrofe* we've had here in the hotel over the years. They're mostly lazy and spoiled."

"He's got a point," said Pepe, chuckling.

"But Signorina Shannon is different," Toto sighed. "I suppose it's because she's Italian."

Mario had just entered the bar, passing through on his way from his office to the small bungalow on site that served as his private residence. "What are you three up to?" he asked. "It's late."

"Signorina Shannon made some brownies," said Pepe. He gestured toward the package. "You're welcome to have one, Signor Agnolini. She said they're for sharing."

Mario gave Pepe a skeptical look. "Signorina Shannon made these, eh? Well, she has a good heart." Seeing the faces of the trio looking at him, he said, "All right, let's give one a try."

Pepe put a square on a plate and handed it to the old man, along with half a glass of milk. Mario looked at the brownie doubtfully. At last, he took a bite, then a sip of milk. His eyebrows rose. He took a second bite, and a third, washing each down with a swallow of milk.

He set down the plate and the tumbler on the bar. "I hope that son of bitch knows just how lucky he is," he sighed.

The three young men nodded in agreement.

In Victoria's suite, Johnny was already in bed. He had just begun reading George Orwell's *Nineteen Eighty-Four* while Victoria removed her makeup. As she did, she asked Johnny if he would accompany her to church in the morning.

"Morning mass?" he said doubtfully.

"Tomorrow is Sunday," she called, laughing. "Mass doesn't start until nine o'clock."

"Well, that's all right, then," he drawled, then shook his head. "I've been sleeping such odd hours this last week, the clock in my head is all out of whack."

He swallowed hard when Victoria walked out of the bathroom in a sheer light blue negligée, thinking to himself he would follow this woman through the gates of Hell. As she climbed into bed, she said, "And now, Johnny darlin', let's see if we can't remind you what Saturday night is supposed to feel like."

32

CORTINA, ITALY—MIRAMONTE HOTEL

SUNDAY, JANUARY 16, 1955
12:30 PM

Church was finished, and it was approaching half past noon. Victoria had already started packing her steamer trunk, mostly with non-essentials. She did pack one suitcase with several days of clothing, underwear, and shoes, in case flights were delayed due to weather over the Atlantic. She decided to pack a cocktail dress, as well; if she had to stay, perhaps she could get in touch with Basil and go out to dinner. Toto had already packed her skis, poles, and boots separately, early this morning.

They had been invited to an early Sunday dinner at Ernesto's house. After hearing about Johnny's sudden weight loss, Ernesto claimed that his aunt Lucrecia would be more than willing to help in that department, and would not take no for an answer. Victoria had grown so fond of Ernesto that she could not refuse.

Dinner was served at one. In recognition of Ernesto's opening his home to a hotel guest, Victoria brought along a gift of assorted chocolates; the American custom of tipping was still considered poor form in Europe, but the dear man deserved something special in thanks for all he'd done for her. She also bought Ernesto an assortment of fine tobacco, which he could enjoy both in his pipe and his hand-rolled cigarettes.

Ernesto's aunt was charming—and not half as feeble as he had made her out to be. Regardless, though she did have help in the kitchen. Esterina Guido, one of the dishwashers from the Miramonte, was always looking to make extra money; she had been set to work peeling and chopping vegetables. Ernesto's cousin Matteo was also able to join the party. Victoria noted with approval that Johnny's Italian had improved significantly—as had her own. Both were able to contribute to conversation quite comfortably.

Dinner was the typical affair with which Victoria had grown up and to which Johnny was becoming accustomed: antipasto, followed by pasta with sausage, lamb, and meatballs in tomato sauce, along with salad and bread. Rather than regular pasta, Zia Lucrecia decided on homemade ravioli to help Johnny with his "weight problem." The plump little squares were filled with ricotta and spinach, rich with the favors of nutmeg and pepper. Dessert was assorted pastries with coffee. Afterward, all three men fell asleep in various seats in the living room. Mission accomplished!

At half past three, the couple reluctantly took their leave; Victoria needed to finish packing, and they were going to meet up with the Three Musketeers that evening for a light meal and a last goodbye.

While Victoria and Johnny were saying goodbye to Ernesto and his family, the Three Musketeers were ending their own recovery session with a Sunday luncheon in the company of three lovely ladies—and yet they could not have been more miserable.

As cavalier as the Alpini pretended to be, the Englishwomen had left their marks on them—Jo-Jo even more than the others. It might have been better if Portia had left things the way they were on Monday morning, he thought, with her seeming to hate him. The apology letter only confused him further. Did she truly care, or was she feeling guilty? Was there anything there, or was she just trying to be civil?

Jo-Jo felt his guts all twisted in knots. What was he supposed to do now? Should he write her? Forget her? Hop the next plane to England? The thought made him squirm. After all, she was engaged to be married. Was her fiancé another Basil, soft, apathetic and condescending? Jo-Jo could imagine himself flying to England and meeting this Cedric fellow face-to-face. It would be nothing like Johnny meeting Basil. Johnny had Victoria there to support him through drinks and dinner and then became an angel of mercy. Would Portia support him in that way? Would she run away with him? Or was Jo-Jo a distraction from the ho-hum life she was destined for? Jo-Jo had to wonder if Cedric was cruel to her; that, he would not tolerate. Common sense told him to leave it alone. But he could not let it go. There was something about Portia; try as he might, he just couldn't get her out of his mind.

He had hoped to find comfort in Donatella Burggoti, a model from the Tedesco modeling agency, a black-haired beauty with deep brown almond-shaped eyes and skin the color of café au lait. She seemed more than eager to be with Jo-Jo. Many of the models were attracted to the dashing, heroic Alpini officers, especially when they came bearing gifts of American chocolates, American cigarettes, and silk stockings.

For Gigi, Teresa Lombardi had little to offer in comparison to Marjorie. From an aesthetic point of view, there was no argument—Teresa was drop-dead gorgeous, resembling Sophia Loren in many ways; but she was vain, dull, and of average intelligence. Marjorie was witty, bright, and empathetic. Gigi could not help to think that someday she would make an excellent physician.

Tony's therapy session was a complete disaster. Several times, he had referred to Antonella Dellacioppa as "Stephanie," which made him blush. Antonella was not unsympathetic; she could tell that the tall, athletic major was trying to forget a previous love, and played along without complaint. Antonella looked like an Italian version of

Maureen O'Hara, with auburn hair and a nose job from one of the best plastic surgeons in Switzerland. She was coming out on the top end of the affair, as far as she was concerned; she could sell the cigarettes and chocolates at a premium price, and the stockings would at least save her a week's salary if she could make them last.

The luncheon could not end quickly enough for the six of them; they were all trying desperately to move on with their lives. With insincere promises to keep in touch, the Three Musketeers started the four-hour trek back to Cortina with two goals in mind: to say a fond goodbye to Victoria Shannon, and to retrieve their good friend Johnny Gillespie.

Mario Agnolini had arranged a private dining area for their party. It was going to be a solemn occasion. He could see that these five had formed a bond not easily broken. He wanted to make it memorable for all involved. He had known Tony and Gigi for over a decade, and Jo-Jo since he was born. Victoria was able to bring out so much in these men; it was amazing. He hated and thanked Sebastian Bossard simultaneously for bringing Victoria into their lives. *Everything happens for a reason,* his dear departed Matilda used to say, and Mario placed his trust in that thought.

Dinner was a light affair: a simple chicken piccata, with nothing more than espresso and grappa for dessert. "Well,

Nurse Shannon," Gigi said, sipping his coffee, "what is your itinerary for tomorrow?"

"I have a reservation with Pan Am. I catch the seven o'clock train to Milan, then a two o'clock flight to London. From there, it's a six o'clock flight from London to New York. I should be there somewhere around eight o'clock Tuesday morning."

"That's a long time traveling," Tony said.

Victoria shrugged. "That's assuming the weather holds."

"Right then, chaps," barked Gigi. "Carlo, if you please."

Carlo entered, pushing a cart with Johnnie Walker Black and several glasses, followed by Toto and Pepe. Toto was carrying a clothing box. Mario followed soon after

"Libations first, thank you," Gigi continued.

Mario joined in the toast: "To live, and fight another day."

"Nurse Shannon, after our conversation on Wednesday, a momentous decision was taken." Gigi was striving for his usual commanding tone, but Victoria could tell he was struggling. "It was decided by the high command that you should be designated an honorary member of the Fighting Ibex Battalion. Toto, if you please."

Toto presented Victoria with the box. Inside was an aviator jacket made of the finest Milanese leather. On the left breast was the Fighting Ibex insignia patch.

Fighting back tears, Victoria stood up and put the jacket on. It fit perfectly. Her face was flushed, but she was beaming.

"Check inside," Tony said, not trusting himself to say more.

Stenciled on the seam of the left inside pocket was her name—and on the right side, the phrase *One of the Boys*.

She was crying in earnest now. She hugged and kissed them all, thanking them for such a wonderful and thoughtful gift.

"Wear it when you go to opening day for the Yankees," Tony said. "Maybe it'll bring 'em luck."

Johnny wrapped a comforting arm around Victoria which seemed to make the two of them melt into one. "My Three Musketeers—and d'Artagnan," she said between sobs. "I'm going to miss you." She pulled out a brand-new address book, and told all of them to write their contact information, with promises to update them all on what was happening with her back in New York.

It was going on ten o'clock. No one wanted the night to end, but everyone had an extensive day of traveling ahead—especially Victoria. They said goodnight, with plans for breakfast in the morning. It was decided during dinner that Pepe would drive Victoria and Johnny to the train station, and the Musketeers would follow them. There would be one last farewell before all the Musketeers headed back to Aviano Air Base, and Victoria went off to begin a new life.

As Johnny and Victoria made their way through the dining room to the lobby, Victoria still wore her leather jacket. It did not compliment her light blue skater dress, earning her strange looks from the male patrons and scowls from the female patrons. Victoria, though, could not be bothered to give a single shit. She was one of the boys.

When they got back to Victoria's suite, she finally took off the jacket and hung it up. "Did you have a hand in this, Captain Gillespie?"

"I suppose I gave them the idea," he admitted. "All I said was, since we all considered you one of the boys, we should make you an honorary member of the Fighting Ibex. They did the rest. Gigi had the jacket commissioned."

"And *that's* why the mysterious trip to Milan," she said. "Friday night party at a modeling agency, hm? I might have known." Victoria stepped out of her shoes; her feet were killing her.

"Oh, no," Johnny assured her. "The models are real enough. They've gone up a few times. Usually, they make a weekend of it."

Victoria sat back on the bed, massaging her aching toes. "Then why did—" Suddenly, she connected the dots. "Did they come with you Friday and tonight to make sure nothing had changed between us?"

Johnny could not meet her eyes. He got up and went to the balcony. She followed him, grabbed his shoulders, spun him around, desperate for an answer. And then she saw it in his face, in his deep cobalt blue eyes: pain.

"My God," she said softly. "Did she hurt you that bad?"

He nodded. The tears sprang up in his eyes, one sliding down his left cheek.

"I'm so sorry," she said, and threw her arms around his neck. "Do you want to talk about it?"

"No."

"Johnny. You can tell me."

"It's not that," he said. There was a catch in his voice. "It hurts too much. And it's our last night together for who knows how long."

Victoria realized that Johnny would talk about it when he was ready—but not now. She held him close. "Johnny darlin'," she whispered. "May God strike me dead if I ever hurt you like that."

The floodgates opened. He crushed her to him, weeping as he had not wept since he was a little boy; years of pain and heartache, locked away for so long, crashed against her like waves. And she held him, and stood firm, and was not washed away.

When he was finally able to catch his breath, he looked at her as if she were an apparition. He reached up tenderly. brushing that unruly lock of hair away from her face. "Are you real?" he whispered.

She kissed his tear-stained face. "Yes, Johnny darlin'," she said gently. "I'm real. Flesh and bones, warts and all, with a slight overbite. Now please, no more crying. Take me to bed."

EPILOGUE

NEW YORK, NEW YORK—THE PLAZA HOTEL

THREE DAYS LATER—
WEDNESDAY, JANUARY 19, 1955
9:00 PM EST

It was a little after eight when Victoria finally got back to her suite. She couldn't believe how much had been accomplished in a little over twenty-four hours. Thankfully Victoria was able to get confirmation of Kip Van Styles's capabilities from one of Joel's fraternity brothers, Tom Romano, who currently worked as assistant DA at SDNY and was using Kip's forensic accountant department to assist in a large racketeering case. Tom also informed Victoria that only about thirty-five people in the United States had the phone number that Johnny had given her; whoever this guy was, he said, Kip obviously held him in high regard. All became clear when Victoria met Kip and his valet, Sam Wolf; both had served in Korea with Johnny.

Victoria could tell that, as with the Alpini, Johnny had a close, strong bond with both Kip and Sam—but would prefer not to speak of those experiences.

Kip was not only helpful in setting up a sound investment strategy for Victoria's newfound wealth, but convinced the Bossards to pay for her stay at the Plaza for the next thirty days while she planned her next moves. In what appeared to Victoria to be flawless French, he had negotiated the deal with Mr. Martin Eisner. When Victoria expressed an interest in making a career of finance, Kip was instrumental there, too. She was now a part-time employee of Van Styles Investments, working with the research team while attending introductory classes at Barnard College. He was even helping her look for an apartment.

The meeting with Scott, Max, and Ira was a little awkward in the beginning. Kip was not joking when he said they lacked people skills; they had barely made eye contact with Victoria when they were introduced. And yet she recognized the close bond among the three of them. In their odd, bookworm way, they reminded Victoria of the Alpini Three Musketeers.

Of the three, Scott was the only one tall enough to look Victoria in the eye; both Max and Ira topped out at about five-foot-five. All three were confirmed bachelors who shared a passion for baseball. Scott, though a Bronx native, was a Brooklyn Dodgers fan, while Ira and Max, both from Brooklyn, rooted for the Giants. Of course, the lively banter began almost immediately as Victoria defended her Yankees. It was all in good fun, but the guys were impressed with Victoria's knowledge of the game. The ice was broken. They also quizzed her on the courses she would be taking, and said that they would be more than happy to assist in any way possible. Kip told all four of them that Victoria would be starting Monday morning at nine o'clock sharp.

At Barnard, she was introduced to Muriel Davis, who had arranged with the registrar for Victoria to start Introduction to Economics and Accounting in her first semester; the classes met on Tuesday and Thursday mornings. Muriel helped Victoria to finish her application and asked her to send an official copy of her transcript from St. Vincent's as soon as possible. Kip wrote Muriel a check, and that was that.

Next it was to the Eldorado to meet with the realtor, Donna Saunders. It was Kip's belief that Victoria should take advantage of the new and growing cooperative market instead of renting. Kip gave Donna a target price of $6,000 to work with. They looked at several apartments in the Eldorado, but Victoria was not bowled over by any of them. They next went to the Beresford; one flat in particular appealed to Victoria, but the kitchen was tiny, and Victoria wanted to be able to cook. Donna raised the possibility of remodeling the kitchen if the apartment was purchased, and Victoria asked her to look into it; she would be in touch the next day.

Over dinner at the Plaza, Kip asked her if she was going to look up any of her old friends. Victoria said no; she was not ready to face them. She was not even ready to tell the story to her uncles and cousins. Victoria wanted to have her life sorted out before she told anyone she was back; she wanted no one's pity, no well-meaning advice, and she meant to sidestep it all.

After dinner, she walked Kip to his limousine and watched him drive off.

Though she was exhausted, she was still excited about the day's events, so she decided on a bubble bath. After changing into her pajamas, she called down to room service for a carafe of red wine and turned on the gas fireplace. There was stationery on the desk; she settled into a chair in front of the fireplace, using her leather folder as a writing desk, and began writing letters to her friends across the pond to update them on how things were going. But the most important letter she saved for last.

d'Artagnan,

I hope you are healthy and fighting fit. I finally made it to New York, as you can tell by the letterhead. After nineteen hours in the air and a full day running around the city, I'm dead on my feet—so this will be just a quick note before bed. I'll write you with the full story in a day or two, I promise.

Thank you so much for introducing me to Kip. He's turned everything around for me in less than twenty-four hours—engineering a monthlong stay at the Plaza, starting me on a new career path, even installing me *as d'Artagnan to my own set of Musketeers. The kindness he's shown me has honestly been overwhelming. He's a remarkable man—I wonder if even you know just how remarkable.*

I saw Basil during my stopover in England. There's something I had to keep from you back in Cortina, for her safety: Beatrix is pregnant with Liam's child. She's about three months along. Basil has put a scheme in motion to protect them and the baby, and keep her out of her Uncle Mortimer's clutches. I will fill you in on the details when I have more time, but please—don't mention any of this to the boys. Things are at a delicate stage, and if it gets back to the girls, it could mean trouble for the two of them.

Speaking of Stephanie, Marjorie, and Portia, we had a chance to meet up, and I've got to tell you—I don't think our Three Musketeers have heard the last of them. Not if they have anything to say about it, anyway!

Before I sign off for now, Johnny—my Johnny—I have to thank you again for your understanding. None of this would have been possible without it, or without you. I can honestly tell you that the closeness we've shared in our short time together is something I never felt with either Joel or Sebastian. I'll write more soon. Keep me in your prayers, and I'll do the same.

Always,
Your Victoria

In the weeks that followed, a large package was delivered to the Miramonte Hotel addressed to Mario Agnolini; inside were several smaller packages of various sizes, each bearing the name of the recipient, and a letter full of news and instructions from Victoria.

Carmella received a luxurious black wool overcoat, which she proudly wore to church the very next morning. Mario received a bottle of Johnnie Walker Swing with its distinct round bottom made for sailing ships, which he displayed with great pride in his office. Pepe was rewarded with an eight-ounce can of Hershey's cocoa powder, accompanied by Victoria's brownie recipe painstakingly written out in Italian. Toto, who was desperately trying to improve his English, received the last six months of the American magazine *Playboy,* which he found highly instructional. Carlo, the avid comic-book reader, received several of the latest issues of Superman, Wonder Woman, and—of course—Batman.

Gigi received a similar package; his gift was the recently published book *High Adventure*, by Sir Edmund Hillary, the first man to summit Mt. Everest with his guide Tenzing Norgay. Along with Gigi's gift were packages for Tony and Jo-Jo. Tony was graced with two ballcaps, with the logos of the New York Yankees on one and the New York Giants football team on the other, along with a note lamenting that Victoria herself would be working in Manhattan, among Dodgers and Giants fans. To Jo-Jo, because of the passion he shared with Portia for the fine arts, Victoria sent a coffee-table book of photographs of the artwork from the Metropolitan Museum of Art.

Victoria remembered that General Thompson had enjoyed James' fine tenor voice and would get a lump in his throat listening to him sing "Danny Boy" on St. Patrick's Day; she sent him a record album of John McCormack singing several Irish ballads. Izzy Robinson had to scratch his head for a moment when received a package with "Medical Supplies" stenciled on it. Inside was a case of Four Roses bourbon, with a note stating that he was in charge of dispensing medicinal amounts during outbreaks and flareups of rheumatism among the unit.

Stephanie, Marjorie, and Portia all received small bottles of Chanel Number 5, and notes asking for any updates of Beatrix and Liam. Basil received a letter asking much the same, along with a copy of *The Complete Book of the Appaloosa.*

For Ernesto, there was a pair of glacier glasses like Johnny's—the hardest of all the gifts to acquire, and one to cherish. How perceptive she was, Ernesto thought, to notice his admiration for the Captain's gear on the day they had all skied together, and how thoughtful to make him such a gift! Thankfully, Ernesto would never know the lengths to which Victoria had gone to procure such a rare treasure—finagling an entry to the Manhattan branch of the American Alpine Club in her tightest skirt and sexiest heels, then putting on her best damsel-in-distress persona for the benefit of three very accommodating junior members.

At his new residence in Vicenza, Italy—some two hundred miles from Cortina, as the crow flies—Johnny was intrigued when he opened his package to find an empty eight-by-ten picture frame. There were instructions attached informing him that he could put in it one of the pictures of Victoria in his bomber jacket—his choice—so he wouldn't forget what she looked like; but she still wanted the rest—and the negatives.

HISTORICAL NOTES

The Brooklyn Dodgers and Giants did not move to Los Angeles and San Francisco respectively until 1957. Growing up in the greater New York City area, I knew several people who had never forgiven the powers that be for allowing such a travesty. One of them was my college calculus professor.

Mickey Mantle did not have his breakout season until 1956.

During the Korean War, there were around eighteen companies of US Army Rangers deployed to Korea. Italy was a member of NATO at the time, but not of the United Nations, and sent only medical units to Korea. There were some combined national units that fought in the Korean war, mostly British commandos and US Army Rangers who operated behind enemy lines.

Made in the USA
Columbia, SC
02 July 2022